OF TOXIN & TEACUPS

OF WITCHES & MEN SERIES

CASSIE SWINDON

Of Toxin & Teacups

Copyright 2025 by Cassie Swindon

All rights reserved.

No part of this book may be reproduced in any form or by any electronic or mechanical means, including information storage and retrieval systems, without written permission from the author, except for the use of brief quotations in a book review.

ISBN (KDP) paperback: 9798282132946

ISBN (Ingramspark) paperback- 979-8-9911519-1-7

Cover Design by: Authortree
Interior Formatting by: Jennifer Laslie
Editing by Desert Ink Editorial (Jessica Julien)

This work is fiction. Names, characters, places, and incidents either are the product of the author's imagination or are used fictitiously. Any resemblance to actual persons, living or dead, businesses, companies, cities, or events is entirely fictional

Dedicated to:

All my fellow North Carolina authors

ALSO BY CASSIE SWINDON

THE LINKED TRILOGY

Scorched

Severed

Shattered

THE FAIRY TALES FLIP SERIES

The Wicked Blue

The Phantom Ink

The Never Hour

THE GOLDEN CHAINS TRILOGY

Break the Stone

Hunt the Storm

Stop the Clock

OF WITCHES & MEN SERIES

[Of Toxin & Teacups]

Of Venom & Vineyards

Of Poison & Pumpkins

please note that prequel short stories are available at www.cassieswindon.com as teasers

ACKNOWLEDGMENTS

Thank you to my readers for supporting me. I hope these stories bring you some joy. I appreciate my newly found local author groups in Raleigh, North Carolina. Shout out to our critique partner group at the library. Honestly, though, I want to acknowledge all the fellow writers out there who find passion and artistic expression in storytelling. Keep going, y'all! You inspire me to not quit.

What humbles me the most is when readers create their own content about my books, whether it's a quote that inspires a social media post or a picture collage. Those little projects keep me motivated to push through the hard times. I feel honored that my work somehow creates more art in this world.

A.A. Warne, you helped me so much as the sensitivity reader for everything Australian. Thanks so much!

Thank you to my kids for their ideas because apparently, they've "written" my books and I'm merely the transcriber of their brilliance. You have the strength and power to burn the world down at a single glance, Piggie. And to my creative mini-me... you have a mind to design entire worlds of your own too. Never stop drawing, Bubba. The ideas and imagery you mold are truly spectacular.

To my author friend, Anna. Without you, I'd be dead. From a chicken. IYKYK

Matt- if I admit that you partially inspired the heroes of my books, would you believe me?

CHARACTERS

Main Characters

> Alouette (Lou) Mae Nkosi - heroine/protagonist – ceramicist
> Jacob Blaine Talksihnn - hero/protagonist – retired professional surfer

Secondary Characters

> Bennet Savion - Ouma's old boyfriend/president of the Fuzer's council
> Dakota (Koda) - Jacob's daughter
> Ivola Steinbeck - ghost/ retired private investigator
> Marquis Nkosi - Alouette's older brother and Jacob's best friend
> Nella Franklin - the mother of Jacob's child
> Ouma (Tariji Nkosi) - Alouette's grandma
> Zola - Alouette's best friend

Barely mentioned Characters

> Cheyenne - Jacob's hammock neighbor
> Erik - Jacob's agent
> Felicity - Jacob's most recent ex
> Grim - the raven
> Hayes - Alouette's dance partner at the gala
> Kolen - giant leprechaun/Ivola's prisoner
> Posh - Jacob's other ex

Rory (the Kwiin) - tarot card reader /oracle
Sal - Dakota's classmate at school
Serefina - Alouette's boss
Sonya - Jacob's other ex
Taco - the turtle who follows Jacob
Ubika Nishal - custody lawyer for Jacob
Willis Nkosi - Ouma's husband
Yuri - tattoo artist

CHAPTER ONE

Alouette

To follow my dream, a passion rooted deeply in the essence of my soul, I need to be brave.

Am I courageous? Debatable. I've managed to create my own path instead of following in the footsteps of my family, but I still hold on to that nagging guilt that I'll always be somewhat of a disappointment.

This morning is too stunning to drown in negative thoughts, though. I bask under the last moments of the sunrise, savoring the way the blues sparkle like a mosaic all the way until the ocean meets the sky. No type of art can fully capture the spectrum of colors in those rays. It's this view, with flocks soaring above, that let me know Ouma still blesses me with her radiance, even though she's gone.

The spectators gathered along the shoreline, watching the infamous RipSilver competition, all applaud in unison. I tune into the sound of the waves crashing, seagulls cawing, and the melody of an ice cream truck. I can almost smell my favorite flavor—coconut.

It'd be nice to cool down since my forehead is sweating a bit. Maybe it wasn't the smartest choice to wear this black dress on the sand instead of a swimsuit. I won't be here for much longer, though. I only came to the beach early for the magical memory-inducing fireworks. I'm hoping to experience a memory involving Ouma, since I will never see her wrinkled face in person again.

Like me, Ouma was a Fuzer. Two of a kind. When I was little, she'd even waste her monthly spells to entertain me with ridiculous magic, like making mailboxes dance when we drove by or bewitching dogs to meow when we passed them on the sidewalk. Goddess, I loved her. After thirty years of her constant companionship, how am I supposed to move on so easily? It'd be nice if I could choose a spell to eliminate this grief, but I doubt the Typs would allow any Fuzer that strong of an ability.

Fuzers make up about one percent of the world's population—those who carry magic in our DNA. Even though we're few and far between, the Typs (non-magical folk) fear us. To ensure balance, Typs approve our magical requests once a month. Every Fuzer is required to declare their spell at the monthly Ceremony. If it's simple and harmless, then it'll be approved by the Typs. It's not like we can do anything insane, like forcing our family to understand our deepest desires at the snap of a finger. Goddess, that'd be bloody nice.

My spell this month increases my reading speed and memory. A skill that is necessary to find what I'm searching for.

In the distance, one of the surfers conquers a wave more gracefully than a pelican gliding in the sky. An announcer calls out his career stats—a surfer named Talksihnn—but I can barely hear over the cheers exploding along Kitesville Beach. The audience applauds loudly for his trick, which looks impossible. Maybe he used a spell, but I bet enhancements are forbidden in such a competition.

My chest tightens at the sight of another wave rolling in. If the other surfers don't start paddling hard to the outside, they'll get rag-dolled. Absolutely terrifying. I squint as the competitors disappear under the water. I hate this moment, the seconds when I don't know if they're safe. It makes me dig my fingers into the sand destroying my manicure, but I can't help it.

A unified gasp erupts from the crowd. One lone surfer shoots out from the barrel, still aboard. Impressive. Excitement reverberates like a live wire down the coast. For a moment, I'm wrapped up in the energy.

"Alouette!" Zola yells from my left.

I turn in time to witness my best friend avoid a frisbee to the head. She ducks between families building sandcastles.

Zola is the main reason I can never spread my wings to leave Calypsa. Not that I'd ever blame her; we've been inseparable neighbors since birth.

"Aloooo!" Zola charges towards me, arms out wide, face covered in glee.

"Whoa! Slow down!"

"HAPPY BIRTHDAY!"

I brace myself for impact. "Zola, you're gonna slam into me!"

We land with a thud, a pretzel of legs in the sand, our entanglement only worsening as she showers me with kisses. I shriek and bat her away.

"Accept my love or I'll give you a lizard kiss!" she threatens.

"No!" I giggle and block myself from her mouth. "You wouldn't dare!"

She sticks her tongue out in a threat and tries to pin back my wrists. I'm not Superwoman, but apparently yoga has worked wonders because I miraculously toss her off me.

"Truce?" I yell.

"Fine!" She smiles that tropical warm smile I love. "Only because you're the birthday princess."

Side by side, both out of breath, we watch the surfers finish their last set.

"You smell weird," Zola says, sniffing my neck.

"Don't ask."

"I do love an epic story."

"No story. Just some guy. And a weird lotion. The end."

"Excuse *him*? Do I need to run a creeper over with my skateboard?"

I sputter out laughing. "Maybe next time."

The surfers wade into the shallows with their boards, causing the paparazzi to swarm. The annual August festival in our beachy town, Calypsa, attracts a lot of crowds because there's always some hot shot celebrity. I've always considered fame overvalued.

A Fuzer points their finger into the air to create celebratory fireworks. This is exactly what I've been waiting for, especially the fuchsia ones, since they have a charmed ability that allows viewers to relive a favorite memory.

I relax, knowing a past scene with Ouma is about to cascade over me. As I grow entranced by the erupting pink in the sky, my vision fades.

In Ouma's cottage kitchen—her baked bread rises in the oven. She sings loudly, with wild abandon better meant for the outdoors. Her sweet smile sent my way has a hint of mischievousness. "How many waterfalls did we see earlier, Little Owl? Five! That must be a new record."

The scene dissolves fast. I'm whiplashed back to the present within a single breath, wishing I had more time. Despite the bright day with clear blue skies, my heart is heavy with the loss of my grandma. Nothing can compare to the pain of not seeing her every day. Honestly, it's been a cynical summer full of twisted nightmares and buckets of tears.

Zola sighs, then lays her head on my shoulder. "I want you to be happy again, Lou."

"I am." I clear the emotions clogging my throat. "Well, I will be. Eventually."

She faces me and holds both my cheeks between her palms. "We all miss Ouma. And she misses you too. I forgot to ask, have you found her cottage yet?"

Even with the magical spell of reading inhumanly fast, I've barely made a dent in my research. Ouma's missing cottage seems impossible to find. Not a single instance has been recorded of a building moving on its own after its owner dies.

Next to me, Zola quietly draws a design in the sand with her finger. My art is pottery, but hers is painting the tiniest, most detailed designs on the teacups I create. Her skills are meant to be seen across the planet, not trapped in Calypsa, where only tourists can witness her talent.

"That's beautiful." I angle my head to get a better view.

"This is a basic sketch of a bird, Lou. You can find charm in anything." She snorts and wipes her drawing away.

"Are you still thinking of that internship offer? London would be lucky to have you."

"I can't leave. You need me here."

"Zola!" I scold her like Ouma once did.

"Alouououou!"

"I'm serious. Quaint Brush needs your decision by September, right?"

She doesn't meet my eye. "Come on. Let's start your b-day! First round is on me!"

I can't help but laugh as she tugs me to my feet. "Wait, Zo, we're meeting Marquis first, remember?"

"Can't your stupid brother wait till tomorrow?"

"He flies back to Sydney tomorrow to give a lecture. Don't look at me like that. I *have* to see him. I mean, I *want* to see him. I do."

"But he's sooo dramatic."

"Hey!" I slap her shoulder softly. "He's simply a bit ... theatrical."

She rolls her eyes and takes my hand, and we stroll towards Moe's Cauldron above us on the pier, our favorite spot for breakfast. I release a giant breath and stare at the clear sky. Divine beauty stares back, luminous and refreshing.

Fortunately, most of the tourists don't know about this local diner and I hope it stays that way. Above, a few fishermen cast their lines over the edge of the pier. Colorful vines climb the rustic wooden columns by the bar, adding vibrant splashes of flowers against the backdrop of the vast ocean.

"Mighty Crone! Look!" Zola points. "There are dolphins!"

I run forward, careful to keep dry. The scars along my back are a reminder of the dangers lurking in the depths.

"Where?" I bump into her by accident. "I don't see them."

"Right there." She points to the spot where they leap.

Dolphins have always been one of my signs of good

fortune to come. Once, when I was a kid, Ouma and I saw an entire pod, complete with calves. What part of my life could this fortune be related to? Maybe my research will finally produce the answers I've been seeking.

"Hey, birthday girl!" Marquis shouts from above. "Get your butt up here!"

My big brother leans over the edge of the pier, waving like a complete dork. Of course he'd wear a plaid bowtie to the beach, with only a matching speedo. I doubt his husband will ever let him forget this look.

"Oh my goddess!" Zola hops chaotically. "Do you *see* him?"

"Unfortunately."

"What? He's sooo hot. I mean, look at him!" Zola squawks and points.

"Huh? My brother? He's a married gay man. Are you high?" I glance between Marquis and Zola.

"Not your stupid brother!" Zola squeals. "Jacob Talksihnn is standing right next to him!"

"Who?"

"The Mackin' Master! National champion in 2019!"

"You know I don't follow surfing."

Zola shakes me like she's out of her mind. "Lou! Listen to me. That white guy with blond hair is Jacob Talksihnn. Surfing legend. Was the best in the world until ... Well, that doesn't matter. And he's standing right next to your brother."

I scan the tall, fit man, and a few puzzle pieces click into place. A few months ago, Marquis had mentioned a friend, Jake, visiting town. This must be him. Since my brother has lived in Sydney for the last decade, I haven't met many of his friends.

I've never been interested in jocks, but holy mother of

the moons, this Jacob guy has a nice body. In fact, I've never been attracted to blondes either, so my reaction is more than a little strange.

Jake's—or Jacob's—blond hair is pulled into a wet bun, dripping droplets down his temple. He's ridiculously tan, as if he lives outside, but his complexion is nowhere near as dark as my and Zola's brown skin. The *surfing legend* lifts a hand to wave as bright camera flashes burst to life.

"Jake! Turn this way!" one paparazzi shouts.

"Jacob! Look over here!"

"How was the water today?"

"Have you spoken with Nella since the scandal broke?"

"What are your comments about her quote in Wave Magazine?"

I meet Zola's eyes, guessing mine are as wide as hers. Do we leave or join them?

CHAPTER TWO

Jacob

All I want is to get away from these cameras and get some tucker. I'm bloody starvin'. I haven't eaten since yesterday at lunch. Twenty hours ago.

The flashes behind me don't help. I hate that these paparazzi have the power to lift me onto a pedestal or destroy me. How others tell my story is all that matters, whether or not it's the truth.

"For fuck's sake, we're knee-deep in shit, mate," I say to Marquis, glancing for an escape off this pier.

"Leave him be," Marquis yells, shooing them away while only wearing his bathers and bowtie. "Get out of here before I call the cops."

"Mister Talksihnn!" one journalist yells. "Did you hear Nella's most recent comment about your choice of lawyers?"

My stomach drops.

"Have you met your child yet?" Another reporter shoves the whole group forward, almost knocking into us.

I step back, unprepared to answer any questions. Though the tabloids and social media call me a playboy, I've never been publicly ambushed about it. It's all because they found out I have a child that resulted from a one-time fuck—with an exotic dancer.

I didn't even know about my kid.

The least Nella could do is tell me if my ten-year-old is a son or daughter. She's hidden the child, unwilling to talk while wanting more money for child support. My lawyers' demand for a verified paternity test is the sole proof I have of the child.

"Do you regret coming out of retirement for the RipSilver event?" a woman hollers.

"How does it feel to compete again?"

I don't dare say that I'd be happier if there was a monetary award today. Instead, I put my head down and focus on my bare feet. My trademark. If I don't have sand between my toes, it might be the end of the world.

More questions fly at me like boomerangs. I have half a mind to jump off the pier and swim with the sharks rather than deal with these mongrels any longer. Thankfully, Marquis is even taller than me and built like a rugby pro, which makes his budgie smugglers that more perfect for this chaos. I stifle a laugh at his choice of outfit, because if I laugh, the reporters could spin it to match any headline they want.

My image matters. Way too much.

A fresh breeze brushes against my cheek while waiters wisp by, balancing their trays. Fuckin' embarrassing, and louder than thunder, my stomach rumbles in hunger. Finally, someone ushers the paparazzi off the pier and out of sight. When the locals return to their meals without a second glance, Marquis pretends nothing happened. Ever since our teens, we've had each other's back—and always will.

I've got to admit the vibe is spot-on at this restaurant, especially with the ghosts swarming above the bar. Who would've guessed that North Carolina's summer air and coastal view could compare to Sydney's?

As I avoid settling onto a barstool, the salty breeze tousles my hair. "Shit, mate." I punch Marquis's shoulder and come up with an excuse to leave early. "I'm buggered. The water was agro today."

He responds with a grunt, then orders four mimosas.

"Four?" I ask while pretending to scan the menu.

Over our long friendship, I haven't withheld any secrets from Marquis, but he doesn't need to know I blew my dosh and currently live in my rental van on the beach. So, there's no chance I'm ordering anything.

"Yeah. Four." He smiles vibrantly and waves to someone behind me. "Remember, we're meeting my little sister? It's her birthday."

"Crikey, that's right," I mumble, not in the least bit interested in socializing.

It's a bit twisted that I've never met Marquis's family. Sure, I've heard about his parents' expedition to the Outback to research bugs, but he's barely mentioned his sister. All I've gathered about her are bits and pieces from their phone calls. From what I remember, she reads and collects obituaries, loves books, and can be highly superstitious. Not someone I'd likely see eye to eye with.

"Lou!" he shouts, voice rising an octave, and pushes away from the counter at hyper speed.

Before I know it, Marquis launches himself forward, arms out wide like a crazed kangaroo ready to attack. I almost choke from surprise.

"Hey! Nice Speedo." A voice rings out from behind him, soft and sweet like a bird's song.

When he finally moves from blocking my view, two women face us, both Black. The shorter, curvier woman's face resembles Marquis's, only she has a cute button nose. She has long, curly hair that falls to her waist.

"You're dirty thirty! I'm buying all your margs later." Marquis bumps into my stool, then slaps my back. "Don't be rude, Jake. This is Lou, my little sister. Lou, meet Jake from Down Under."

"G'day, mate, how ya goin'?"

As I scan her black dress with bits of pink around the edges, my attention drops to her feet—bare, like me. I lift one foot and wiggle it at her awkwardly. She does the same with a cute smile until our big toes touch in greeting.

"Weirdos," her taller friend says.

"And what's your name?" I face the one with a ballerina figure.

"Don't mind me. *This* is the birthday girl," she says, pushing Marquis's sister towards me. "Alouette."

Alouette. Not a name I could easily forget. It rolls off my tongue like a song as I repeat it, "Alouette."

She studies me with an intensity I'm not used to, like she's digging for a secret I didn't know I'd buried.

I clear my throat. "I bet you don't want a stranger to spoil your party, so I should head out."

"Oh, that accent!" The tall one claps her hands together and blocks my path for the exit. "I can't get over it. So sexy. Say something Australian!"

"Uh, we both speak English."

Next to her, Alouette bites her lip to keep from laughing, but she doesn't save me from this catastrophe. In fact, she gives a little gesture as if welcoming me to take the stage. Fine. I'll play their game before I head out.

"Uh, okay, how about ... put some snags on the barbie."

Not even a hint of a smile crosses Alouette's face as she silently shakes her head.

"Lou, I saved y'all two stools." Marquis's southern accent makes a rare appearance.

Lou? The nickname doesn't fully suit her. She seems fancier than that. Not that I'm sticking around to chat about her deepest desires and darkest secrets because I need to head to the Fuzer's Sanctuary soon.

This month, my spell stocks extra food whenever I'm at the homeless shelter. This way, not only does it look like I'm helping a charitable organization, but I get free food. No one's going to stop a prior Olympian medalist from stealing a sandwich or two when I volunteer most of my non-working hours at their center.

The shelter's most heartbreaking aspect is that most Fuzers there have lost their magical abilities—either through curses, genetic illness, or bans. When magic is taken, there's usually a rapid decline in mental health and cognitive function. I couldn't imagine losing my core identity.

"Well, I'm gonna shoot through. Happy birthday." I nod to Alouette, who is much too pretty to be a rellie of Marquis.

"No, no, you must stay!" The tall one yanks on my arm.

I pull away immediately.

"Woah, sorry." She gapes, dropping her hand.

I gulp and my gaze lands on Alouette again. Something in her knowing expression sees right through me like I'm water myself.

"Yeah, come on, Jake, stay a while," Marquis adds. "We need to catch up anyways. I fly out tomorrow."

My gaze stays on Alouette's, as if I'm waiting for her permission to leave. Maybe I am.

A slight twitch tugs at the corner of her lips. What does her true smile look like? She nods and kicks my stool out for me to sit.

Hesitantly, her lips part. "Yeah, stay. Call it my birthday gift. I could use a change of pace from these two. All Zola and Marquis do is bicker."

"That's not true," Zola exclaims at the same time as Marquis says, "Yeah, that shit tends to happen."

I hold Alouette's dark brown eyes for a few moments too long. Their depths have entranced me like they hold stories I immediately want to hear. It's not every day I have this reaction.

I refuse to sit. "So, you're both Fuzers?"

The girls nod. Zola sips her mimosa as Alouette inspects hers like it has a story to tell. When she looks up at me, there's a twinkle in her eyes.

"You're a Fuzer too?" Alouette asks.

Suddenly, I realize why she's acting differently than most people.

"You don't know who I am, do you?" I ask.

"Nope." Her fingertip glides around the rim of her glass, collecting all the sugar, then she sucks it off with an audible *pop*.

Immediately, I get a stiffy. Nope. No no no. Attraction is not an option. Bloody hell. What is wrong with me? I stand and head inside the restaurant so quickly, I give everyone whiplash.

The doors fling themselves open automagically, enchanted of course. Inside, the lively chatter echoes off the walls. The smell of food is torture to all my senses. So hungry. I try not to stare at each customers' plates. Ugh, my mouth is watering.

As I pass the kitchen, a dirty plate sits at the corner of a counter. I glance around to make sure no one's watching, then grab a few bites, shoving them into my mouth. They're soggy, but I don't give a shit. I snatch a few more, then duck around the corner into the dunny.

Empty. Good. I stare at myself in the mirror and rub a hand down my face. Surprisingly, there aren't bags under my eyes. I shake my head and snap myself back into the situation. I'll leave now and text Marquis that I'm sick. It's only a mile to the shelter, and it doesn't close until eight. If I run, I'll make it in time for the last scraps of breakfast.

The bathroom door soars open, slamming against the wall.

"Holy Abyss, these doors have attitude." Marquis laughs as he enters. After one look at me, he stops cold. "You okay, man?"

"Bloody oath, I'm good."

The intense scrutiny of his gaze from head to toe makes me squirm.

"You look guilty as sin. Why'd you run off?" He joins me at the sink, watching me in the mirror.

"Nothing, mate. I'm gonna head out."

He's quiet for far too long, an accusation lying on the tip of his tongue.

"I'm not buying it. You're leaving 'cuz you like her."

"Bro!"

"I knew it. You're into her and don't want to be tempted!"

Heat spreads across my body and a tingle zings in my stomach. Maybe it's more than hunger affecting my body.

"Nah, she's your sister, I'd never—"

"Woah, woah, woah." Marquis waves his hands and his easy-going smile vanishes. "I meant Zola! Oh, my goddess, you're into Lou? Nope. Not okay, man, it'll never happen."

He's right. Even though I haven't had sex since I found out I have a child, I'm not willing to sleep with another woman until I can meet my kid and figure all this shit out.

"Pull ya head in, mate." I raise both hands in surrender. "Don't be a drongo."

"Who you calling a drongo?" His eyebrows furrow together in the way I've only seen when he's defending me.

For the first time in our long friendship, Marquis stands offensively against me, ready for a fight. Even his fists are curled at his side, tight and threatening. I'm shocked; this is a side of him I've been fortunate enough to never experience. And his mood shifted so abruptly that I can barely process the change.

"I'm out," I say.

"Nah, you're staying. The only reason you'd leave is if you feel guilty about something. But you won't ever pursue Lou, and you definitely aren't attracted to her. AT ALL. Which means you're staying. Am I right?"

I return his stare without making a sound. This is foreign territory for both of us.

"Great. Well, now that's settled. I'm gonna take a piss," he says and strides away. "I'll see ya out there."

Not wasting a moment, I let the door swing open for me and I hustle out. In the lobby, a bachelorette party surrounds me, and I'm momentarily assaulted by roaming hands with "oohs" and "aahs" cooing from each woman. It's like that terrible night, years ago, all over again.

My heart rams harder than a rough current, and I need a breath of fresh air. I stumble outside onto the front porch and into the parking lot. I bend over, put both hands on my knees and suck in a giant inhale. It's useless. My vision clouds over anyways.

I was twenty-one years old, at my first strip club, surrounded by my buddies who were all laughing, tossing cash onstage. Since I was the only endorsed athlete among us, I didn't drink. But they were all legless within the hour.

A woman with a ruby red wig approached me and straddled my lap. She whispered something in my ear, but the music pounded too loud to hear. Instead of replying, I nodded, which led her to believe I wanted a dance. Some raw animal energy possessed me that night. Our lips tangled together, and she eventually led me away from my friends. Her freckles were the feature that captivated me. They made me believe I could trust someone who looked so sweet. But I was naïve. Appearances certainly deceive.

It started as simple fun in the back room, charmed with floating chandeliers and sex toys. Her hands and body took us to another level, and I ended up fucking her like my life depended on it, exploding inside her without a condom. Never had I been so reckless, so stupid.

"You okay, Jacob?"

My eyes snap open and I stand straight, too fast. Dizzy. The world zooms in and out of focus. "Alouette?"

Someone braces me as I sway.

"Woah, you're turning paler than that ghost," she says, but her voice sounds far away.

"I think I'm gonna pass out."

"What's wrong?"

"I'm okay," I say. "Just hungry."

My knees give out and I sink to the concrete.

"Do you have a food allergy?"

"No, nothing."

"When did you last eat?"

Unsure if I respond, I'm immediately grateful when she presses something between my lips.

"It's a protein bar. Open up."

Eyes trained on her, I bite down and let the granola and chocolate settle on my tongue. The mixed consistency is hard to chew when my jaw has decided to malfunction, but her soft persuasion convinces me to swallow.

"That's right. Almost done." She breaks off another small piece and eases it between my lips. "Let's get you home. I'll call a driver."

She helps me stand then supports me since my feet feel like lead.

"Woah, you're heavy." She taps on her phone a kilometer a minute. "I need the address of the hotel you're staying at. Where to?"

"Don't have an address."

The way her brows pinch together might be the most adorable feature I've seen on any human face. Unfortunately, that's when my knees decide to buckle again.

"Okay, okay, easy there, big guy. I'll take you to my place."

CHAPTER THREE

Alouette

The ghosts in the parking lot looked more alive than Jacob, and I wondered why he almost fainted. Since he wasn't coherent enough to give me an address, I had no choice but to bring him home.

If Jacob didn't look so weak, it'd be quite comical to watch the staff carry his six-foot ass upstairs to a spare room. Honestly, it'd be pointless to offer to help since he weighs fifty pounds more than me.

Footsteps thunder down the hall until Zola arrives by my side. With a curious tilt of her head, she joins me in watching the three centaurs support Jacob to the second floor.

"This is a strange turn of events," Zola says. "What happened?"

"I dunno. He almost passed out. He was super pale, but when I gave him food, some of the color returned to his face. The entire car ride he sat with his forehead pressed against the window like all the energy had been sucked out of him."

"So ... no birthday breakfast?"

I sigh and head towards my studio. "Honestly, you know I'd rather stay home. Marquis is the one with the big celebration ideas and who dragged me out," I say, checking behind her. "Where is he anyways? Parking the car?"

"Oh, no. He made some new friends and decided to meet us later for drinks."

We enter my favorite room of my parents' estate—my pottery studio. Through the tall windows, morning light streams in, casting long shadows across the wooden worktables. The earthy scent of clay and glazes fills my lungs with each deep breath, even as the stress-inducing whiteboard on the far wall catches my eye; its numbers a reminder of the thirty pieces still needed by Friday.

Though, it's not duty that forces me here on my birthday. Even if Jacob hadn't needed my help, I would've made some excuse to return home. His dilemma happened to give me the perfect excuse to hibernate in my safe space.

I walk to my usual spot, my footsteps echoing, and tie on my worn canvas apron. The phone in my pocket buzzes with another message—Marquis, wondering where I went. Truth is, celebrating today doesn't feel right without Ouma. Last year, I hadn't known it was my final birthday with her. I should've saved the voicemail when she called at exactly eight AM, her voice crackling through the phone in excitement for her surprise. Will the heaviness in my heart ever leave?

Beside me, Zola moves with quiet grace, humming as she heads to the shelves lined with finished teacups and teapots waiting to be painted. She tests each paintbrush against her palm, her dark curls pulled back in a messy bun, which tells me she's ready and willing to work by my side all day if needed. I'm very glad she isn't asking questions about why I've hauled a possibly anemic stranger to my home.

Turning to my own task, the wire tools and wooden ribs from my kit find their precise places on the splash pan around my wheel. Cool and promising, the clay feels alive against my palms as it emerges from its plastic wrapping. After patting it into a rough ball, the wedging begins—push, fold, quarter turn, repeat. The motions mirror Ouma's hands kneading bread dough on Sundays, her wedding ring catching sunlight as she worked. What I'd give to taste her delicious treats again.

From the glazing station, Zola's voice drifts over. "Should I try that new flower pattern I showed you?" she asks, already mixing colors on her palette. "If I can finish six pieces today, we might actually get ahead of schedule." A pause, then softer: "Though we could always take a long lunch break, you know. It's not every day my best friend turns thirty."

"Nah, let's just stay home," I pause. "Please."

"Whatever you want, babe," Zola says, then turns on some music from her phone.

Muscle memory kicks in as I center the clay on my wheel. The date looms in my mind, burdened with heaviness I don't want to articulate. Our work session isn't as fluid as usual, but it's not because of the pressure of production quotas and deadlines.

After dipping my hands in the cool water, I pull up the walls that will become my teacup—the first of many needed to satisfy the growing stack of orders. My fingers curve to create the lip that transforms a simple piece into art.

"So, you think the Mackin' Master is hot?" Zola asks.

"Who?"

"Don't act stupid," she says. "We're not doing that game today."

"I mean, he was only third in line for the cover of Wave Magazine. Plus, he's definitely not my type."

"Your type needs to change. Every guy you've dated walks all over you and takes advantage of how sweet you are."

I snort in response. "Sweet? Since when have you thought of me as sweet? Have you forgotten a certain pillow fight a few nights ago when you called me a stubborn rat-bitch because I wouldn't share my chocolate with you?"

"I said what I said." She smiles, while nodding along to the beat of the song. "You're a chocolate whore, the end. It's quite simple, so you should accept it."

"But, I bet Jacob would be the kind of boyfriend to buy his girl all the chocolate in the world and not ask for a single bite," Zola says with a dreamy sigh. "And when you have a little smudge leftover in the corner of your lip, I bet he'd slowly reach over and swipe it away, then lick his finger clean with a devilish, suggestive look. You know the one I'm talking 'bout, right?"

"Zola, no one ever knows what you're talking about. Now be quiet so I can focus."

"Oh, my goddess! I knew it!" She throws her paintbrush down and storms over, pointing a finger in my face. "You DO think he's hot. Let's go upstairs and ask if he's single."

I yank her wrist down, forcing her to plop on the stool next to me before she can run off. "As birthday queen, I forbid that. Now look at this and tell me if we should make the next set this size or bigger."

After a second pause, Zola smashes her hand down over my clay to flatten the teacup.

"Hey!"

"I will continue to support you during this rough patch, Lou, but as your BFF, I will never stop pushing you towards joy." Zola tucks some of my wild hair behind my ear. "You're stuck, baby boo. Ouma wouldn't want you drowning like this. I know you miss her, but you've gotta find some sort of life again, okay? It doesn't have to be today, or tomorrow, but find something, anything, that's outside this room and just try. Please? Promise me?"

"Yeah, okay ..." I glance at my smushed pottery. "You didn't have to kill it, though."

"Forget the stupid clay. You're a pottery wizard and can fix that in one second. Listen to me." Zola turns my chair to face her, the legs screeching against the floor. "Every soul alive knows you're hard working and intelligent and dedicated to your pottery, but I need YOU to know that you're also fuckalicious, and fan-fuckin-tastic and all the things your Ouma would yell at me for saying."

I laugh and feel hot tears pooling.

Pulling me up, Zola starts moving my arms as she sways her hips rhythmically. "You didn't promise me. So, your punishment is dancing with me."

"Zola ... quit it," I say, mid-laugh, letting her flail my arms about chaotically. "You're gonna dislocate my shoulder, then who will make all the teacups?"

"Promise me! Promise me you'll leave this studio at some point in the next fifty thousand years!" Zola starts singing her commands in tune with the melody. "Prooooomiiiiiiise meeeeeeeeeee!"

"Okay, okay!" I pull my arms away. "I promise, on this day, in August of 2025 that you have my word."

"That you'll do … what exactly?"

I huff in exasperation. "That I'll … start living again."

"Oooooh, coco-bitch! I couldn't have said it better myself!" She twirls around, then starts twerking. "You've died. That's what happened. When Ouma died, you did too!" she shouts, then jumps on one of the tables, with her hands in the air. "Come back to life, Lou!"

"Okay, I will. Now get down before Mariah and Chad run in here thinking there's some emergency."

Zola hops off the table with a grumpy groan. "Or maybe you want a different special someone to come check on you?"

"I don't know what you're talking about," I say, gathering the clay into a pile again. "Now, get back to work. My new life starts tomorrow."

"Tomorrow." She nods and slips back into her chair.

Tomorrow. Zola's right. I can still grieve Ouma without my entire personality revolving around wallowing in this weight. Tomorrow. Yes, when I wake up, I'll turn a new page, to start a fresh year as a thirty-year-old. Tomorrow.

CHAPTER FOUR

Alouette

The next morning, I wake to the pleasant sound of birds chirping outside my window. My favorite raven, Ms. Grim, pecks her beak at her back to groom. I swear she tells me that I slept like a corpse. I've never chosen a spell to speak to animals, but I'd bet my favorite pottery wheel that I accurately guess what birds are thinking most of the time. It's like we speak the same language.

Morning sun peeks through my curtains onto my bed. Though nothing in my parents' mansion truly feels like mine. I've been lucky enough to live here rent free for years while they explore different countries in search of rare bugs. Never in that time have I felt any ownership of this space. They're the ones who selected the high-end fabric and furniture that don't match my taste.

I guess the art studio is my safe space here. Mom and Dad have never set foot inside it. Everything in there belongs to me. In a house fire, I'd save the first teacup I created after going into business with Zola. The thought of her makes me grope around for my phone under my pillow. Twenty missed texts from her.

> Tell me you & the surfer hooked up?

> I need deets now. Are Aussie's bigger down under? Hahahahha. do they have wild sex tricks inspired by wallabees?????

> Omg you already have some dirty nickname for him. Did you shout out "wallabee!" when he gave you a massive O

I throw the phone on my blanket and stare at the newly dusted dreamcatcher. Not that it should be a surprise, since the staff keep this place as tidy as the Nkosi museum.

As a kid, I barely spent any time in this house, except for when my parents were in town for a conference. They'd drag me along and brag about how my quiet introspection made me well suited to be a stellar scientist. Only Ouma understood my artsy side. She never roped me into fundraisers or black-tie events. I may never know if she fully understood me because we shared the magical gene or if was something else.

In her cottage, where I was raised, plants grow at an outstanding rate, curling in through the windows and wrapping around the lamps and leg chairs. I loved Tuesdays especially because it was when the sunflowers often leaned towards me like I exuded light. A palette of cozy grays, creams, and greens of every shade decorates my missing home, the one I've spent day and night trying to find. It's where the palm trees sing, and dragonflies are royalty—if only I could find the damned place. Which is why I need to get back to the library to continue my research.

Every free hour I've had here has been spent researching how a house can vanish.

Peeking out the window, I take in the greens of the trees, then zip my attention to the fountain where all the birds usually gather. I gasp. A shirtless man is upside down, completing a Pincha Mayurasana stance on a yoga mat.

Not just any man.

Jacob.

Gravity moves his shorts to expose more of his toned quads. I should look away. Should move from the window. But one little glimpse won't hurt anything. He's clearly off limits, as Marquis's friend.

Hidden from view, I scan the dips and curves of his muscles and the jagged scars along his legs. I bet all my tarot decks he earned those while surfing. There's beauty in his scars, though, a map of passion etched into his skin.

Behind him, lush foliage creates a tapestry of green, punctuated by bursts of August blooms that dance in the breeze. At the garden's heart, the fountain gently gurgles, its water harmonizing with birdsong.

A blackbird lands on Jacob's foot, which rocks his balance, and he rolls to the mat. Another bird lands on his butt. I spurt out a laugh, then cover my mouth, but it's too late. Jacob's attention snaps up and our eyes meet. I duck low under the windowsill.

"Damn it!" I whisper and slap the pillow.

I squirm flat on my bed like a worm until I topple over the side to crawl across the floor. There's no chance in Abyss I'm letting him see me again. As fast as possible, I grab fresh clothes, flummoxed that everything is organized differently than usual. It's not even laundry day. Did Mariah hire someone new to help her?

Fumbling with my favorite black sundress with the bubblegum-colored skulls, I manage to slip it on without breaking a leg. If I hurry to the library, I can act as if I've been in there for hours. I rush past the insects preserved in jars full of amber fluid, and down the hallway full of framed moths and butterflies pinned on display.

Since I'd never dare to offend a centaur, I grab a cinnamon roll as I zoom past the kitchen and holler, "Thanks, Chad!"

"No problem, sugar!"

As I step into the home library, I am enveloped in a cocoon of knowledge and imagination. The earthy scent of paper and leather is as comforting as the glow of fireflies that light the towering shelves.

Sunlight paints a golden hue over Mom and Dad's wooden furniture. Whispers of stories trying to escape their pages fill the air in here. Each book promises a sort of adventure or insight I can experience. The library is my second favorite room of the house after my studio.

Unique vases sit on the mantle, all done by famous ceramicists that I admire. The only object in here that haunts me is the empty frame that has my name engraved underneath. Unlike Marquis's, mine isn't full of a prestigious certificate or title. It's as empty as a gnome's brain. Apparently, what I've accomplished thus far hasn't earned a spot in my framed space yet.

Every tourist who hears my last name at the pottery shop stops me to ask a thousand questions. If it were up to me, I'd ignore all the inquisitions about my lineage of scholars who have won countless scientific awards. Ouma, known as Doctor Tariji Nkosi, had published dozens of international journal articles of her finds as an entomologist. Unlike my parents, who bonded over fossils, I've always disliked creepy crawlies. I've avoided holiday gatherings since the family discussions about butterflies, leaving me to hide in the corner. Even Marquis is obsessed with bugs. How thrilling.

I sink into my favorite reading chair and scoop up a book. I'd already written a note that shows: *'leprechauns deal in trades ... often enjoy witnessing worst fears... Last resort is to ask a leprechaun for assistance ...?'*

That sounds like a terrible idea. I pick up a nearby book called *Of Magic Buildings and their Ghosts.'* Half the page is highlighted, so that won't be helpful if I can't narrow down the details. I push the book against my forehead in defeat and groan like a dying animal.

"Is the story *that* bad?"

I throw the book across the room at the source of the deep voice. "Holy Goblet!" I shriek. "You scared me."

I dip out of the chair to collect it at the same time as Jacob moves toward me. I brace myself for impact but what I expect to happen is not the outcome. Instead of our skulls crunching together, somehow my body lands in Jacob's arms, which creates the most confusing three seconds of my life.

"What are you–?!" I yell.

"Woah! You okay? I didn't mean to grab ya there, sorry."

"I'm fine. You can let me go. Please."

"Right, right. Sorry, again. I would never want to touch your tits ... well, I mean they're nice ..." He scrunches his nose and I wonder if he's aware of how distracting the small movement is.

His face turns so red that I pity the man for a second. I

try to ease the tension with the only joke I can think of. "Think fast ... why should you never race against cats?"

"What are ya talkin' 'bout? That came out of nowhere," he says, but because of his grin I continue.

"Cuz there's always one cheat-ah," I say, feeling my face flush warm. "Um ... when I'm nervous I may or may not make weird cat puns."

His smile is a tiny bit crooked, but gorgeous all the same. One meant for the front of a magazine—not that I've stalked him on social media to discover he's been on the cover of no less than twelve over his career. That one picture of him in the navy swimsuit left little to the imagination.

He points to the book. "Marquis once told me ya like thrillers?"

"Yeah, horrors too. But this isn't a fiction. I'm doing research. I've been in here all morning, in this chair, the whole time. Reading since dawn."

Jacob flashes another devastating smile. I swear yesterday his eyes were a light green, but today they look more blue. There's a towel wrapped around his neck, but his hair is wet and clean, not full of sweat.

"Did you shower?" I ask.

"No, I ran through the garden sprinkler." He runs the towel over his loose hair. "The one by your ... window."

I swallow the rock sized ball of guilt in my throat.

"You need a ride home. I'll get Raphael to drive you."

"I can't skip brekky!" Jacob moves with the grace of someone who is accustomed to rolling with the waves, shifting forms to shape what life throws his way. He settles into the chair next to me and picks up a book.

"Ah, well, you can head to the kitchen and Chad will feed you on your way out." I bury my nose in the book. "It may be a better idea to call your *people* to pick you up. I wouldn't want to be accused of kidnapping a celebrity."

"You don't like me much, do you?"

I peek around the binding, noticing his book is upside down. "I trust Marquis's judgment. That doesn't mean I want paparazzi showing up in my garden to snap pics of yoga poses."

He bolts upright, a lively smile on his face. "I *knew* you were watching!"

"What?" I raise the book again. "Watch who? I mean … what?"

"Yeah, okay, I'll let this one slide."

There's a knock on the door and Chad enters the library with two plates on his tray. "Hungry, Lou?"

"Thank you, Chad. I appreciate you. Mister Talksihnn is taking his to go, isn't that right?" I glare in Jacob's direction, hoping he doesn't complicate things, or the staff will talk.

"And refuse your hospitality? I'd be rude to ignore that sanger with avos."

"I didn't understand half of that. You're gonna have to Americanize your words."

Silence, broken only by cuckoo clocks, fills our mealtime among the bookshelves. The cinnamon roll melts on my tongue like a dream, but I try not to devour it in front of a man who has a type of surfboard named after him. Jacob saves no manners for my benefit and finishes his plate before I've had four bites.

"So, I have hours before teaching my first lesson. What're we researchin'?" he asks.

"We?"

"Yeah, I'll 'av a go. Beach bums can add the ABCs too."

My body is more tense than it should be. I focus on relaxing my shoulders and loosening my grip on my fork.

"I have it covered. What lesson are you going to? More yoga?"

His eyes flash with deviousness, and a smirk plays on his lips this time. "Since I'm retired, I'm a surfing instructor now. The little ankle biters sure love the water. I'm stoked 'bout this one boy who's rippin'. He can already do a cutback."

Is he patient with his students or strict? What if a kid is afraid of the water? Does he ease them into it or force them to conquer their fear head on?

He turns the page of a book, pretending to read, though it's still upside down. With a huff, I lean over and flip it the correct way. His cheeks flush a sweet shade of coral that matches the skulls on my dress.

"Well, I better get back to work." I glance towards the door and wait for him to leave.

"Alright, I can take a hint, but … please don't tell Marquis I was here. Not that it matters."

I raise a hand to stop him. "Don't worry about it."

He still hasn't made any move to leave and looks quite comfortable in his chair. If he is still recovering, the least I could do to let his body heal is let him stay in my air-conditioned house until he goes to work. Even though my magical spell enables me to read at an inhuman pace, I could use help.

"Fine. Skim these for anything mentioning 'bewitched cottages' or 'charmed homes', then highlight the paragraph."

He starts immediately, serious and fully concentrated.

After I've read the same page for the third time, I squeeze my eyes shut. Sure, Jacob is what some people would consider attractive, but that doesn't mean my brain needs to obsess over questions like whether he sleeps on his side or stomach? Because that only makes me picture him in bed, which is a terrible path to tread.

"*Why* are we researchin'?" he asks casually.

"I need to find my grandma's cottage. After she died recently, it ... moved."

"Fuck me dead! You're lying!"

"Am not. It's like the house gained legs and walked away during her funeral, and I have to find it as soon as possible."

"Why do you care about the cottage if you have this place?"

CHAPTER FIVE

Jacob

"*Why* I'm searching isn't your business." Alouette's soft voice doesn't match the fire in her eyes. It's like she's two pieces split in half, each battling to take the main stage. Is she a bookish mouse or an inferno?

She certainly senses my focus on her because she keeps biting her lip.

"Getting a good look?" she asks sarcastically.

I scan my attention to where framed bugs sit like trophies on a bookcase, up to where ghosts hover above the top shelf of the library. Somehow, the enchantments here have magically pushed new vocabulary words into my conscious. Fancy terms like risible, blithesome, rhapsodic, and ebullient bob around like floating buoys in my mind. Strange. There must be more residual magic built up in Calypsa than anywhere I've ever traveled. Wonder why.

Anyone with eyes can see that Alouette's mansion is bonkers. I woke early this morning to explore, and the chef gave me some snacks. Chad seemed thrilled to cook something different for once. I've eaten internationally since I was seventeen, so I like cuisine from around the globe and will try anything at least once. Although, these days, I'm just grateful for a full stomach because budgeting hasn't been easy. After sending money to Nella, the rest of my savings went to the PR reps, social media experts, and lawyers. To make ends meet, I even sold my collection of sunnies. That broke my bloody heart.

Since I don't have enough money saved, my sister has been adamant to pay for a private investigator service. It's my last option for learning about my kid. Since she's in the military, my sister can access databases and methods to find anyone, regardless of whether they want to be found, so I trust her intuition. Whenever she sends me an address, that's my next stop.

"Hurry, tell me your biggest fear," Alouette demands.

"What?"

"This book won't open until you answer." She caresses its spine in a rhythmic motion.

"Uh ... crowded places?" My body tenses at the thought.

"No, it's not accepting that," her words spit out louder. "Hurry, there must be something else you're more afraid of?"

"Why *my* fears? Can't you give it your own?"

"It's asking for yours!"

"Uh ... uh ... I don't know!"

"Please! I desperately *need* this book."

I swallow the nervous lump in my throat, squeeze my eyes shut and blurt out, "Never meeting my child!"

As we lock eyes, her book opens. She stares up at me, jaw dropped. "You have a kid?"

I run a hand through my hair, tugging at the roots. "Crickey, you don't hang out on social, huh? Haven't you heard any stories about Nella Franklin?"

"Nope. You wanna tell me *your* side?"

"My side?"

"Yeah, I bet you're tired of the world believing whatever's been posted."

Wow. She's giving me the chance to speak, and she doesn't have a hint of judgment on her face. I've pictured this moment a thousand times, and I'm ready to deliver my prepared speech. I never imagined actually saying it to anyone because no one cared about the truth.

"Okay," I say, taking a steadying breath as I move closer, waiting for a sign that she doesn't want to know. But as I lower myself to the couch and sit on the edge of the seat, I gather my thoughts. "I was young." I gulp. "Twenty-one. It only happened once. In Indo during a comp. I never met Nella before that night and haven't seen her since. Things got out of hand quickly ... I swear she didn't tell me she was pregnant. There's a solid chance that if Nella walked by on the street, I wouldn't even recognize her."

"I can see that hurts you."

"If I can't remember the woman I made a baby with, how would I recognize my only child? I would've been there this whole time. I would've tried to work somethin' out. But I didn't learn 'bout the kid 'til recently. At first, I thought it was a scam so I got the lawyer involved, but Nella didn't back down, kept commentin' online and eventually she got a reporter to tell her story, saying I've refused to help raise our child. But I didn't know!"

I stop myself as heat rushes to my cheeks. "The stories they ran about me ... they ruined my career. Sponsors dropped me. No one wanted my name attached to their brand. Competitions banned me. There's a word Americans use—canceled. That was me."

"That sounds so hard."

"I've only talked to Nella through lawyers," I say, wanting to hide my face from her, but force myself to look into her eyes.

"How do you even know you're the father?"

"That was the first step. Lawyer ordered three paternity tests done at three different labs to be sure, but other than knowing I am the father, I have zero other information. Nella won't tell me anythin'. I don't know if it's a boy or girl, their name, or what they're interested in. The only thing my lawyers have been able to confirm is they live in one of the Carolinas, which is why I moved here. I've begged Nella to meet, but she refused. So, my sister gave me money to hire a PI."

"Where is this PI?"

"Thornwitch Isle."

She turns towards her cuppa and takes a long sip, deep in thought.

"Can we ... can we not talk 'bout this anymore right now?" I ask quietly, finally dropping my gaze.

"Yeah, of course," Alouette says, nodding. "Sounds like you're close to your sister. She the only sibling you got?"

"Nah, I have nine sisters and they live all 'round the world. We've traveled my whole life. I bet I could fool ya with any accent."

Her hands fiddle with her black dress. It's a bit adorable how she runs her fingertips up and down. What color knickers does she wear? Fuck, I shake my head to erase the thought.

"Portuguese," she says with a challenge.

"Vegemite is nasty," I say with a Portuguese accent.

"Woah! That's cool. I've never traveled. Never even been on a plane."

"Seriously? Where'd ya most want to see?"

"Egypt. But I bet you've been there? Or your sisters? Wait, did you say you have nine?" Alouette leans back against the desk and crosses her arms.

"Ah, yes. Full sisters, half- sisters, stepsisters, and our pet turtle of course … she counts." I salute Alouette awkwardly. I don't even know why I did that. "Mom is American and Dad is Australian. They split when I was eleven. Jen and I lived with Dad. Jules and Jess lived with Mom in Portland. That fucked me up for a while.

"Mom remarried before I went pro, which gave me Ashley and Havanna, but I barely ever saw them. Then Dad and his girlfriend moved in together, but they never got married. Had three daughters. That'd be Beks, Stef, and little Mils."

She studies me longer than normal. "Can I ask how you got all your scars?"

"So, you're admitting to spying on me earlier."

"You've check out my cleavage more than enough times to make it even."

"Have not!"

"Don't lie."

"I'm a terrible liar," I say, smiling.

"That's something only a good liar would say." This time, she smiles back, adding to the glow of the room.

"I got these ones from surfin'. I wiped out. Your bro saved my life that day, but …"

I think back to senior year of high school when I skipped class to hit the water. A guy with a 'U of Sydney' t-shirt was the only other one on the beach early.

"Current took me under. Marquis saved me. End of story."

For some reason, I worry about her response. Does she view me as weak now knowing that my own sport almost killed me. Luckily, I don't have to find out yet since my phone buzzes in my pocket. I half slide it out and glare at my agent's name.

"G'day, Erik. how ya goin'?"

On the video screen, my Aussie friend looks tired as Abyss, with dark circles against his pale skin. "Fuckin' shite, mate. Nella's trying to charge ya with attempted kidnappin'."

"For fuck's sake?!" My stomach drops. "That's bullshit!"

"I know, I know, mate. But I had to tell ya she's already posted it all over the internet and people are gobblin' up her claims."

"Argh! This is the worst."

"Shit, ain't it?"

"What am I goin' do?"

"I'll tell ya what ya not goin' to do. Don't go online. Stay low, and don't do nuthin' stupid."

I groan and raise my arms out wide. "All I've done is work and surf."

"Doesn't matter. My bet is she saw the pic of you with that chick on the beach."

"Wait, what chick?"

"... got jealous."

"Who? I wasn't with anyone."

"That girl in the black dress. Long, curly, dark hair.

She's starin' straight at ya in the picture like a blood lovesick puppy. It's gone viral."

My eyes whip to Alouette's, where she stands silent in the middle of the library, listening.

"Wait, is that her?" Erik looks down at his watch. "Ya slept there?! Jeez, Jake, I thought you pledged no women till we figure this shit out."

I shake my head at the same time as Alouette says, "No, we're not together. He's leaving."

A beat of silence passes, then another, until Erik smiles. "She's way too beautiful for you, mate."

I hang up before he can embarrass me any further.

"I'll see ya round but I've got work to do," she says, turning away, giving me a front row seat to scars carved into her shoulder blades.

Where did she get those and when? Phantom pain scorches my skin where my own scars have haunted my nightmares. We may have more in common than I thought. Realizing I'm staring too long, I clear my throat, preparing to defend myself when my sister's message pops up with coordinates for the PI. It's not even far from here.

"Paparazzi might be outside. Stay in here, 'kay?" I slip out the door and wait a few steps before I sprint down the hall.

With any luck, I'll have that PI working for me within the hour.

After dodging the paparazzi and running three miles to the pier, I finally reach my van. Muscles screaming, I chug a bottle of water. My turtle friend, Taco, perches on my foot as I catch my breath.

"Adorable little guy," Cheyenne says.

Today, my neighbor wears an oversize rock band shirt that compliments her golden tan nicely. Cheyenne's not like the other bludgers who also live under this pier. Her water-sports business is thriving. Some people simply prefer to fall asleep to the sound of waves crashing against the shore.

"Hey. No time to chat. I need your boat. That good?" I ask.

Cheyenne leans against my bumper-sticker covered van and says, "Yeah, you can take her. But I need her back by one. A family rented her for tubing."

"Ah, perfect! I'm fuckin' rapt. You're a saint."

"I can be whatever you want, Jake. Saint or devil." She gives me a wink. "Just ask Abby."

Like me, Cheyenne thrives in a committed relationship. Other than the one night with Nella, I've always been a tie-me-down-for-life type of guy. A few wild nights with a tourist would only leave me feeling empty.

Cheyenne gives me the keys; I sprint to her boat, still in my swim trunks, trying to ignore the burning sand. The water splashes up my legs, refreshing and cold. I dive under to cool off, then climb up the ladder. I rev the engine and plug in the coordinates my sister texted me. Over the first set of waves, the boat bounces hard, but I don't slow.

The faster I go, the harder the harsh wind whips my face. Fucking love it. Pelicans soar ahead and the sun beats down on my skin, already drying me off from my dip. It would've been a perfect arvo to surf. I doubt my passion for the ocean will ever die.

A stretch of green land grows larger as I accelerate. After

waiting for this chance, there's no way I'll delay a moment longer.

I'm a nervous wreck, sweating profusely, even before the island's palm trees come into view. A few ramshackle cottages, half collapsed, line the beach, otherwise, there's only an ominous forest. Easing in the shallows, I check the depth, ready to anchor, when a shadow the size of a unicorn looms over the boat. Odd. They don't usually take to the sea. I glance up and gasp. Two people fly, hand in hand, a few meters above my head.

"Fuck! What ya doin?!"

It's Alouette and her friend. Apparently, her friend has chosen the ability to fly as her spell for the month. They glide over me as I turn off the engine. In a heartbeat, I jump off the boat and swim to shore; the waves doing half the work for me. When I emerge, I wipe off the salty ocean and march towards the women who are talking out of earshot, hands chaotically pointing to the forest.

"What's goin' on?" I glance between them.

Apparently, Alouette had time to change. She wears a purple sports bra with matching sporty shorts that fit her curves like a joey fits in a kanga's pouch. Her untamed hair is windblown, and the only reason I notice how long her eyelashes are compared to this morning is because of the guilty look she throws my way.

"I need that PI," she says. "Sorry, but after you left, I realized how much more help I need to find my Ouma's cottage."

"Ya followed me?"

"No hard feelings?" She winks—bloody winks—then waves goodbye to Zola who is already flying away.

Women. Curse them all. Serves me right for spilling a secret to someone I barely know. There's no chance the house she's searching for is more important than my child. I'm competitive in nature, and there's no way she's gonna win.

"Tell ya what ... Ya find the PI first, you can have her." I smile.

Immediately, I rush into the shrubs that scrape my shins. I'm shit outta luck for not having any shoes. Alouette hollers after me, and I hear the crunching of her steps on the leaves. But it doesn't matter cause I'm faster.

CHAPTER SIX

Alouette

I f there's one sport I excel at, it's running. Ahead, Jacob pounds across the ground, scaring any dwarves within a mile's radius. I rush past countless trees, chasing him. How can the PI live out in this mangled forest?

We sprint through a plethora of spiderwebs. Ouma would've loved to inspect every single insect here, but there's no time for that. Heart hammering, already sweating, I'm thankful the canopy of leaves above blocks the afternoon sun. I'll have to return here when the leaves turn colors soon.

With each step forward, I swear the breeze sings my name in a humming harmony. The forest buzzes with overwhelmingly beautiful raw magic, and it's been on the news that ever since we crossed into 2025, Calypsa has harbored a lot of untamed magic. It's obvious this island overflows with enchantments. I can even taste it with each breath, sweet as honey. Where is all this abundance coming from?

I slam straight into a tree. Nope. A man.

"You okay, mate?"

Hands catch me as I tumble to the ground.

"Yeah." I look straight up into those deep blue-green eyes that swirl with forbidden temptations.

Jacob winks, then without so much as an 'are you okay?' he leaps onto a massive log. That's when I notice the rushing river below and freeze. Paralyzed. I try to convince myself that rivers aren't the same as oceans. There aren't huge chunks of debris that could make me bleed out.

Jacob's halfway across the makeshift bridge already, balancing like an acrobat on steroids. I don't want to watch but I also can't look away. If he falls, there's no way I'd be brave enough to help him.

When he lands on the other bank with a loud triumphant call, both hands held in the air, I exhale the air that'd been trapped in my lungs. He weaves between more trees, leaving me alone and stranded. I guess this is it. I'll have to return empty-handed and wait by his boat. Jacob will find the PI, hire them, and find the child he's been searching for. Good for him.

Except Ouma would have hated that fear is dictating my life. Fear of the water. Fear of moving on without her. Fear of creating art. Fear of starting my own business.

I force myself to continue. On shaky legs, wobblier than ever, I step onto the hard, thick log. I can do this. I move at a snail's pace with my arms out like helicopter wings, serving as a balancing tactic.

Don't look down. Don't look down. The smell of fish and the roar of rushing water invade my senses. Don't look down.

But I do.

Through the clear water, I see something metallic. Shit.

My foot slips. Body sways sideways. I teeter over and a scream parts my lips. Strong arms envelop me.

"I got ya, little owl." Jacob scoops me up and cradles me against his chest.

My heart clenches at the nickname. Only Ouma called me that, and I adored the endearment. The phrase slipping past his lips feels right—like I've needed to hear it, only I've been waiting for someone specific to say it.

He hesitates and lowers his eyes. "Is little owl an okay nickname? Guess I should've asked."

When the log makes a cracking sound underneath us, I cling to his body tighter. Hold my breath.

"I said I fuckin' got ya," he teases, smiling, and tightens his grip around me. "The nickname? It's okay?"

I nod, forcing some ease into my voice. "Yeah. I can tolerate it ... I guess."

He moves like I'm a feather as he hops across easily. On the other side, safe and on solid ground, he gently sets me down where brittle leaves tickle my ankles. It takes all my self-restraint not to worship the earth I stand on.

"Uh, thanks."

Jacob gives me a little smirk, then points to a decaying chapel, overgrown with vines and ivy. "Think she lives in there?"

I pretend like my body isn't trembling and march forward. "Only one way to find out."

Picking up a long stick, I use it to push away foliage and thorns. A few still slice my arms, but I've never been sensitive about pain. In fact, a few days ago, I was telling Zola I want to get a tattoo soon in honor of Ouma. I haven't decided yet between a blackbird or a coffin with a rose design. Or maybe a moth.

"Alouette? I think you're in shock."

"Hmm?"

"You've been starin' at that bug for about two minutes. At first, I thought maybe your spell of the month had to do with communicatin' with insects, but then I remembered you mumbled somethin' in the library earlier about superhuman readin'." He reaches forward and plucks grass from my curls. "So, I'm guessin' you're not having a conversation with that butterfly?"

"Uh, no. Sometimes I space out. I'm, uh, working on it."

"Why? Daydreamin' is cute."

I stare at him, utterly surprised. Not once has my lack of focus been viewed as a positive trait. Throughout school, my teachers would hound me and my parents to improve my attention. No type of punishment had ever been successful in preventing my mind from wandering. Even the tiniest detail of the grain in a wooden desk could entertain me for hours. I'd trace the lines of it with my finger like it was a maze meant for ants to find an escape.

Around us, the forest is quieter than a crypt. Eerie. I glance around. It seems like even the breeze has stopped blowing. Suddenly, a blood-curling whistle pierces the air. It's unlike any bird call I've heard before.

Jacob's hand automatically grips my waist and brings me in close. His voice is a whisper as he says, "There's someone else out here."

"Obviously. We're trying to find them."

"No. Somethin' else. Somethin' dark."

Instead of letting fear overtake me, I reach out, but the chapel door swings open automagically. It creaks loudly; a sound designed for a horror movie. Damn, I love watching terrifying movies behind a fortress of pillows, a blanket over my face, the only light in the room from the screen portraying a villain about to deliver a jump scare.

Horror films were something Ouma and I watched together.

"Stay behind me." Jacob's grip drops from my waist, but he finds my hand.

As his fingers wrap around mine, a tingling shoots down my wrist and spreads over my whole body. Does he feel it too? This visceral response doesn't make sense. I shouldn't be this affected by *any* guy. And Jacob is forbidden fruit. Marquis might not like that I was interested in his best friend. It doesn't take a genius to realize he's compartmentalized us. He wouldn't want me to sully Jacob's reputation further and drag him through the mud because of my disappointing career. Jacob's suffering through more than enough drama.

I can still think he's attractive. Secretly. Without admitting it to anyone.

"Woah." Jacob's grip on my hand tightens. "What's that?"

I scan the interior of the chapel. It's cast in shadows, with anomalous light twisting in odd directions. Jacob points to a podium holding a strangely shaped art piece made of glass shards glued together. Our reflection within is disorienting and jagged, showing only part of our faces and bodies when we shift our weight.

Tools sit on a counter. A red liquid drips from the tip of a glue gun. On high alert, I wish my spell choice had been a defensive one, especially when I see other more ominous tools, from doohickeys to axes to menacing knives.

"Please tell me your magic involves fighting off bad guys," I whisper to him.

"Nope, penis extension," he deadpans.

I snort, and my free hand flies to my mouth to stifle the sound.

A sinister shadow moves across the window.

"Did you see that?" I ask.

A loud noise thumps on the roof.

"Is this place haunted?" Jacob asks.

"Yesssssssssss," says a high-pitched chilling voice.

I shudder, and all the tiny hairs on my arm rise on end.

"Where is the voice comin' from?" Jacob whispers.

Then she appears—a dowdy ghost, as transparent as the glass artwork, her tragic death accented by a tattered noose around her neck. Her sullen energy saturates the room with an oppressive weight.

"Are you the private investigator?" Jacob asks. "Ivola Steinbeck?"

"Yesssss, but you have come unprepared," she hisses. "I can ssssssssmell the rotten cash in your pocket, boy, and desire no sssssssuch payment."

"Is there something else you want?" I ask.

"Blood. I need blood. Fuzer sssssssacrifice ssssssserves as the bessssst glue for my looking glassssss."

Blood. My mind is torn in another direction, to my past, as a child caught under the surface of the ocean waves. There was so much blood in the water. Sharp edges of debris had cut and wretchedly carved my back. I could barely swim to shore. Blood had trailed after me throughout the entire struggle.

"It's all good, mate. I'll do it." Jacob steps forward.

"No, then she'll be working for *you*." I swallow the selfish feeling creeping up my throat. "I need her skills as much as you do."

Jacob's eyes narrow. "A house is more important than a kid?"

Suddenly, the door bangs against the wall, and a middle-aged man with glasses and a long gray beard runs in. He's holding out a jar full of crimson liquid sloshing around.

"Which of you is Ivola?" He glances between me and the ghost. "I have the blood payment. Please! Our top oceanographer went missing while studying an underwater storm. Can you find him?" His eyes are wild and frantic.

Ivola whooshes down to the newcomer. The breeze she creates makes Jacob's hair flutter against his cheek. A few freckles dot his face that I hadn't noticed before.

"Not the time to check me out, little owl." Jacob smirks without turning.

I realize we're still holding hands, and I yank mine away.

"Give that here." Ivola snatches the bottle in her translucent hands. "Yessss, thissss is good." She pours the blood into a bowl on the podium.

"That's it? You won't help us?" I stomp forward with half a mind to knock the bowl of blood to the ground.

"Correct. You came unprepared. Thisssss will take me a while. Come back later."

"I can't wait," both Jacob and I say simultaneously.

"Leave!" she hisses as a horrible, unearthly roar bellows from outside.

I jump and grip Jacob's arm again. Whatever howled that loudly must be larger than a giant troll.

"What is that?" I beg, heart ramming wildly, though it can't compete with the booming footsteps outside.

Boorish stomps shake the earth. Every boom increases my fear of being trampled to death. Coming here was a mistake. Another ear-splitting roar explodes outside the chapel. Trapped. I lunge across the small room and grab the axe I noticed leaning against the wall.

"Jacob ..." I stutter. "Wh-what do we do?"

He bends over until we're eye to eye and lifts my chin. "What did I say earlier, Alouette? I've got ya. Understand?"

All I can do is nod. The intensity of his eyes bears into mine, like he already knows my soul.

"Is that *your* creature out there?" Jacob flings an arm at Ivola. "Call 'im off!"

She ignores us. For a moment, I pray to Skies that we can hide in the corner of the chapel until it leaves. But with a nasty snap of Ivola's hand, our bodies are flung out the door and into the forest.

I gasp. A goliath leprechaun stomps forward. His leathery skin could repel bricks, and his heavily muscled fists could crumble boulders. We drop into a crouch position. Jacob holds one finger in front of his tightly sealed mouth to signal 'quiet.'

The axe I'm holding won't even make a dent in the leprechaun's toe. Frozen, I swallow my fear. Count to ten. Another deafening wail shakes the trees. I cover my ears and flinch. Then feel Jacob's hands, covering mine to help block out the sound. Well, shit. He's helped me three times now.

The leprechaun's feet create craters as it staggers around. We leap out of the way, and Jacob shields me with his body; as if we wouldn't both be flattened if a foot landed on us. Stupid chauvinistic gentleman. Why can't he be an asshat?

Then the leprechaun spots us. It bends over, huge hands zooming towards us like a hammer ready to pulverize.

"No! Wait! Stop!" Jacob screams. "We can give ya somethin' Ivola has never offered."

The leprechaun pauses, flops to the ground on its butt, and leans forward. "What you give?"

I see the chains for the first time, wrapped around the leprechaun's waist and extending into the forest. It'd want the same thing every human does. Every Fuzer or Typ. Man or woman. We all want freedom: to be who we want, to live without limits or expectations.

"Freedom," I say and point to his shackles.

"How?" he roars.

I exchange a glance with Jacob. He nods, encouraging me, though I have no plan.

"What's your name, big guy?" I ask.

"Kolen."

"Okay, Kolen, at the next ceremony, we can request a spell that will release you."

"Noooooo!" Kolen stands again and throws a tantrum in place. "Free me now!"

Each stomp creates a new deadly divot in the soil.

"Okay, okay, mate!" Jacob throws up both hands in surrender. "What do you want?"

"Cut chains! Now!" Kolen moves closer and closer, fists high.

Ivola appears next to us, making Jacob jump in place.

"This monsssssster is mine to control. Only I can sssssssave you from being eaten. But my favor has a cosssssst. It'll void your magic until the next ssssssseremony"—she smiles wickedly—"or you can try to outrun my leprechaun."

I wince, and Jacob cringes as Kolen charges again.

"Okay, fine," I rush out. "Hurry."

"Deal." Ivola shuts her eyes and waves her arms. *"Traslatio majikcae trolodytam!"*

Instantly, I feel a crushing blow to my chest, as if

someone ripped my heart out. I collapse to the ground, only to see Jacob's body convulse and fall next to me, his eyes wide, in shock, gasping for air.

"Oh, and one thing I forgot ... a little sssssstipulation to my asssssssistance." Ivola snickers. "Whatever you came here for ... you have to help each other find before midnight on the thirteenth, or your powers will never return. Good luck."

The last hazy detail I see is Ivola turning more solid, no longer transparent. Her features look more human than spirit. Something about the magic here is wrong. I try with all my might to keep my eyes on Jacob. But my world goes black.

CHAPTER SEVEN

Alouette

"It's gone," I say. "My magic ... it's empty. It's gone. This can't happen." My voice elevates. "Our magic wouldn't leave."

I feel as if I'm choking on something. Can't get enough oxygen. There's a tingling in my body and I'm about to puke.

"You look like you're gonna pass ouagaint," Jacob says, swaying on his feet.

My pulse skyrockets and I'm sweating, my chest feels like it's going to explode. A sudden and overwhelming sense of dread racks through me. "This doesn't make sense."

"We need ... we need to calm down," he says, panting. His hands clamp down on his head, and the veins in his neck bulge. "Everythin's gonna be okay. We'll be okay. It'll be alright."

"What! How?! Our magic is GONE!"

His eyes go wide and wild. Jacob grabs both my

shoulders and makes me stare straight at him. "Take a deep breath, Alouette. We can't freak out."

"I don't know how I'm going to live without magic." My voice is shaking. "Okay, okay ... We need to form a plan. But we only have twelve days and I've been researching for months. There's no other account of a home that moved. This is impossible!"

At least I can still feel the enchantments on this island. The energy in the air crackles with an intensity I hadn't felt during the run inland. Somehow, I can even taste and smell the charms floating in the air like edible dust specs. There's a hint of a rich, buttery pie crust scent in the breeze that invites me to take a deeper breath. I don't, in fear of catching a whiff of Jacob's cologne again. Whatever he wears must be a designer brand, because it's intoxicating.

He stops in place, turning to block me from continuing. I have to admit, it's nice to have a break. We're obviously lost in this damned forest, though both of us are too stubborn to admit it.

"We can do this. Think of it like a treasure hunt." He pauses and his brows furrow together. "Cheyenne is clever with this stuff, she can help."

"Who's Cheyenne?" A strange heat burns my belly and rises to my chest.

"My ... roommate."

"A girlfriend?"

"No. Jealous much?"

"You wish." I cross my arms.

We experience the worst omen when a lizard crosses the dirt path in front of us. I don't dare mention it out loud to Jacob. It'll only manifest terrible misfortunes. While we walk back to Jacob's boat, it'll be better to focus on things that calm me—like obituaries.

"Did you know Jane E. Tonkef died last week from an amulet strangulation?" I ask, but there's no chance Jacob will find this interesting. "She was 102 and was found with all fourteen of her cats lying on her body."

Jacob marches a few strides ahead to clear the path for me. Sweet, but unnecessary.

"And Gertie Tedeug died the same day in 1925. She was found with twenty rings on her fingers, all glowing bright magenta, but back then Fuzers weren't accepted, so the story was buried."

"You okay now?" Jacob asks while peeking over his shoulder.

"Yeah."

"That makes us both shitty liars."

A few more cardinals have joined our trek and one lands on my shoulder. "Sorry, bud. I don't have any food. I'd do anything for a cheeseburger, though."

"Not a veggo?" Jacob asks.

"No. Why?"

Jacob gestures to my body up and down. "You look healthy as Abyss. I assumed you—"

"Don't assume anything about me. I'm not someone you can label or put in a box."

It's the first time I've snapped at him. A thoughtful look crosses his face before he begins clearing branches from our way again.

"You have more zest than I realized, Miss Nkosi."

I poke a finger into his back. "I told you not to assume anything about me. Just because you carried me across that damn log doesn't make me weak or pathetic or undeserving of a—"

"Woah! Hey, I was jokin'. It's all good, mate."

"Good? What's good about being stuck out here in the

jungle? And all my life I've been..." I stop the words from coming out of my mouth.

Jacob stops and faces me. "You've been ... what?"

I turn away and put some distance between us so I can breathe.

"Alouette," he says softer, coming up behind me.

"Never mind. A loved celebrity like you wouldn't understand."

"Me? Loved?" He snorts in disbelief.

I swing around at his pained tone, then push past him.

"Okay, we're not leavin' till we get this sorted. If anythin' Ivola said back there is true, then you and me"—he gestures between us—"we're partners now, whether we like it or not. We gotta trust each other. You have some sort of problamo with me? Go 'head, let it out. Give it to me. I can handle it."

He adopts a broad stance, hands on hips, as if he's bracing himself for a massive blow. For a moment, I feel bad for giving him crap, but he deserves it because ... well, he ... shit, I don't have a good reason.

He raised his eyebrows, and it's enough to release the floodgates.

"You've had an easy life full of supportive people who helped you rise to the top and encouraged your dreams. You excel at everything you do, and it's nauseating." I blow out a loud huff. "I'm not like you, Jacob. I never will be. As a kid, I was made fun of for being part of a family who was obsessed with bugs. They called me the poisoned ladybug until high school. Then I eventually became the idiotic girl who didn't want to follow in her family's footsteps when it was obviously the correct career path, full of opportunities. You'll never know what it's like to let others down." I pause, in shock that I'm disclosing so much personal information. "I want to start over. The only place I want to do that is Ouma's cottage. I have a plan; will even change my name. I bet you can't even imagine doing something like that when everyone praises the Talksihnn name."

He leans against a tree on the other side of the path and waits. Patience. This man has more of it than I gave him credit for. When my body fully relaxes, he finally moves.

"They treated you like crap as a kid," Jacob starts. "That's not fair. I hate bullies."

More tension in my chest uncoils.

"Feelin' like a failure sucks ass, I get that," he says.

He does? I look him up and down. A person of his caliber likely had to make many mistakes to reach the top.

"Change can be good," he says. "Starting fresh is a good dream."

When it seems like he's finished, I realize I've been waiting for him to either become defensive, deflect, or call me out for being wrong. Jacob did none of those things. Maybe I am in shock. He listened and responded without making it about himself. I've never had a boyfriend do that before. Not that he's my boyfriend, let alone that I'd want to date him, but this conversation is foreign ground.

"If ya want, gimme the names of who called ya poisonous and I'll deliver a box o' dog shit to their address."

I explode with laughter, unable to hold back.

"Don't shake your head like that. I'd totally do it."

"Oh, I believe you."

He pushes off the tree and holds out his hand. It's an invitation to meet him halfway. He's right. If we have to solve our problems together without our magic, there's no time to bicker.

So I listen to my gut and stand by his side. The

expression he gives me is full of understanding. Maybe I finally have someone on my team other than Zola.

"Zola!"

Jacob twists around. "Where?"

"No, I never checked in." I grab my phone and check my messages.

> If you're not dead, I'm gonna kill you!

> Unless you're making out with Jacob, then I need to know your rating scale from zero-fudge yeah.

> I better be your maid of honor when you two get married.

> OMG. Lou! Where are you!

> Show proof of life.

> Sorry. I'm okay. Headed to the boat now. Lots to tell you.

Jacob starts chuckling softly next to me. He's scrolling through his own phone.

"Look at what your stupid brother sent me," he says and shows me a video of a kangaroo pack on the airport runway, delaying other planes from landing. When it's done, he presses the button to turn the screen off and stares at it. "Um, we should probably keep our cahoots quiet. Wouldn't want Marquis gettin' the wrong idea, ya know?" He shifts his feet, then finally looks at me.

"Agreed."

Whimsical mushrooms with polka dots randomly sprout from the ground and form an aisle for us. I'm guessing their magic is pointing us toward the boat. Jacob jogs ahead, body loose and chill. As the winding path brings us back to the beach, I take a moment to commit the scene to memory. Spellbinding clouds curl and dance with a flock of griffins. The divine blues of the sea shimmer, attempting to allure me with a siren's influence. Not gonna happen. I'll never swim in the ocean again.

A dazzling diamond-scaled tail flips over the surface. Then a second and third. Mermaids! My heart rate spikes, and I rush forward until my toes get wet. I haven't seen a mermaid since I was a kid.

"Ready?" Jacob already stands in the boat, arm outstretched.

I back up, realizing I've stepped into the water. In a blink, the mermaids are gone and I'm alone on shore once again.

"Hold on. I'll come get ya."

Jacob splashes into the water and makes his way to me. Once he's a foot away, he holds out both arms.

"Hop on. Free ride." His smile is genuine but holds a tinge of knowing ... knowing that fear tingles on the back of my neck.

I sigh, shaking my head. "No way. I'm not letting you carry me again."

"Well, it's either this or I throw you over my shoulder. We gotta get on the boat. How ya do that is your choice."

How dare he be obnoxiously helpful. It's perfectly acceptable that I'm scared of the water. However, imagining wrapping my legs around his waist is a different kind of fear altogether.

"Turn around," I say, twirling my finger.

"Yes, ma'am," he agrees, pivoting. I can no longer see his face but hear the smile in his tone, softer than the beach sand. He crouches low so I can climb on his back. This angle doesn't help much since his back is sculpted with thick muscles that lead to broad, capable shoulders.

I try to focus on my next set of teacups and teapots I plan to make, with a wider rim and deeper set than the last order. It's not working. My brain continues to fixate on Jacob's forearms hooked around me. A few splashes of water wet my legs as he moves, but at least no harm will reach me in the safety of his arms.

Before I know it, I have my feet firmly planted in the boat. Jacob readjusts his soaked clothes, but they cling to his skin, anyway. He starts up the boat and we zoom away. Already, my hands hurt from clenching the seat tightly.

"Let's play a game. You guess if I'm tellin' the truth or lyin'," he offers. "It'll take your mind off the loop that's obviously playin' in your head." He doesn't give me time to debate. "There's a turtle named Taco who follows me 'round at the beach. Truth or lie?"

"I don't wanna play." I squeeze my eyes shut.

"It'll help. I swear," he insists. Then his voice softens as he adds, "You're safe with me."

I let out a deep breath, keeping my eyes shut. I ignore the rumbling of the boat on the water and listen for the soft bird calls above.

"Now tell me if Taco is true," he says.

"Yeah, I believe you."

"You're right. Next, my favorite childhood memory is visiting the Sydney Opera House."

"Lie," I spurt out, confident.

"Two for two. Nice job. Fave memory is actually teachin' my sisters how to surf ... okay, let me think. Oh, I never went to college."

This one makes me pause. Perhaps he took college

courses while traveling to surf professionally, but that's not his style. I peek one eye open and study his face.

"True, but you're smart enough to take classes if you want."

He meets my pirate-eye and winks before I clench it shut again. "Oh, this is a good one. The last time Marquis and I went to the bar, he spilled a drink on his lap, right on his crotch. Epic." His laughter drips with honey.

"That has to be true."

"Actually, he spilled *two* drinks. Back-to-back. It was a bloody disaster."

Ocean spray whips my cheeks and the boat rocks. I grasp onto the handle tighter. "Are we almost there?"

"Yeah, close. Your turn. Make me guess."

I decide to lay it all out there for the sake of our new truce. "I'm jealous of you. Growing up, I only had Marquis and Ouma. Whenever I presented in art shows, they'd be there in the first row, next to two empty seats saved for my parents. Now that Ouma's gone, Marquis is all I have left. But he's in Sydney. Even you've had more time with him than me. Basically, you took him from me. My brain is a mess. He didn't deny it at all or downplay my feelings.

"I've never broken up with anyone. I've had four serious relationships, and they all left me. The first one said I traveled too much. Posh never told me her reason. Sonya couldn't get on board with my public sex kink, and I'd rather not talk about Felicity."

I choke on my spit. Coughing as my face warms and my eyes water. "Public sex kink?"

Behind the steering wheel, he glances over at me and winks. "Truth or lie?"

I can't answer. A warm tingling zips up between my inner thighs. What is this reaction? I can't imagine sex with

Jacob. Anything between us would lead to disaster. Plus, we don't have time to flirt and mess around when we both have a goal.

Though, the possibility of Jacob's hands roaming my body sounds like a decent distraction. I'd only offer the proposition as a physical stress reliever.

"It was true." The boat slows and Jacob heaves the anchor overboard. "Your turn."

For some insane reason, I have a desperate desire to share more pieces of myself. Like a strange compulsion out of my control. Maybe it's the excess magic that has accumulated in Calypsa recently that's drawing out secrets from deep within. This is no longer a game.

"I believe in love at first sight, but have never been in love—yet. The cruelest thing I've said to a boyfriend was that I was too good for him, which I didn't even believe. My first ever kiss was at the Calypsa county fair when I was sixteen and it was slow and hesitant and kind of boring. And the last time my heart was broken was when Ouma died."

"That was a lot. Can I give you a hug?" Jacob asks.

I don't like being the reason for his smile to disappear, so I nod. "Sure."

"Nope. Be confident," he begs me on his knees. "Come on, I need a hug."

"Oh my Goddess, fine!" I stand on unsteady feet and shuffle my way across the boat like a penguin and lean into him.

Before I can wrap my arms around him, he locks me in a tight squeeze. I'm pretty sure he sniffs my hair, but I can't judge him since I'm also absorbed in the scent of his wet skin. Salt water and man and hunger. I'm aware it's not possible, but he smells of a craving, a hopeful starvation. What is it that he needs?

His child. Of course.

Every second we waste chatting or embracing is a moment he remains separated from his kid. We don't have time to linger and play games. I pull away harder than is socially acceptable and pretend not to see the confusion on his face.

"Sorry, I'm not much of a hugger," I lie, then stare at the bit of water between our bobbing boat and the coast.

"You can jump on again. I won't bite. But it'll cost you ten thousand bucks."

In front of our eyes, bewitched logs roll from the other side of the dunes. In a mysterious way that Zola will never believe, a bridge begins to form. One piece of wood at a time extends over the water, stretching closer to our boat. Jacob looks as stunned as I feel. There aren't any Fuzers in sight on the beach. There's no way the residue magic is this strong. Earlier when I had found all my socks already matched and asked Mariah if she switched laundry days, she had denied being in my room that day. That type of low magic is unexplainable, minor enough to disregard. However, this much surplus is consequential and needs to be reported.

When it's finished, Jacob steps on it first to assess its safety. He jumps up and down, hard and heavy, but the bridge stays strong.

"Race ya to the other side." Jacob throws me a wicked grin, then speeds away.

I chase after him, solely for the reason of not wanting to be alone over open water. On the sand, he keeps running, creating more and more distance between us. I could stop to inspect the hundreds of seashells underfoot or lie on my back to admire the shifting clouds. But every part of my being wants to stay as close to Jacob as possible. I need to get a hold of this lust before it overwhelms me.

Breathless, I finally arrive at the pier and find Jacob leaning against a van covered in bumper stickers. Next to it are about ten hammocks hanging from the rafters. A few people mingle and chat, all with sun-kissed skin and chill vibes. Some play a card game while sitting crisscrossed on their surfboards. And there's a damned turtle. Well, there hello Mister Taco.

"What took ya so long?" Jacob teases, then gestures to his van. "Welcome to my home."

At first, I don't process what he means. I glance into the windows of the van and notice how it's jam-packed full of belongings, like someone who travels with everything they own.

"Wait. You *live* in there?"

CHAPTER EIGHT

Jacob

The next day, I stand inside the Fuzer Sanctuary, a bland community hall with boring beige walls. At least the cheeseburger aroma wafting through the air has some life to it. As usual, I hand out paper plates with questionable meat, but I still sneak a few bites.

I watch the others eat and wonder if this will be my future since my powers have also been stripped. Usually, the first person I'd go to for advice is Marquis, but I'm avoiding his calls. It's not that I'm guilty; these feelings towards Alouette are only lust. He'd murder me if I pursued his younger sister. Obviously, he'll never understand her qualities that turn me on—her serious expressions that fail to hide her awkward, quirky layers. Not to mention how she's always walking around in her own dream world, constantly entranced by the smallest details. Seriously. Yesterday, she was going on and on about the different shades of pink in a single flower. How does she even notice that? The whole time I had to keep from smiling.

"I got you a new pair of sunglasses. Since you sold your collection." A familiar voice I hadn't expected has me turning.

Cheyenne stands with a volunteer apron on, both hands on her wide hips. Before I knew about her wife, I had considered fooling around with her a bit to ease some tension, but it's been a good thing that I've stuck to my promise of not screwing anyone till I find my kid. Plus when Cheyenne smiles, it doesn't warm me from the inside. Sure, she's nice enough, but there's something missing. I glance at her feet, where black thongs separate her toes. For some reason I was hoping she'd be barefoot.

"Woah, what's wrong?" Cheyenne's eyes narrow. "You look like someone snapped your board in half."

"Nah, it's all good, mate." I scrape the ladle along the bottom of the metal tray and slop another scoop onto a homeless man's plate. He nods his thanks and moves down the assembly line.

"Flaming fates, you look like shit." Cheyenne hip checks me and grabs a spatula. "Scoot over and tell me why." She leans closer and I can feel her scrutinize the heat creeping up my neck. "Or WHO? Hmm, it's that quiet girl from the beach, isn't it? I saw the way she looked at you."

"Who?"

She waves me off. "Oh, shut up. You like her. And she's obviously into you. Be a man and step up."

"Don't know what you're talkin' 'bout, mate."

"Bullshit. I give you two weeks max before you sleep with her."

"Never gonna happen." I pause as she scoffs, but I ignore it. "Need your help, though. Do ya know any old Fuzer 'round here who has mystical powers like readin' minds or tellin' the future?"

"Lemme think." Cheyenne piles another hefty portion into a woman's bowl.

As I wait, two men at a nearby table laugh and knock their plastic cups together. Will the sanctuary have enough food now that my spell was taken?

Cheyenne faces me. "There's this one person, Rory. They claim themself as neither king nor queen, but *Kwiin* of the oracles. You can find them at the Black Cat Market after midnight, but it's not easy to get there. It's a mile hike into the forest. Then you gotta go under a waterfall, inside a bat cave. Anyone's welcome, even Typs, but the vendors don't want the Council to find them. I guess their shops break a bunch of rules and they'd get shut down." Cheyenne shrugs. "Also, since it's in the middle of the night, it's damned hard to see. You could bring an ever-light, though. That'll help."

I tap my pocket. "Or a phone flashlight."

"Sure. What about your future are you worried about?" Cheyenne playfully bumps me again. "If that girl will be *the one*?" Her laughter is as smooth as fine liquor. "Oh, wow, I was kiddin' but your face is bright red, Jake!"

"Need to find somethin' important. Runnin' out of time."

"Maybe I could help." Cheyenne's eyes soften like a momma wombat's.

I glance at the clock, then tell Cheyenne, "It's all good, mate. Actually, I need to head out." I whip my apron off and leap over the counter. Before leaving, I whisper across the barrier, "Will ya text me where to find that night market?"

"Yup, and we're still on for surfing tomorrow morning, right?"

"Bloody oath. Tomorrow." I nod and spring out the door to the fresh air.

Sun-drenched beach umbrellas rest against the side of the building, all faded from the years of use. A soft breeze brushes my face and makes the umbrellas' fabric flutter. I run across the street as an ice cream truck song plays on repeat. In less than a month, the days will start to shorten and the season for ice cream and smoothies will end. By then, my magic may be gone forever. But that's not the motivation driving me to visit this night market. I could handle a Typ-life. What I can't process is never meeting my kid.

In the distance, past the lighthouse and tide lines, the turquoise sea calls my name, begs me to come surf, but for once there's something more important than riding the waves.

My phone vibrates with a message from Cheyenne; a pinned location for the market. I'll go tonight, but not if this weather doesn't improve. A family scurries along the sidewalk, shrieking and holding their hats down. Thunder rolls softly, followed by a lightning strike. Need to hurry, but I don't have enough cash to fill my van with gas. At least I can afford to rent a bike. As I jog past a group holding paddle boards, the wind picks up in speed, almost knocking one kid to the ground.

"Woah, easy, mate." I catch him and push him between his taller friends.

At the bike station, one cycle rises off the ground. No one else seems to notice.

"What the fuck?" I mumble.

No natural storm could accelerate this quickly. An electric scooter rises off the ground too. It hovers, then spins in a chaotic circle, before crashing through a storefront's window.

"Woah!"

The sky darkens too fast. Another bike is violently launched into the air, smashing against the store's brick wall. Bent and broken, the bike lies in a tangled mess on the ground. My hair lashes at my face and blinds me for a moment. I use my hand as a visor since my eyes water from the thrashing wind. Thunder roars. A group of fairies fly away from the seaside towards the closest restaurant. I should find cover, too. This is insane.

I wedge myself in the alley between two buildings. Something isn't right about this storm. It smells of driftwood and the echoes of wicked laughter. I hear a loud bang and see the heavy lifeguard tower has blown over.

My phone rings.

"... Jacob? ... hear me?" Alouette yells on the other line, urgent and fearful.

"I'm at the beach! There's a bonza storm!"

"... and ... house ... lightning ..."

"What?"

The line disconnects. My shoulders tense, and my breathing turns ragged. Is Alouette hurt? I flinch at a savage boom behind me. Kites and water coolers sweep through the alley. Who knows what might roll through the street next. I focus on the bike stand. Only one bike remains chained.

I glance left then right for flying debris, then jump out of the alley. The intense wind smacks my face. Need to get a bike. I struggle against the turbulence until my hands grope against the bike rack. Sweat drips down my back.

The second I slide onto the bike, the storm stops. A strange twilight glow instantly replaces the gray skies. Seagulls call above as if nothing happened, and the gentle lapping of the water behind the boardwalk makes me feel like I'm losing my mind. Did I imagine it all?

No, everyone else is just as confused. Fishermen help tie each other's boats to the dock, chattering loudly with curse words filling in the gaps. Picnickers chase after the remains of their belongings that have spread out far from where they were sitting. Sandcastle builders stare at the wreckage of their sturdy creations.

"What the fuck was all that?" I say to no one, then ride straight towards Alouette's house, as fast as possible.

CHAPTER NINE

Alouette

I cower in the corner of my pottery studio, wedged between the wheel and side table. Hesitantly, I rise and peek over the counter. All clear. Slowly, I drop my arms from where they'd been shielding my head from flying wreckage. Shattered glass lies from the broken window, and now only a gentle, salty breeze blows in, rustling my black curtains like a caress. Each steadying breath I take smells of wild magic.

"What the acorns was that about?" I ask my feathered friend Ms. Grim, who sits on my windowsill as usual, unphased.

Like always, the raven only blinks, but I swear she mentions something about worms. I glance around at the mess of tools. Most are scattered on the ground, though my scraper and caliber are wedged into the wall like darts.

Of course, the project I'd been working on is now a lopsided pile of clay. At least my wheel looks unharmed.

The door swings open in a flurry and Zola rampages in, hair windblown and out of control.

"You okay?" She skitters over, eyes wider than the hundreds of teacup saucers along the wall, some of which fell off their shelves.

"Think so. You?"

She nods. "That was crazy. Never seen anything like it. I was driving here and a whole flock of fairies zipped by my windshield. You know the group that lives on the north side who always wear top hats? I've never seen them travel during daylight. After I passed them, a massive herd of unicorns ran by in a stampede! When I glanced up, the sky was as pink as a flamingo! Did you see it?"

I realize my hands are shaking, so I hide them behind my back. "No, I was working in here. And had my earbuds in. Didn't know there was a storm 'till *that* broke my window."

Zola follows to where my finger points.

"No way! Is that ... is that a tombstone!?"

"Yup. I'll be looking up their obit later."

"That could've killed you if it hit your head! Are you bleeding?" She tugs me forward and checks my skull for injuries. "I give up. You have too much hair, girl."

"Really? I wasn't aware." I pick up scraps again, tossing them into a bin.

That was no ordinary storm. Where did it come from, and why? How did it stop? How far did it spread? Did anyone get injured?

"It's good most the teacups survived," I say. "Or we'd be owing Serafina half our paycheck."

Zola freezes, body stiff. What'd I say wrong? I try to meet her eyes, but Zola stares at the framed selfie of us from a few summers ago, smiling in front of the apothecary shop downtown.

"Lou, there's something I need to tell you." She keeps her back towards me.

There's an empty feeling in the pit of my stomach and I grip my stomach. Wild Sage, is she dying?

"Quaint Brush called this morning. One of their scholarship recipients had a family emergency and backed out of the program. Their budget opened. They're offering me room and board, too."

"You're going," I say and set down the tools I'd gathered onto the counter. "You must!"

"I can't!"

"Why not?"

"Because ..." she looks everywhere but me. "Serafina will have a hard time replacing me. And you ..." her voice cracks, letting me know she's already decided to take the job. "You'll be alone, Lou. I can't leave."

My mind races through the possibilities. I have enough inheritance to not work for years. The only reason I went into partnership with Serafina was for Zola's sake. I can afford flights abroad and will promise to visit. Or maybe there's a chance to move with her. No, Zola needs to find her own footing and I'd only hold her back. While I've been stuck in my grief all summer, she's eager to break free and start living again, to make new friends, and find new adventures.

"You are definitely going. I'll be fine. Plus, I have Ouma's cottage to find, remember? I'll be so busy searching, I won't even notice you're gone."

Zola turns, eyes filled with tears that start streaming down her beautiful face. She runs across the room and crushes me in a hug. "You're a terrible liar, Lou. How am I supposed to live with myself knowing how lonely you'll be?"

I pull away from her until we're nose to nose, then wipe the tears from her cheeks. "Stop it. You're going. And I'll be thrilled to not be distracted by your gossip. I won't have to hear about what couple was recently seen at Kalan's Haunted Shack." Traitorous tears trickle down my cheek too. "And I'll lose a few pounds without being forced to share your raw cookie dough addiction. But we have to live stream TruDeath together, because if you find out which vampire Corey ends up with before I do, then I'll run a stake through you myself!"

She laugh-sobs, then embraces me again. Our wet cheeks meld together, sticky and warm. She mumbles something I can't understand.

"What?" I ask.

"I leave tomorrow."

My breath is stolen from my lungs. "Tomorrow?"

"Yeah. They bought me a ticket and booked my flight. It leaves at noon."

We both dab our eyes with our t-shirts, then laugh at our twin-like move. There's so much to say, but Zola already knows my heart. Plus, it's not as if we'll stop talking.

"I know you'll be busy, but you better send me updates." I take out my phone and look up the time difference.

She blocks my phone and lowers my hands. "I won't forget about you. This is a path I need to explore. Like that one time you found a gold glitter trail that led you to that wild unicorn stuck in a trap. Remember how your gut knew it was something you had to do?" She sighs, then straightens, tightening her stance. "I need to go pack. Don't offer to come over. You're such a minimalist that you'll convince me not to pack anything. Then I'll be in London with nothing but a pair of underwear and my vibrator."

"Hey!" I poke her waist. "I'm always a vibrator advocate."

"I know. And I bet Jacob would go to the Kink Dungeon store with you."

"I'm going to pretend you didn't say that."

"What? You two would be adorable together. And the way he looks at you is ... intense. If you hook up, I want the details."

"We won't."

"Whatever." Zola pulls something out of her back pocket. "One more thing. Please, don't hate me for keeping this a secret, but this is for you. Don't open it until I'm gone, 'k?"

It's an envelope with my name in loopy cursive. Ouma's handwriting. The top corner shows a date from a week before she died. Zola had it this whole time? Has she read it? I turn it over. Sealed. No, she doesn't know what's inside. I wonder what it says.

I glance up to ask a thousand questions, but she's already a whisp in the wind. The studio, filled with my teacups, feels empty without her by my side.

Unable to wait, I tear the letter open and immediately wish I still had my magic ability to read at sonic speed to devour Ouma's words faster.

My dearest little owl,

I love you dearly and have enjoyed my time watching you from my new home among the stars. The moon is gorgeous here, so don't bite your pretty manicure from worry. How can I describe such a place to someone who captures bits of beauty everywhere? One day when you were five, and I was driving you to school, you were staring at your window and said, 'Ouma, I think most people would want those telephone poles to disappear. But I think they're beautiful because they give the gremlins a place to play and hop from tree to tree.'

Looking into the rear-view mirror and seeing your thoughtful brain at work was such a wonder.

I see you shaking your head right now, darling. It's time for you to accept compliments and believe them. You're such a warm, delightful spirit, so own up to your strengths and let them shine. It's quite boring to watch you sulk. Give me some entertainment and live a little.

I know you're struggling with a few internal battles, so I have a proposition for you. My idea will help you start fresh. Hear me out. Ultimately, it's your choice since there's nothing I can do about your actions from this side of the realm.

Option A- continue your life as is ... (boring!)
Option B- throw a wrench into your life
Quit your job with Serafina (you deserve better anyways)

Go on a scavenger hunt. Your Mom has the first clue. She knows what to say.

I may have conveniently forgotten to mention that your parents' estate will soon go to the centaurs. So, this is the perfect time for an adventure

Believe me, I'm still keeping an eye out for you. Until you find my second note, all my love, forever and always,

Your Ouma

I flip the page over, hoping for more as a teardrop splashes on her name and muddles the ink. Quickly, I blot it dry with my shirt.

Before I can stop myself, I email a short letter of resignation to Serafina. After I push send, I collapse into the paint-stained couch in the corner and hope that Ouma's second letter will magically fall from the ceiling.

Too many emotions swirl like a tornado in my chest. Zola's leaving. Depending on how soon the house sells, I won't have a place to stay. Zola must know more than she had said.

> Why did you give me the letter today?

Ouma made me promise.

What's it say?

> She wants me to do a scavenger hunt. Which starts with calling Mom

Do it

> The last thing I wanna do is disturb her. She's busy.

> Do it or I'll never come home to visit

>> Harsh

> You love me anyways

>> Maybe. Maybe not

Goddess, I'm going to miss Zola. As I lay my phone down, my finger stings sharply. When I look down, my nails have all been bitten short. Damn it.

A sudden sensation of being strangled overwhelms me. My studio is too small. The shelf-filled walls too consuming. I rush out, down the hallway, past the framed awards and displayed butterflies and science articles hung on the wall.

The back door to the garden swings open. Light pours in. I leap into the fresh air, breathing in a new moment, when suddenly someone steps into my path.

Jacob. A sempiternal moment stretches across centuries as we lock eyes.

"Are you okay?" he blurts, concern etched in his voice.

"Yeah."

"You sure? When you called it sounded like you—" He searches me quickly for injuries.

"Promise I'm fine." I laugh, but then notice the worry lines around his eyes. "What about you? You look frazzled."

He waits a beat and I swear he's about to declare something deep and meaningful. Thankfully, when his breathing returns to normal and that far-away look in his eyes dissipates, he says, "I haven't been able to think straight since we left Thornwitch Isle." Desperation lines his words. "I need ya help to find my kid. Please, mate."

CHAPTER TEN

Alouette

After hiking for an hour, we stand side by side in a dense forest. How do we keep getting ourselves stranded together? I'm more out of breath than Jacob is, but that's because I've had the torturous view of his gloriously toned calves. Because it was almost pitch dark out, I kept my eyes on his ankles so I could follow his steps.

Who in their right mind finds calves sexy? It's simply skin over muscle and fat and blood and bone. There's no reason to want to run my fingertip over them and up his thighs.

Ahead, the water landing in the pond could compete with the greatest of symphonies. Despite how terrifying it looks, the sight is Mother Crone's work at her finest. Jacob must be certifiably insane if he expects me to follow him under that waterfall.

"I'm not going in there," I bite out as Jacob yanks off his first shoe.

"Okay. The night elves won't devour you under a crescent moon," he says with a smirk he doesn't bother to hide.

I glare at his deviously attractive face while he yanks off his other shoe, followed by his socks. I don't raise my attention to his thick quads. Or higher. I don't.

"You can take a peek." He grins and tugs his shirt slowly up, over his abs, his chest, his shoulders.

I swear to Luna that he holds his shirt over his face for an extra second or … twenty. I could throw my backpack at him. That'd teach him to play games. Or I could imagine what it'd be like to brush my lips over the strong curves and dips of his body. Fine, it's a fact. Jacob is sexy as sin; but he's off limits.

In only shorts, that more-so resemble a swimsuit, he wades into the pond. Or is it a lagoon?

"Don't let the fire breathing mushrooms get too close while I'm gone." His teasing tone doesn't keep me from checking out his sculpted back. If only the shorts were a little loose and dropped lower. "And keep an eye out for mini crocs. You must know the legend of their spiked tails," he finishes with a laugh.

"Hmph! Your jokes are worse than a soggy hot dog!" I march towards the bank, letting my shoes get stuck in the mud as I step out of them.

He swivels around, grin plastered over his face like a kid at a playground. Arms out wide, he must expect to carry me through the water. Like Hex will I let that happen.

I tear off my socks first, careful not to fall on my butt.

"You've perfected the strip tease, little owl." Jacob chuckles, but his eyes turn to fire when I reach for the bottom of my shirt. "Maybe keep that on, mate."

"Don't think so. We'll be on equal grounds," I say, then

whip off my shirt and shorts until I'm standing in a bikini in front of him.

Jacob gestures to my chest. "Well, then you may as well take off those little triangles."

"Oh, grow up!" I yell, so flustered that I march into the water until it's up to my waist.

Something swivels past my ankles and I yelp, grabbing onto Jacob's shoulders and climbing his front like a ladder. I manage to lift myself until my thighs are right by his mouth, close enough so his soft stubble brushes against my skin. I'm half aware that his hands clutch my ass tightly. He's shaking from laughter, which does nothing to help my mood.

"I'm not goin' to say a thing."

I smack his shoulder, which only makes him laugh harder, then wiggle out of his grip until I'm back in the water.

"I. Don't. Like. Water."

"I couldn't tell." He holds out his hand like a peace offering. "Come on, I'm scared of tons of shit, too."

"What are *you* scared of?"

He swims like an expert, barely having to work to keep us afloat. "That I'll die young without meeting my kid. Or that I'll die in pain. Or havin' to quit surfin' someday from an injury. Or my kid wouldn't trust me to let me teach them to surf."

"What's your favorite part about surfing?" I ask right when my arm grazes his chest underwater.

His eyes dip to where we meet, but he ignores it. I'm unsure how that's possible since my skin turns hot where we touch, and all my nerves fire a warning message to my brain. He's half naked. Nonsensical tendrils of desire twist through my thoughts.

"Surfin' is ... freedom. There's nothin' the same as bein' on top of a wave. And my job is absolutely perfecto. It doesn't matter that I'm not competin' anymore. I love passin' along what I've learned to the sweet little ankle biters. Shit, maybe I'll coach one of 'em to break my records someday." He slows our momentum as we near the falls. "I could teach ya to surf, ya know."

I can't respond because he moves us closer to the waterfall. Its volume is steadily rising. My heart is pounding. Fear threatens to suffocate me. Body tight.

The thunderous white water pounds close to our heads. Jacob's face fades in and out of focus, then turns fuzzy. "I can't do this. I can't go under the water."

"Yes, ya can," he urges, water splashing his face. He pulls me closer until we're chest to chest, skin to skin. "You can do anythin', Alouette. You wanna get answers or not? The oracle is on the other side of these falls. They might know where to find the cottage, alright?"

I nod, afraid I'll cry if I speak. Though it wouldn't matter, since water rains over my face anyways.

"Trust me?" he yells over the booming water, concern weighing down his tone.

The genuinely thoughtful look he wears is enough for me to nod in permission. If the only option is to go under that waterfall, then we need to work as a team.

"Drag me. Please," I yell. "I need you to ..."

Before I can finish, Jacob pulls me underwater. Fully submerged, I squeeze my eyes shut. The battering water punches above us with the strength of a titan. My body is in his control. And, yes, apparently, I trust him because I'm not fighting against his hold.

On the other side, we break the surface and I snatch a lungful of air. After moving my soaked hair from my face and gaining my bearings, I realize I'm still plastered against Jacob's chest. Actually, my legs grip his hips with iron-like strength.

"Do I need to change your nickname to my little koala?" he asks.

There are a hundred ways I could say thank you, but Jacob's large, hard erection pressing against me abducts the moment as I slide down his front.

He shrugs nonchalantly. "Can't blame me for being a guy, Lou."

"Don't do that."

He tilts his head. "Don't do what?"

"Everyone else calls me Lou."

Jacob licks his bottom lip. "You don't want me to be a part of *everyone*? You want me to be somethin' different? Someone special?"

"Th- that's not what I meant."

His eyes drop to my mouth and I bet a million amulets that he tastes like summer popsicles.

A scintillating light suddenly flickers behind his head. That's when I notice our surroundings. Majestic grimoires couldn't describe a scene this poetic. We're in a dark cave, though it grows brighter by the moment. Sconces in the shape of crescent moons turn on, one by one, creating a path into the unknown.

"What in the holy herbs is this place?" I whisper.

Sheer intrigue wins out against any remaining fear. I wade through the shallows towards the bank until the crashing waterfall behind us dims to a low purr. As I step out of the water, the ground is solid, black rock, possibly even obsidian jasper. The trail looks worn, flat and smooth, surrounded by jagged stalactites spearing the air at all angles. Above us, the pitter patter of bat wings is as soothing as a lullaby. One detail I didn't expect is the musty, thick scent in the air that smells similar to post-sex in a car, when the windows are all fogged over.

I turn towards Jacob in time to see him tying his wet, disheveled hair in a high bun, his biceps flexing as he twists the band around, hypnotizing me.

Stop staring. I need to focus on anything else. Teacup designs—hamptons, avons, and malverns. Nope, that's not doing the trick. I'm still shamelessly gawking at the muscles, running my eyes along the V, following it down to the point towards his crotch. Birds. Think about birds. Ravens have a wingspan of 45.5 to 46.5 inches. They live ten to fifteen years and are known as Corvus corax.

"Eyes up here, Alouette." He chuckles.

"I … we …" I shake my head, refocusing my thoughts. "Let's go."

With each step on the hard surface, magical gold glitter marks where we step.

"How far do you think this tunnel goes?" I ask him.

"Not sure," he replies, eyes scanning the corners of the cave.

With a nervous hand, I take his, our fingers interlacing. In an instant, I can feel his gaze on me, but I don't dare look up.

"Need another distraction?" he asks.

I nod and try to collect saliva to swallow because my mouth has turned dry, epically fast.

"My favorite food is cheese. Any kind. If I could have a superpower, it'd be to hold my breath forever. I can be too organized. My most treasured possession is a surfboard given to me by a gold medalist."

"Why are all these tidbits about *you*? There are other

ways to distract me, like ... what kind of birds are native to Australia?"

"I'm telling you about myself, so when you ultimately fall in love with me, you'll have been warned about my flaws and quirks."

My feet stop moving. Accidentally, I jerk his elbow back.

"Ow! What's wrong? You see a rat?"

"Reverse. Back up." I drop his hand and point in his face. "What do you mean *when* I fall in love with you? You're crazy! That'll never happen."

His eyes shine with mischief. "Fuck, you're fun to mess around with."

The scoff that parts my lips is borderline embarrassing since I sound like a disgruntled teenager. "Just you wait. I can plan an epic revenge. Maybe not tomorrow, or next week, but one day, when you least expect me ..."

"What's your threat?" He laughs. "You'll climb up my face again? Yes, please! I accept."

I stomp ahead and refuse to engage as he asks me question after question about pottery, my other hobbies, how I met Zola, how often I see Marquis, if I've ever visited him in Sydney, what I was like in high school, and how often I practice yoga. I ignore every inquiry, no matter how curious he sounds, even when his questions become harder to ignore, like what's my favorite horror author and have I ever saved any obituary clips. The answers are on the tip of my tongue, but I charge ahead into the glow of brighter lights.

Along the path, lanterns are added to the sconces. Soon, fireflies twinkle in the air and I catch sight of incandescent fairies.

A mushroom bursts from the jasper rock directly in

front of me. Right as Jacob is about to step over it, I clothesline him fast, his body racking against my arm.

"Woah! What's wrong? You okay?"

His look of concern is endearing, adorable, even whimsically enthralling. Ugh. This is a crush, and I can squash it faster than a coven can cast a jinx.

"You almost stepped on a mushroom. That's bad luck. Wait, no, no, step on the right side of it, not the left. This way, follow me."

"Phew, you saved my life."

Soft, light-hearted singing echoes off the onyx walls, and a few shadows dance high, then low.

"The lanterns turn around that corner." Jacob points. "I think we're almost there."

My skin prickles. He must be right. If the stories are true, we're about to step foot in the wistful Black Cat Market. As we walk quietly, I smell the spiced cider first, followed by juniper. I imagine the possibilities—booths with tapestries, candles, and crystals. As distracting as the market will be, our main goal is to find the oracle.

I suck in a thrilling breath and turn the corner.

CHAPTER ELEVEN

Jacob

Badass pink skulls and candles line the cave's path, leading toward arches that welcome us into the Black Cat Market. Thousands of twinkling lights hang over people and creatures of all sizes. Mini ogres and giant fairies and unicorns all bustle around booths. If there are any Typs here, can they taste and feel the enchantments coating every surface? I've never been surrounded by such an abundance of magic.

Next to me, Alouette seems frozen in a state of awe as she absorbs the scene. I follow her gaze to the massive vases of pink flowers that must have been bespelled to grow in the dark. In fact, those could be night orchids; their petals only open in the moonlight. But how can the moon penetrate a cave? In answer, a breeze tickles my skin. I gaze upward to see that the cave in this section is actually open to the starry sky.

"Stunning," Alouette whispers, jaw hanging loose.

I think of those romcom movie scenes when the female

character checks out a beautiful view and says 'gorgeous' and the guy agrees, but is implying that she's the beauty herself.

Even if I wanted to date Alouette, it's not as if she'd be interested in being with someone whose life is plastered all over the internet. My rep as a quick and fun fuck isn't the type of guy Alouette would settle for. I'd never be lucky enough to land a woman as smart and sophisticated as Alouette.

Her hair—soaked from our adventure—drips water down her bikini. Part of me wants to buy her a sweater, but my feminist sisters would tell me to support Alouette in whatever she feels comfortable wearing. After all, I'm half naked myself. Hopefully, our bathing suits won't attract much attention compared to some of the costumes others are wearing.

Between the outfits and the bats, this place resembles Halloween night. Aussies are bred to not fear rare and dangerous animals. Bats might give me goosebumps, but I'll be the last to run if it charges. I doubt they'll be an issue though, given the amount of cats lounging on the rocky slopes in the background. One watches me as if it can see my soul.

I follow Alouette's lead as she meanders past soap carts, booths displaying gems and necklaces, and artists of all kind. A legend-teller on the corner sings a ballad about how he has beaten the battle against mortality. I drop a dollar into his bucket as we stroll by.

"If you got a tattoo, what image would it be?" I point to an artist drilling ink into a woman's hip.

"One for Ouma. Maybe a moon with a rose? Or her favorite quote: 'To understand the world, listen to the bird's silent flight.'"

"What does it mean?"

"She never told me. But I like to think of it as trying to slow down our busy minds and pay attention to what is around us. Or maybe to make room for the quiet."

I nod and try to shake off the imagery of where Alouette might place a tattoo. Her bikini isn't doing me any favors.

"Oh, look!" she says, then guides me to a tent. Alouette jumps in place, then moves to a pottery booth with pieces in the most peculiar shapes. "Maybe I could open a booth here someday."

Her energy blazes more vividly, full of passion here. Sharing this moment with her, I feel raw, fully alive for the first time since ... I can't remember. Her excitement is intoxicating, infectious, even. I can't deny that I want to learn what makes her tick. What does she like to do on lazy Sunday mornings? How can I make her smile more often?

What would her fingertips feel like against my skin? Is she a clawer? Would she dig her nails into my back if I satisfied her enough? Fuck, what has gotten into me? I haven't fantasized about someone real, in the flesh for years.

There is an irresistible pull toward her, a feeling so intense that fear I may explode if I don't put my arm around her waist or breathe in the scent of her hair. I want to fall asleep with her head on my chest. No! Fuck, fuck, fuck.

"I'm gonna look over here, mate."

I need to ignore her intoxicating scent. Her citrus shampoo gives me an aching hard-on every time I get a whiff. As I move away, two laughing women stumble into me, spilling alcohol from their goblets that barely misses me. I weave through the crowd, able to see over most of the bobbing heads. The phantom taste of apple juice in the air makes my mouth water. Each step brings me a stronger delicious flavor infused with magic.

At the end of the line of booths, the oracle sits alone at their table, eyes already locked on mine. Waiting.

I jostle through the bodies until I stand in front of the oracle's booth. A black and red sign reads *Kwiin Rory* but doesn't list the price, so I hope I have enough cash left. My hand taps my pocket as if it can count the value based on how thick the bills are in my shorts. Since my phone is on the other side of the waterfall, I can't use any apps to pay for their service.

"Don't worry. For celebrities, my readings are half off," they say, then itches their eyebrow piercing.

I pay, then fumble with the stool. Its metal legs screech against the rock floor. Kwiin Rory is the first Asian Fuzer I've seen after moving to Calypsa. I'm jealous of their cropped black hair and would switch my blond for theirs any day.

Rory shuffles one of the seventy-eight card tarot decks stacked across the table. I've never had a reading, but my sister once taught me about arcana and trumps, the forces and virtues.

"Think of an open-ended question, but don't say it aloud," they say with a serious face. Their eyes are different colors, one purple, one silver, and I wonder if it's natural or from contact lenses.

During our hike here, I had considered what to ask. How can I persuade Nella to talk to me? Where is my child? What is the best way to find my kid?

But now that I'm here, none of those questions feel right. A new one settles into my heart and pushes away any other option. *Is my child safe, happy, and healthy?* I think, and the oracle gives a slight nod, understanding I'm ready.

They gesture to the cards. "These symbols and stories are part of our collective unconscious. There is a psychic power in all of us; it's universal, and part of the natural gift from Mother Crone herself. Are you a believer?"

"I'm open to any help you'll give me, mate."

"Timeless truths will speak to me and help you find your way," they say. "First, pick a deck that calls to you."

Three decks are stacked face down with an artistic design on each, one shows endless swirls that make me dizzy, the second looks too abstract and creepy, but the third speaks to me, a pink pattern that resembles the crest of a wave. I tap on that deck and a little tug pulls at the corner of the oracle's mouth.

"You're here with someone," they say with a knowing gaze.

I shrug and guilt immediately tugs at my heart 'cause I abandoned Alouette in the chaos of the market.

"Three card spread," they say quietly, yet their voice is crystal clear like we're in our own bubble, oblivious to the chatter surrounding the booth.

They flip over an image of a black swan looking up into the sky.

"There's a woman," they say.

"Nella. She's the mother of my child."

"No. The woman you need is here, divine like this swan, the woman with long hair wilder than the sea, but she doesn't belong in the water like you."

"I don't need to find Alouette. I need to find Nella, and my child."

They point across the way. "The woman with the spirit of a bird currently lives in a cage of her own making."

"A cage?"

Turning over the second card, they frown deeply at the

split image of a sun and moon above the ocean. "What does time mean to you?"

If I had my phone, I'd reach for it to check the time. "Uh, that ya close soon and I need to hurry before Alouette realizes I'm missin'."

They shake their head. "No, in the grand aspect of life ... what does time symbolize to you?"

"That there's no point in wastin' time doin' what ya don't care about or bein' with people who don't love ya back. The purpose of life is to find what ya love and do it as often as ya can with friends and family ya trust."

"You'll see Nella this week if ..." They hold up their hand to stop me from interrupting, then brush their fingers over the back of the last card.

Once it's turned, I tilt my head to try to interpret the image. A human couple lies on a beach, entangled in each other's arms, surrounded by fireflies.

"You'll see Nella this week *if* the swan woman initiates a kiss with you before the cuckoo clock strikes midnight ... three nights from now."

They sweep all the cards away before I can inspect them further and start packing up their decks.

"That's it?" I stand, fists clenched by my side. My sudden movement makes the stool screech against the rock. "I need more. That didn't answer my question. Is my kid safe? Are they loved? Why does that need to happen three nights from now? What if the swan card doesn't represent Alouette? How will anyone kissin' me bring me to Nella?"

After they enclose their materials in a bedazzled suitcase, the oracle sighs, then scans me up and down as if making up their mind about me. "I don't usually do this.

But your kid is a girl. Your daughter is safe and healthy but she's ..."

I leap forward, almost crawling across the table. "She's what? Tell me."

"She's searching for you. Events are all connected to each other. There are paths between this moment we're living right now and what could happen next week. If you want to save Dakota, to keep her from running into danger, the cards say that your Alouette is the key."

My heart spasms, threatening to break free. "Dakota? That's her name? What kind of danger?"

Squeals and screams echo off the stone walls. My attention snaps to where I left Alouette. Something large and black swoops to the ground and parts the crowd.

"What's going on?" I ask the oracle, but when I turn back, they're already gone.

The shouts multiply. Grow louder. More frantic. I shove through the stampede, moving in the opposite direction of where I'm headed. What are they running from? The market is shattered by a loud crash, then a shriek and a terrifying howl cut through the air.

"Alouette!?" I yell at the top of my lungs as a nearby booth collapses in a heap.

Ahead, I spot her, ducking under a vendor's display table, covering her head. Then the most unexpected scene enfolds between me and the woman I apparently need to seduce.

CHAPTER TWELVE

Alouette

A trio of fierce black cats attack a bat as large as a bike. Eyes fixed on me, it swerves left, evading two cats before flying straight at me.

"Alouette!" Jacob calls, the crowd splits from his shoving. "I'm coming!"

I should be terrified, trembling even, but that specific sexual phrase he yells through the market only makes me laugh. Unfortunately, I'll never be the one to pleasure Mister Jacob Talksihnn, ladies' man of Down Under.

I've never seen him look so distraught before, and honestly, it's not my favorite look on him. There's no reason he should be this concerned. Sure, the monstrous bat has freaked me out, but I've seen worse in Ouma's garden. Plus, it's not like this is a shark ambush.

The cats pounce and violently claw at the bat until it's pinned and stops moving. After the ruckus has died down and the dispersed people regain their sanity, Jacob joins me under the table.

"Did you see that?" I ask.

"Why are you laughing?" Flipping my hands, he checks if I'm injured.

"I'm okay."

Although I'm only wearing a skimpy bikini, my skin is warm where we touch. Make these desires go away. Please. The air crackles with energy between us when our eyes meet. It'd only take a little lean forward to press my lips against his.

"Market's closing, you two." The vendor nods to the graceful arches where we had entered. "May wanna head out before the bat's mate returns."

I sneak a closer peek at its body while Jacob averts his eyes. "Witches tits, that's gruesome! Aradia, Ravenna, and Fiona are murderous little devils, aren't they?"

"Of course you named the cats." He smirks. "Why do I have a feeling that you want to say a few words on the deceased's behalf?" Jacob asks.

There's a strange tumbling in my stomach at his thoughtful suggestion. Maybe he does know a few things about me after all. Eyeing Jacob, hiding his face with his hands, I create an obituary for the bat.

"Black Opal entered eternal life on Tuesday, August fifth, 2025. Its spirit is most likely carried on by a multitude of children that reside in this cave. The world was blessed to learn valuable lessons from Black Opal during its lifetime, among them: Never attack a trio of cats, fly only to the west of the moon, don't eat the blossom butterflies, and if a skunk enters your space, choose another spot to scavenge. It is survived by its mate who will grieve this monumental loss. In Opal's memory, donations may be made to The Black Cat Market. Goodbye to our dear bat, you will be missed."

"Oath," Jacob says and puts an arm around my waist.

I linger, only for the chance to relish in his large hand on my skin. As if he's testing his boundaries, Jacob slowly rubs a finger up and down. I should stop this, protest somehow, but I hate the word, '*should.*' It implies a suggested standard of how others think I *should* behave, how I *should* talk, *should* act, *should* feel. Perhaps I'm not supposed to enjoy Jacob's company, but I obviously do.

Slowly, I lift my arm and gently rest it across Jacob's lower back, too. His whole body immediately stiffens. Well, that wasn't the outcome I hoped for. He stares down at me, lips parted.

"My love language is quality time. I hate onions," he says quickly, "The worst spell of the month I've ever chosen was to be constantly horny; blame that one on the brain of a seventeen-year-old." He talks faster. "My biggest pet peeve is families who don't watch their kids in the waves. I never went to college, and I've been in love once. Maybe once we spend more time together, you'll follow through on that kiss you want."

"I don't know what you're talking about." The instant heat in my cheeks gives me away.

"Sure, you do. Earlier your eyes were like this," he says making a face like he's constipated. "Wait no, more like this, the face that models make when they're angry but turned on."

I move towards the exit. "You're officially insane. Let's go."

We follow the leftover crowd, though I wish we had more time here. As the skulls and candles guide us out, I peek over my shoulder at the booths once more: incense and chakra stones, book stands and palmistry books, pendulums and offering bowls. This place is a sanctuary, a dream come true. Whoever founded it is a genius of epic proportions. The magic here reminds me of Ouma: ubiquitous, everlasting, and bold. I especially like the way the moonlight glints off the orbs—a positive luck charm.

I turn to Jacob and ask, "I assume you found the oracle when you deserted me so callously? Some people would call that neglect or abandonment."

When I see his anguished face, I immediately regret my words. My statement replays in my mind. Realization hits me like a slap in the face. I stop and pull him towards me.

"Shit, Jacob, I'm sorry. I didn't mean that."

His head drops low and heavy. "It's fine."

"No, that was insensitive. I'm sorry."

He sighs. "I'll never forgive myself for not being there for Dakota. She deserved much more. The worst thing that can be done to a person is to be left and forgotten."

His situation is a disaster. Jacob didn't do anything wrong and he's suffering from something he can't control.

"Look at me." I raise a hand to his cheek, not wanting him to carry this weight alone. "Her name's Dakota?"

A slight spark lights his blue-green eyes again. "Yeah, the oracle said she's a girl, but what if they didn't know what the Abyss they were talkin' bout? What if it's all bullshit? What if the reading isn't true?"

"What else did they say?" I search his face for any clue, but he stays quiet.

After a beat, I drop my hand and nod toward the exit. "Come on. We should get back to our clothes before anyone steals them."

Overwhelmed by the new information, my mind feels foggy as we enter the water, plunge under the falls, and resurface in the woods. What did the oracle tell him? Was it helpful? I'm still in a daze when we find our belongings behind a bush and Jacob wanders off with his backpack to change. Shivering, I squeeze the water from my hair.

The temperature must've dropped ten degrees while we were in the cave. While I wait, I take out my phone and hover my thumb over Mom's number.

Her pout in her contact picture mirrors mine, but I've never thought we resemble each other. Maybe it's because I saw all my characteristics as coming from Ouma. Even though I share more DNA with Mom than Ouma, my hands only know pottery because of my grandmother. Ouma's extraordinary bedtime stories inspired all my wildest dreams. She raised me and I'll never be more grateful for her presence. Why did she have to leave?

Her letter mentioned options. Choices. Ultimately, my destiny is up to me. But really, there's no debate at all. I'm going to try every possibility to hold on to her memory as long as possible, and that starts with the cottage. I need to find it before her perfume dissolves and her most prized possessions become coated with dust.

Hesitantly, I push Mom's name. I quickly calculate the time difference in western Australia. It's close to two in the morning here; we're thirteen hours behind, so she should be wide awake, nearing the end of her workday.

She picks up immediately and static crackles. "Lou? What's wrong?"

"Uh, hi, Mom. How are you? How's work?"

"Oh, your father and I are fine, dear, but why are you awake? Are you in trouble?"

"No, no," I say, standing and pacing. "I'm fine, couldn't sleep and I have a quick question."

"Okay, hold on. Let me put this stuff down."

Loud metal clanks echo through the line and I have to pull it away from my ear. "Sorry, okay, I'm ready. What is it,

Lou? Do you need money transferred over? Your father can—"

"No, I'm fine. Ouma left me a letter..."

Silence.

"It said you're selling the house in Calypsa soon?"

Nothing.

"And that I need to ask you for my first clue."

"Lou, are you sure this little game is a good idea? She's gone. I know you two were close, but there are more important things to focus on, like—"

"Please, Mom."

A beat passes. Finally, I hear a heavy sigh.

"Okay, but I don't want to hear complaints later if this doesn't live up to your expectations. She said you need to set up a meeting with Bennett Savion. Your Ouma said he has the key."

"THE Bennett Savion? But he's the president of the NFA. How am I supposed to contact the most powerful Fuzer in the country?"

"If you want it badly enough, I know you'll find a way," Mom says, and the compliment almost sticks until she continues, "But are you sure her cottage is what you need? There are plenty of apartments by State. I could pay your rent if you enroll in a biology class next semester."

There's no chance I'm starting over in classes with students twelve years younger than me. If she hasn't learned by now that I'm not following in her footsteps, then she'll never understand.

"We'll talk about that another time," I say.

"Okay, hun. We have a new expedition tomorrow. I may not be near my phone," she says, sounding hubristic.

I wait a beat, stoking myself up to ask her if she'll come home to visit soon. "Hey, Mom?"

But her side of the line is already dead. Shame boiling my blood, I amble around the trees to find a spot hidden enough to change into my dry clothes. In the darkness, a blurred shape moves slowly in my peripheral. I hold in a panicked scream and twist around. My bare foot snags on a sharp twig and I lose my balance. I run into someone; bare skin pressed against mine.

"Alouette?"

"Jacob!?"

My cheek is squished against his ... I don't even want to know ... hopefully his chest? I grope around and try to balance, when my hand swipes against something long and thick and warm and hard.

"Hey! That's my—"

"Ah, sorry!" I reel away and turn my back towards him. "WHY ARE YOU NAKED?!"

"Why are ya spyin' on me?"

"I didn't mean to grab your ..."

"My manly broomstick?" His chuckle sounds like sin in a bottle.

"Damned demons! This isn't funny!"

"It's a little funny," he calls out as I storm away to find a place to change.

Once I'm sure I'm far enough away, I strip faster than a griffin can fly and don my leggings, sweater, and sneakers. The hour-long hike back to the car might be torture if he brings up that unfortunate incident. I take a moment to sit on the nearest boulder to sort through the situation alone.

I've somehow managed to make a complete fool of myself by touching the penis of an internationally known athlete. Though, he didn't seem to mind. Of course not, he's a dude. And why was his dick hard in the middle of the forest anyway!? What goes on in the other sex's brain will always remain a mystery. Who cares if I have gained a little crush on the guy? It wouldn't be breaking any law.

My palms grow slick at the thought. Do I like him enough to try for more? I collect the traits I've learned about him: his silly nature, his willingness to help others, his determination to find his daughter, his patience with dealing with the press' obscene lies, his friendliness, trust in his beach friends, his devotion to his students, his crooked smile that washes away my worries.

I like him. *Shit*. A second passes when my world drops from under my feet, like the times when I'm at the top of the stairs and know I'm about to miss a step and stumble all the way down.

I drop my head into my hands. I like Jacob.

"Fuck!"

"Blimey! Don't think I've heard you swear before. It's gotta nice ring." Jacob shuffles on the other side of the trees. "What ya cursin' for?"

Without glancing up, I scoop up my backpack and march towards the path with a prepared lie on the tip of my tongue. "Because I need to talk to Bennett Savion. Which is impossible."

"Who?" he asks while we walk side by side, our phones illuminating the dirt path. "Wait, I know that name. Isn't he—"

"The president of the USA's Fuzer Association? Yup."

"He's booked with meetings for the next year. And his bodyguards will kill ya if ya step outa line."

"Wow, that's incredibly helpful, thank you."

"You're welcome," he says, his step snapping a twig as we trudge ahead.

"Better hurry. Only have nine more days."

"Nine? You plannin' my murder already, little owl?" His

deep chuckle sends that delicious tingle up my spine—the one I'm starting to crave.

"Jacob, listen." I stop, and he halts beside me. "We're being forced to work together. Tell me what else the oracle said. Maybe I can help interpret the message."

His face is unreadable, but he doesn't blink as he replies, "I'll tell you what they said on Saturday."

"What? Why wait till Saturday?"

"I—" he begins, and even though it seems he wants to answer me, it's like the words are caught in this throat. Shaking his head, he exhales sharply. When he looks at me, I see a flicker of an internal battle in his eyes, but then he licks his lower lip and I forget whatever we were discussing. The thought of his tongue sends my world spiraling again. *Shit.*

CHAPTER THIRTEEN

Jacob

The next day, one of the centaurs buzzes me through Alouette's front gates. The paparazzi shout my name. With two bags of the best smelling takeout cheeseburgers in hand, I stroll across the courtyard, through the front door, and down the long corridor. Gilded frames display Alouette and Marquis at different ages. It's intriguing to watch her spark wither as she ages. The older she looks, the more she fades into the background of the photographs until I spot a unique picture of her with a wrinkled woman, both laughing with their heads thrown back. This. This is the Alouette I want to experience.

"Hoo! Hoo! Little owl? Where are ya?" I shout down the hall, guessing she's in the pottery studio she once mentioned—if only I can find it in this maze. This place is a fuckin' castle.

I turn left but run into a door that leads to a toilet, then backtrack.

"Alouette? Say somethin', or I'll eat your burger."

A door flings open to my right. Entering cautiously, I inspect the bedroom furniture and notice black crystals, dreamcatchers, and a giant painting on one wall. I'm about to step out when an image on a laptop grabs my attention.

My face—wet after exiting the ocean—fills the screen. It's a video with a reporter after my last competition two years ago, paused mid-interview. Apparently, someone has been getting snoopy. I glance around the space again with newfound awareness, eyes landing on a few plants, the open window where she spied on me doing yoga, then the messy bed. *Her* bed.

My body goes on high alert and my cock twitches. Fuck. Not now. It was bad enough she caught me rubbin' one out in the forest last night. It's not my fault. Damn near impossible to spend time around her without imagining how soft her skin would feel or the sounds she'd make from my touch.

My phone rings, snapping me out of the torturous trance.

"Erik! G'day mate. How's it goin'?"

"May as well oil my balls up cause yer gonna love me forever, mate. Got good news."

I freeze. My heart ricochets. "Spit it out, would ya!"

"I pulled some good ones, let me tell ya. A custody lawyer is friends with Maggie's brother. Anyway, I got an in for ya. She's willin' to meet off-the-record to chat about Nella."

I can't breathe. This is perfect.

"The brother spilled the beans a bit. She's all about the ritzy fancy type these days, so ya gotta impress her at a charity gala."

"Okay."

"It's a black-tie event, Jake, so no bare feet," he yells, then takes a breath and a swig of somethin' before continuing. "Ever been to Outer Dunes? Oh, of course, ya have. That one competition in 2016, remember when we took that boat out?"

"Erik, hold up, man. When's the gala?"

"Friday night. I'll text ya the address and book ya a hotel room on my company card, it's no worries, mate. That's a two-hour drive, or four-hour unicorn ride, but I think they banned rentin' them. Ya may wanna look up the rules for—"

"Yeah, mate, I'll take care of it. You're a fuckin' legend. Anyone tell ya that?"

"Not today."

When he hangs up, I jump straight up and punch the ceiling. "Yes!"

A soft breeze whips through the window, reminding me of the cheeseburgers still smelling as scrumptious as ever. I prance down the hall like a pony on steroids. This gala is my chance. I can feel it deep in my bones. In the distance, light glows from one open door and a vibrating humming sound spill towards me.

"Owlette!?"

The second I turn the corner I stop in my tracks. With her back to me, Alouette dances, uninhibited, headphones blaring music only she can hear. Her hips sway wildly, and I can't help but trace the curves of her form where her crop top meets skin. I find comaraderie in the fact that we both have scars. Hers are more spread out, peeking out from above and below the hem of her tight shirt, spanning the entirety of her back. Someday, a guy will kiss that trail to erase any leftover trauma from what she's suffered.

I lean against the door, not wanting to interrupt her

moment of joy. Barefoot, as always, her sleek, toned legs glimmer in the sunlight. I follow the rays that bounce off her round ass, shaking every which way.

With every other beat, she bends forward and messes with the clay on the wheel, which gives me an even better view. I need to let her know I'm here without frightening her, so I start waving the bag of cheeseburgers in the air.

It only takes a few moments for her to turn and face me, surprise quickly replaced by something I don't want to name. She shoots me a look teetering between desire and curiosity.

As much as I want to try, I know a relationship with her is impossible. I can't become the person she wants. I have nothing to offer Alouette. No money. No real career. No home. No consistency. If everything goes according to plan, I'll be living near Dakota soon—wherever that is.

"Cheeseburgers!" Alouette swipes off her headphones. Salsa music continues to pulse as she tosses them onto a paint-stained couch.

The air carries the comforting scent of clay mingling with wood and fired ceramics. Shelves line the walls, displaying an array of tools and materials as well as colorful teacups and teapots. Unfinished clay creations sit on worktables scattered around the room, awaiting transformation. Sunlight filters in through the broken windows, casting a soft glow over the studio.

"What song were you listenin' to?"

"Every cats' favorite: "You Kneaded Me," she lies, evident in her the lack of a poker face.

How is she so adorable?

She rolls her lips in then nods to the window. "I thought you bailed on lunch when I saw the camera crew out there."

I watch her rip into the bag and chomp into a fry like a mighty croc.

"What you smiling at?" She gestures to the dented bench. "Sit. Eat."

"Yes, ma'am," I say, and dig into my own bag.

She smirks, then jerks up a hand. "Wait! That one's mine."

"How do you know?" I ask.

"You hate onions, right?"

I stare. How did she remember that?

"We can't have you turning into a grumpy muppet."

Holy Abyss, yes. This silly version of Alouette is the one I want to spend time with. Mayonnaise goops out of her burger and spreads across her cheek.

"You've gotta little somethin' here," I say, then thumb the white smudge on her face to wipe it off.

She munches another bite like a wild, famished animal. I survey the scene in hopes of learning a little more about her. Teacups are magically rearranging themselves in different stacks along a shelf while dirty tools wash themselves independently in the sink.

"Thought we lost our powers?" I nod to the enchanted items.

"Yup. Don't know how that's happening, honestly. It's like my parent's house comes more to life every day. Earlier, my mismatched socks were finding their pair and my underwear ... never mind." She drops her chin and avoids my eyes.

I reach over, lift her chin slightly to make her look at me.

"Don't ever hide from me, little owl. Understand? Tell me all the bits and pieces of you, underwear and all."

Her beautiful, big brown eyes widen, then drop to my

lips. Even though the oracle said I need her to kiss me, that doesn't mean I should let it happen.

"If I didn't say it before, this house is amazin'," I tell her. "But it'd freak me out to live in such a big place."

"The beach is a pretty big place."

I shake my head and shove my hand to the bottom of my bag, expecting no fries to be left, when five more randomly appear. Interesting.

"You know what I mean. I like my van, but I wish it had space for a fridge, so I don't have to share with Cheyenne."

Her chewing noticeably slows. "How did you and Cheyenne meet?"

"Oh, she's my wife."

She spits out a wad of food and it splatters to the floor. "What!?"

"You should see your face right now." I bend over in laughter. Wiping a tear, I take time to regain my composure. "I met Cheyenne 'bout two years ago out on the waves. She heard my accent, offered to get drinks with me and introduced me to her partner."

It's adorable the way Alouette's shoulders noticeably relax.

"Back then I still had a condo, a kayak, and everythin'. Over time, I've sold a lot and lived off the basics: food and clothes, oh and treats for Taco. That crazy bastard turtle."

"As long as you don't give them to him on a Tuesday," she deadpans. "Bad omen."

"Why?"

"Three T's. Treat. Taco. Tuesday."

I finish the last of my fries, and as I start to crumple up the bag, I realize it weighs more than it should. When I peek inside, at least twenty fresh, steaming fries wait for me. Is someone playing a trick?

"Mmm, that was delicious." I have to avert my gaze as she licks her fingers individually.

"Ya gonna teach me how to use that thing?" I point to a machine, trying to distract my mind.

"My wheel?"

"Yeah. Can you teach me to sculpt?"

"It's called throwing. It's a type of ceramic work that refers to objects made from clay that have been shaped, fired, and decorated or glazed. But sure, I can teach you."

"Did you memorize that from a dictionary?"

"Smart ass." Her brows knit together. I happen to prefer when she lets her tongue slip with the occasional curse word. "You wanna learn or not?"

"Yeah."

She sits on a low stool; legs spread and leaning forward a little. I have a direct view down her shirt and immediately notice she's not wearing a bra. Holy deities. Look away. I stare at the window, where a bunch of birds perch on the windowsill.

"Come on, sit next to me and do what I do." She taps the stool beside her.

"On that? It's for a toddler. I can't fit on there without breakin' my back."

She sighs like I'm indeed a child and shows me her posture. "Look, put your elbows here and it'll support you, plus it'll help you naturally use your body weight."

I lower myself onto the stool and follow her instructions. Our knees bump, but she doesn't move away.

"You're right-handed?"

I wave it dramatically.

"Okay, good. First, we cut a pound with the wire." She holds up a long string type device. "It's not floss." I follow her steps again, wishing she'd slow down so I don't look like an idiot.

In high school, I was always the jock, never the artsy type. "What are all these?" I point to tools she has laid on her station.

"Wooden rib." She raises one at a time. "Needle tool. Sponge. Wooden knife. Jacob, are you paying attention?"

"Uh, are you gonna test me later?"

"Maybe." She smirks, and it's the genuine kind of smile that sends my heart racing. "This platform on the wheel is called a bat. It helps if you want to move your piece to keep it from getting distorted."

I nod, waiting for further instruction.

"First, we pound the block of clay with your palm into a ball." Taking my fist, I strike the clay. "No," she says, lifting her hand to demonstrate. "Use the base of your palm so you don't hurt yourself." Adjusting my position, I try again. "Yeah, like that!"

The clay is smooth and easy to mold in my hands. I squish it a little and form an indent. It's oddly satisfying. My blob of clay is warped compared to her perfect sphere, but I soldier on, entranced by the passion in her tone.

"Now we throw it onto the bat like this." It lands with a loud smack.

When I toss mine, it splatters gunk, landing on her exposed belly button. Of course, my traitorous brain starts wondering if clay is edible.

"Down by your foot is the pedal. The harder you push, the faster it goes, but you don't need to keep pushing to keep the pace going. Let's test it out. Push down. Release. Good." She bends low and repositions my foot higher on the pedal. "Now, if you put your heel down, it'll stop the wheel."

I test it out, surprised by how little pressure the pedal needs.

"Good, you're actually listening."

"Bloody oath. I've gotta impress ya somehow."

Hands covered in clay, she swipes her phone so the music plays from a speaker instead of her headphones. Dried clay coats her screen. This messy version of Alouette is utterly hypnotizing. Every side of her, serious or playful or passionate or curious, are all puzzle pieces that form who she is. Each new part she shows is like a mini gift, making me fall just an inch further than before.

The hour flies by and she teaches me how to shape the clay, pressing my fingers at certain angles and applying varied pressure. Every time I add more water to the slippery mess, I want to rub some on her like a mud bath. Half of what she says is too complicated and detailed to remember, but I watch her hands work like it's my life's mission. Since pottery is what makes her smile, I need to create the most beautiful bowl-cup thing a novice has ever thrown.

We finally call it quits when her vase could be sold in a store and mine is too contorted to be worth glazing.

"Good job, for your first time."

I lean back in a huge stretch. "Wow, my back is killin' me. How do you tolerate that?"

She shrugs. "Guess I'm stronger than you."

"Obviously." As much as my back will scream at me tomorrow, I don't want to leave yet. "Is that it?"

"Is that *it*? That's all you have to say?" A crease forms between her brow, but her eyes glint with an edge of playfulness. "Damn divination! What a way to boost a girl up."

"Ya know, I didn't mean it like that."

"No, that's not *it*, jeez. Next, I trim a foot on them, then dry them all the way. The time for how long that takes will depend on the weather. It might crack if I dry it too fast."

She mentions a few more steps, but I can't focus when all I want to do is to pin her against the wall and discover what her lips taste like. I bet something like strawberry popsicles or sweet lemonade. But I can't.

"... I'll do the bisque firing later. When it comes out of the bisque, you can come back to glaze it." She points to a row on a counter. "See, those teacups have been glazed."

"Why do they look chalky?"

"Because they need to go into the kiln again. Then it's ready to be painted."

"Shit, that *is* a lot of steps."

"Not to mention clean up."

"Now you're speaking my language. I'm a cleaning wizard."

Alouette puts both hands on her hips and studies me with a calculating stare. This woman. Damn. She's summer's peaceful stillness twisted with the threat of a wildfire. Patches of golden sunlight shine through the window, highlighting her cheeks in a warm glow. My skin prickles in desire at the sight of her; it's so ethereal.

Her shuddered exhale sounds resigned, like she has made up her mind about something—maybe about me. I hate how I'm viscerally aware of the transformation humming in my veins, how I want to muddle the clear boundary between us by peppering her neck with soft pecks.

"Okay, Mister Show-off. Toss your tools into your bucket and meet me at the sink."

Both covered in splotches of dried clay, we take turns under the one faucet. I clean one tool and dry it off while she cleans one of hers. And then we switch; her drying while I wash. I'm hyperaware every time our wrists brush against one another. Or how I want more contact each time the back of her forearm glides against mine.

I reach towards her bucket, swipe up a blob of wet clay and streak it across her nose. "Whoops."

"Jacob Talksihnn! How dare you!"

Fuck it. Slowly, I reach over, as if I'm about to wipe her clean, but instead spread the smudge further, up and over her forehead.

Her glare would be murderous if she weren't smirking. There's a nagging gut feeling that begs me to invite her as my plus one to the gala, but to witness Alouette in a striking gown might be the death of me.

"We should get to researching, but thank you for teaching me, little owl." I poke her nose to decorate it with another clay blob.

"Thanks for the cheeseburgers," she says, her nose scrunching up in the cutest way known to planet earth.

Fuck. Me. I'm done.

My phone rings and I expect it to be Erik, but Marquis's contact image shows up on the screen—one I've saved from ten years ago when he's taking a body shot off a guy who now is his husband. A thousand times he has hassled me to change his picture, but I refuse.

"Be right back. Don't clean anything without me."

She laughs as I hop out of the studio and answer my phone.

"Why are you with Alouette?" Marquis spits out before I can say a word.

"What?"

I scan the hallway ceiling for cameras.

"You're plastered all over the internet outside my parents' house. This article's title is *'The Mackin' Master plans to master another sweetheart.'* Oh, and this one says *'Talksihnn has sights set on bigger game-Nkosi scholar.'* So, I'll ask again, why are you with Lou?"

"We're only workin' together, mate. Helpin' each other out, that's it."

He pauses. One. Two. Three beats. "I didn't tell you my spell this month, Jake. Wanna know what it is?"

I swallow and my chest tightens.

"I can detect lies. So, I'm calling you out on your bullshit. We've dealt with a lot together, man, but don't touch my sister. Leave her alone. You understand?"

"Yeah, mate. It's not a problem, but I gotta ask ... why?"

"You'd delirious, right?"

I'm glad an ocean separates us. "You'd destroy her. I love ya, man, really, but you two will *never* be okay."

"Righteo."

Who Alouette dates is her choice and maybe that person could be me.

CHAPTER FOURTEEN

Alouette

The next morning, I run towards the sea faster than the sun can rise over the sparkling water. My toes sink into the warm sand. It's too early for swimmers, volleyball players, and shell collectors, but the surfers wait in their line for the next wave. I spot Jacob quickly, magnetized by his energy. He doesn't know I'm here, yet I still throw my arms up, waving wildly to get his attention. Stopping before the whispering tide touches my toes, I inhale the salty ocean breeze, then shout his name at the top of my lungs.

The crashing waves collect my voice and send it to the seaweed.

"Turn around!" I yell.

He needs to know that the spirits sent me a message in my dream last night. The second I awoke, I did their bidding and Googled 'Bennett Savion events,' a charity auction was added to the list. By some miracle, it's in the Outer Dunes. Better yet, it's in two nights. I refuse to use the Nkosi name to call in a favor to attend the gala, but maybe a certain surfer celebrity wouldn't mind using his status to our advantage.

The downside: I'd be Jacob's date. The upside: I'd be his date.

Tangy sea spray skims my face as I watch Jacob in action. He must know how to consider the size of the swell, the speed of the waves, the length of time between sets and the height of the tide. Me? I crack my knuckles and pray to the Goddess above he isn't swept away by Crone's mighty sea.

Within a quick blink, I miss him rising to stand on his surfboard. He's already balancing atop and rides the wave all the way to the shore. Faint cheers erupt from the rest of the surfers and Jacob sends them a pumped fist in the air.

I expect him to rejoin them, instead, he's moving closer, the sun haloing him in light. The urge to find shelter in his hug is overpowering and, to say the least, terrifying.

"Owlette? What ya doin' here?" He shakes water from his hair while positioning his board against his side.

"I found something," I say quickly, an adrenaline rush shooting through me. "I couldn't wait to tell you."

A beaming smile lights up his face, his aqua eyes twinkling. I pace, unable to stay still, until he reaches my side. "You're literally bouncin'. Tell me before you explode."

"Bennett Savion will be at a party in the Outer Dunes this Friday!" I imagine all that could happen that night, the information he might tell me about Ouma. "Can you do me a favor and get us tickets? Pretty please."

His bubbly smile disappears in an instant. "Ya wanna use my status for your gain? Is that all ya see me as?"

"Oh no, not at all. Um, I was hoping ..."

He laughs, and hops forward, poking my waist. "Fuck, it's okay. I'm goin' anyways."

"You are?"

He nods towards his van, and I match his stride across the sand, our footprints side by side. If anyone else sees us, they might even assume we are holding hands.

"Yup. A lawyer will be there I need to chat with. Would've told ya last night, but ... guess I forgot once we started throwin'.

Planting his surfboard in the sand, he crosses his arms and leans against the van.

"I'll make ya a deal. Take a swimmin' lesson with me, and I'll bring ya as my plus one."

"Okay, I'll check my calendar and pencil you in."

"Nope." He tosses me a wetsuit from a rack. "Now."

I hurl it back at his chest. "I don't think so. Pick something else."

He chucks it at me again. "If I have to face my fear for this event, it's only fair that you do, too."

"Fear?" I search his face. "Of what?"

One hand runs through his hair as he looks into the distance, then scrubs down his beard, which is growing longer by the day. "Marquis. He ..."

"He what?" I immediately assume the worst of my brother. There's a pounding in my ears and I see red. "What did he say?"

Jacob's wandering hand clings to the back of his neck. "I shouldn't be sayin' this." He plants his feet wide apart, as if bracing for an argument. "Your brother is one of my closest friends. Sure, we give each other shit, but I'd jump in front of a truck for that man."

"And?" My veins strain against my skin. I hold my breath and hope he doesn't say what I expect him to.

"He saw a picture of us in the tabloids and lashed out. Said we couldn't hang out. I don't wanna fuck anythin' up."

"You won't. Let me worry about my stupid brother."

My throat turns dry and there's an edgy, twitchy feeling crawling through my body. I get tunnel vision and want to pound Marquis with a pillow until he sees stars. His protectiveness of Jacob was expected, but his deep-seated shame in me, preventing his best friend from being seen with his low-achieving sister, is the final straw. It had been naïve of me to think Marquis was on my side all these years. Apparently, underneath his sweet nature, Marquis has been as disappointed in my life choices as my parents.

I grip the wetsuit tighter. "Where do I change?"

Jacob's eyes widen to the point of bulging. "You don't have bathers under that?" I catch him scan my black dress up and down.

"Nope."

Silently, he points to the van, and I climb in. It smells of salt and coconuts, thanks to the multiple air refreshers on his dashboard. Unable to resist, I glance in the back, shocked by how much space there is to move. Everything is crisply organized in labeled bins. He wasn't joking about being a cleaning expert. The seats have all been taken out and there's enough space for a six-foot man to sleep. Clear containers full of folded clothes create makeshift dressers that double as a table. Hmm, someone has been watching episodes of Tiny House.

Still infuriated with Marquis, I strip to my underwear and bra, shove on the wetsuit that fits too snugly, and march out to Jacob with fake confidence. The best way to convince me to do something is to say that I *shouldn't*. My brother will learn that I control my own fate and make my own choices, whether or not he approves. If I want to spend the entire night at the gala, latched to Jacob's arm, by Seer's Sight, I will.

"Ready," I warn Jacob as he's watching the other surfers.

He turns, saying, "That was fast, do you—" His gaze drops to my curves in the tight spandex material and a low rumble vibrates in his chest. That sexy knot in his throat rises and falls slowly. Yeah, there's no denying he's attracted to me.

"I'm puttin' ya in a life vest the first time." He stands closer and wraps the straps around me. "Alouette, you're shakin'. We don't actually have to swim. I'll take ya to the party, I swear."

"I'm goin' in with or without you." I unclench my jaw that keeps clamping tightly from nerves.

"Okay, okay, wait, I'm right behind ya.'" He jogs after me until water washes over the tip of our toes. "I'll keep ya safe. Don't worry. We can stop anytime. Do ya wanna hold my hand?"

I glance down at his hand, held out in offering, and shake my head. I need to have enough faith in myself to believe that I can swim. Maybe if I can conquer this, then I'll believe that I can also find Ouma's cottage and start my own business.

I suck in a deep breath and take a step forward. Ankles disappear below the surface. Zola would faint if she saw me now. Forward. Shins soaked. Too fast. I want to sprint as far away as possible. My legs wobble and my knees buckle, but I straighten before Jacob can catch me. Thighs wet.

What if there's sharp, hidden shrapnel down there in the murky water? What if I lose a foot and the pain is unbearable?

"Hey, little owl. Breathe with me. In. Out. That's good."

His voice is faint, far enough to be in another world. "You're doin' great. Keep goin', you can do this."

Water rises to my waist. The waves slam into me in warning.

I can do this. I will.

I tackle the hardest part head-on, powering through the swell of the wave which takes my feet off the ground. At the ocean's mercy, I paddle like a deranged cat to where the water is calmer. On the other side, I'm out of breath, shaking, pulse racing, but when I lock onto Jacob's eyes, the pride present there erases my fears.

"You did it!" Jacob pulls me into him so my vest is pressed against his chest.

"Only because you're here," I say, glancing at the coast.

A wave empties its last energy onto the sandbar. On this side of the wave, it reminds me of watching Ms. Grim fly in the garden, wild and fierce. We bob, face to face for far too long, until I can see tiny golden flecks in his turquoise eyes. Finally, he clears his throat and points to where his friends still surf.

"To us, the water is energy, a soul, each droplet representing little intimate fractions of life. It's a force to feel, to unite with."

"Mr. Talksihnn. You didn't tell me you're a poet."

"Nah, I'm not brilliant like ya."

He thinks I'm brilliant? My cheeks warm, but hopefully it'll only look like the sun has kissed my face.

"Watch. See the bulge in the water moving towards them? We can feel the size and strength beforehand, well at least I can. My favorite part is the sudden slope then leapin' onto my feet."

The universe chooses that moment to shine brilliant rays on Jacob, illuminating him with an aura that could only be explained by magic. Goosebumps slide along the back of my neck, and I feel fully awake for the first time in weeks, maybe months. Every shade of color in the water intensifies, but it's the way Jacob looks that enchants me, full of wonder and awe or even enlightenment with the way he gazes at the horizon. That euphoric state is a sensation I feel only when in my studio. It dawns on me that we've both shared a meaningful piece of ourselves already. Maybe I know more about him than I realized. And I don't want to stop sharing anytime soon.

"I want to tell you how I got my scars," I say.

"Here? You sure? Maybe once we get back on land?"

"No, this is the purrrfect time."

"Purr?" he asks.

"When I'm nervous—"

"You make cat puns. I've noticed." He smiles, giving me time to decide.

I bite my lip. "I was eight ..."

"I'm listenin'," he says whole-heartedly, while treading water so close that I can see specs of gold in his eyes.

"I've always loved the beach, but I wouldn't say I was the best swimmer. And I was crazy for any seashells I found on the ocean floor because they were way better than the ones washed up on the beach.

"One day, I was diving under to grab shells from the bottom. It was only four feet or so, nothing too dangerous..." I take a steadying breath before continuing. "But I almost died that day."

Jacob's eyes go wide.

"I saw the metal before it hit me. It barreled towards me so fast, all ragged and rough around the edges ..." I pause, focusing on his arms squeezing me. It's enough to keep me going. "I tried to swim away but a sharp corner sliced into my back. I screamed and sucked in a heap of water. It burned my lungs and then the waves toppled me head over heels, and carried me out of control. Every time I flipped and twisted, the metal followed, carving fresh gashes in my back. I had never been that scared. I couldn't even explain the pain. It felt like being ripped open."

Jacob wipes away my tear. But it's the swelling lump in my throat that needs tending to.

"The water tousled me around with such fury I didn't think I'd ever see the surface again. I don't remember making it back to the sand. It's all a haze until the lifeguards were rolling me over and their hands came away bloody."

"You went into shock," Jacob states.

I nod. "I was in the hospital for days." Taking a breath, I gaze out at the glistening water. " I don't know how you're brave enough to go out there every day with the risk."

"Sometimes the scariest things are worth fightin' for," he says quietly, drawing my attention back.

A vital tectonic plate shifts in my chest, giving space for the expansion of the unknown. I'll always remember conquering my fear today, but I want something to fully ground it. I memorize the rhythm of Jacob's breathing; a steady pace that will help me stay calm in the water, and perhaps in other frightening situations, too.

Jacob has helped me conquer my fears. Like being in his presence brings something new and brave out of me. I wouldn't mind keeping him around longer. What's the worst thing that could happen?

CHAPTER FIFTEEN

Jacob

The scent of pizza deliciously spreads through the Fuzer Homeless Sanctuary as I finish showing my surfing students how the shelter serves dinner to those in need. All ten kids happily volunteered. Just because my magic doesn't work anymore doesn't mean I'd abandoned the shelter. The sweet kids smile at each person and remember not to ask anyone to show off their magic, since most here have been stripped of their powers. A shiver runs up my spine as I realize that I may be among them soon. I have less than a week to find Dakota and the cottage, or I'll never feel magic in my veins again.

Alouette and I have to succeed. There's no other choice. But first, she needs to kiss me before midnight tomorrow. It feels like an impossible task. I didn't see her at all yesterday as she burrowed away in her library. One spell showed promise, but we'd need rare ingredients and someone who is crafty with potions. And that is not my expertise.

The number of cameras following me have become so

intrusive that Erik has hired centaur body guards. It's excessive, but necessary since Nella posted her new false claim.

The paparazzi wave from across the street. Thanks to someone's spell, a protective dome surrounds the sanctuary. No matter how many flashes burn my eyes, no one will get a decent photograph.

Marquis's face lights up my buzzing phone. I step away from the tempting pizza and make my way into the alleyway out back. Thankfully, no cameras jump out at me from behind the dumpster.

"Hey, you rotten bastard," Marquis says, smiling. "How's the weather?"

"Fuck the weather, mate. Yesterday, it was sunny and birds were chirpin' and the next minute the sky turned pink and we were all expectin' another storm rush that never came."

He nods on screen then winces. "Yeah, it's all over the news. Only happening on the east coast of the States right now. Wonder what's going on? All that global warming and crap." He checks something on his desk, then looks up again. "I heard Erik hired bodyguards. How are the centaurs working out?"

"They're as professional as your ass in front of a lecture hall full of students."

He laughs. "Ah, I don't know if that's a compliment or a dig."

I kick an empty soda can across the pavement with my bare feet like it's a ball. "It's a good thing you're in Sydney hiding."

"Alright, big mouth. Prove it on the thirteenth. You'll still be in Calypsa for the ceremony?"

"You're flyin' back?" My body tenses, but I need to act like I don't care. "Lucky me."

"Fuck, you, bro." Marquis chuckles and starts writing again. "I'm goin to support Lou. She said this ceremony was special and I need to be there."

Despite his calm approach, a thick tension suspends in the silence between us. If Alouette hasn't told her brother there's a chance she'll never be able to use another spell again, then it's not my place to inform him.

"Right, mate. We'll have to get some coldies, unless you're still on your virgin daiquiri phase. No judgment here."

He laughs so hard he slaps the table. "Remember my senior year when we went to that lake house with John's crew? Now *that* guy knows how to mix a cocktail."

Memories flip through my mind like a reel of that weekend. We practically lived on the dock, falling asleep with our toes dangling over the edge into the water.

"Yeah, mate. I'm getting' too old for all that. I have a ten-year-old daughter, for Christ's sake."

He pauses, brings his phone closer and stares seriously. "She's a girl?"

I can't help but smile. "I think her name's Dakota."

"Congrats, man!" He jumps out of his chair and nearly falls into the bookcase behind him. "Finally you found some answers! Fuck, I wish I could hug you right now. What's she look like?"

"Haven't seen her yet."

"Then how do you know her name?"

"An oracle."

Marquis frowns, returning to his seat. "Jake ... that doesn't make it true. Whoever read your cards could've created any story for a few extra bucks. Do you have any proof that Dakota is her name? A birth certificate or school records?"

"No." My heart sinks. "My lawyer has told me Nella home schools."

Marquis sighs. "This situation sucks, man. I can't believe how little they've been able to find out. It's almost as if your kid doesn't exist."

This time my heart clenches so tight my chest might burst.

"What if Nella fabricated the paternity test somehow?" Marquis asks. "Maybe she has a friend in a medical lab who can create fraudulent papers."

I stare at the soda can I've been kicking. When I originally heard of my child, I had been in denial for months. Since accepting it, Marquis's suggestion has been my biggest fear. My entire being would be crushed if my child didn't exist. That would be less forgivable than Nella hiding her.

"Sorry, man. Shouldn't have said that," he says, voice low and sullen. "I have a class soon. Take care, Jake. See ya next week."

"Oath, thanks."

His face disappears as I hang up. Every cell in my body burns with frustration. I'm damned stuck. Nella has the media eating out of the palm of her hand with every social media sob story she posts online. Doing the exact opposite of what Erik has advised, I log into my anonymous account and search for Nella's name.

Fuck. She has 200k followers. Yesterday's post starts with a picture of Nella in front of an ice cream truck with the quote: 'There were harsh trolls after my last post that implied my child doesn't exist. Here ya go world: here's proof. My baby gets to pick any flavor they want and as many scoops as they can eat once a month. Even a hard-working single mom remembers what it's like being a kid with a sugar craving. Today's choice: strawberry.'

I swipe the image and gasp. It's an image of a little hand holding an ice cream cone. Of course, this could be any child, not Dakota. But what if it *is* real? This is the first time I've seen a piece of her. Faster than I can process, I click on and swipe all of Nella's past images I've never seen to check if any had pictures of a child with her. Nope. None. This was the first.

I need to hire better lawyers. I don't know shit about what information they're allowed to gather about Dakota. Maybe if I tell them what the oracle said, they'd have leads on how to research more?

"You're thinking so hard your brain might explode," a sugary voice says near the back door.

I turn to see Alouette leaning against the brick exterior. As usual, she wears another black dress. This one has a line of pink roses along the bottom that brushes against her knees when she moves. Her hair is more unruly than usual, like she's gone to war with the humidity.

"G'day, how's it goin'?" I pick up the can quickly and toss it into a recycling bin in the alley.

"Nice shot." Alouette nods, then picks up a bottle cap and throws it straight into the trash too. "I have a dress fitting appointment next door for our da—" she looks to the ground, then mutters something under her breath. When she lifts her head, her big brown eyes lock onto mine. "For the gala tomorrow. I wanted to stop by to see if you were here."

I move closer, placing one hand on the wall next to her head, and lean into her ear to whisper, "Miss me?"

Do I need her to kiss me? Yes. Would I want her to

anyways, without the oracle's premonition hanging over my head? Yes. But rushing it feels like a trick, like a lie, like something forced and unnatural.

"I thought about you all day yesterday," I say.

"Me too." A soft breath escapes her lips.

"So why'd ya hide from me?" I ask her.

I hear her audibly swallow. "I was busy, Jacob. You know that."

When she half-heartedly tries to move out from under me, I put my free hand against her waist and gently pin her to the wall.

Hoping she can't see me squeeze my eyes shut, I whisper, "And I thought about you last night too, before bed, when I was in the shower."

A tiny gasp parts her lips, but she remains still. I can feel the fight within her, the battle of deciding how to respond. What I know about Alouette is she's full of contradictions. She's a shy woman with a tiger's spirit. A cunning, creative soul who has no confidence in herself, yet somewhere deep inside she knows she could obliterate any competition.

I lean even closer, so my words are a breath against her skin. "I mentioned I have a little fetish for PDA. Anyone could walk by the alley and see us in the heat of the moment."

"Jacob!" This time she pushes against my chest and escapes. "Where is this coming from?"

I drop my head and scrunch up my face. "Sorry, I'm into you and I came off too strong. I should've–"

"Should've?" She cuts me off and her voice changes. "Tell me, what would you do right now if the word '*should*' didn't exist?"

"I'd kiss you," I say to the brick wall. "But I can't. Forget it."

She's quiet for so long that I'm sure she has left. I ready my fist to punch the bloody dumpster when a quiet sound slips from between her lips. Lips I'm afraid to turn around to see. Because if there's fire in her eyes like when she taught me how to throw pottery, I may not be able to resist myself.

"Jacob ... it's best if we stay focused until the ceremony. There's too much at stake to get distracted."

"You're right," I lie, fighting the urge to face her. "I'll see ya tomorrow."

This time, I'm hyper aware of her confused energy behind me. I want to apologize for being a douchebag, but she beats me to it.

"I'm sorry if I've created any confusion, Jacob. It was never my intention. I'll have a driver pick you up at four tomorrow, but I'll take a separate limo," she pauses. "After all, if I only have six more days to use my parents' fortune, may as well take advantage of it before I go out on my own."

Silence follows, and then I hear the door swing open. The pads of her feet patter down the hall. Of course she'd be barefoot. We're two of the same kind, but she doesn't want me in the same way as I want her.

CHAPTER SIXTEEN

Alouette

Barefoot, I stand on a raised platform surrounded by mirrors in the dress store. The scent of fresh flowers flutters like unicorn sparkles in the air.

I *should* be grateful that the manager of 'Mess of a Dress' recognized me from a Nkosi family portrait in the Fuzer Times and let me into her shop without wearing mandatory shoes. I *should* be. Instead, I'm irritated that I took advantage of the perk connected to my last name. Once I find Ouma's cottage, I decided my new last name will be something average like Smith or Parker. Alouette Jones sounds magnificent.

I check out every angle of my ass in this gorgeous gown. The black sheath is practically painted onto my curves. It's not my usual style, but I had to choose this one because of the pink trim detail on the upper half, which accentuates my boobs marvelously. If I have one chance at being Jacob's date, I want to blow him away.

Soft music plays from a speaker, and I hum along, not

knowing the words. All the magic in the store is clearly focused on a bride sipping champagne. Enchanted veils, purses, and belts fling themselves across the aisles for a chance to be worn.

The friends and family surrounding the bride show a fleet of emotions more varied than a circus act—from jokes to sobs to sharp opinions. I haven't decided if I ever want to have a wedding. To me, marriage looks like a religious way to restrict women. Committing to a life partner verbally, without all the legalities, sounds more romantic than following a set of documents and policies that are expected from society norms. Another *should*.

I keep my distance from the group and remain next to the one window facing the Fuzer Sanctuary. That way, if Jacob leaves, I'll get to sneak one more look at him before the big gala tomorrow.

My mind is in a flurry from his confession in the alley. He had acted so primal and desperate, in a way I never thought I'd be attracted to. That's one more way he has surprised me. His carnal desire confused the Abyss out of me.

Clearly, he wanted to kiss me. That much was evident. I'm pretty sure a part of me was disappointed when he backed down. Did I want him to try harder? To fight for a chance?

His other admission about getting caught in the moment plays on repeat in my head. Why does this imagery make my heart pump faster, like it's my personal addiction? Standing that close to him felt like the morning mist in my garden, like a ballad on the radio that I can't help but sing along to.

This is nonsense. What I need is for Zola to talk some

sense into me. She's supposed to call any minute now to approve my dress selection.

A sprite employee flies closer, needle in hand, and begins pinning spots in my dress that need altered. I turn when she motions, doing my best to position myself to still see out the window. Will he glance this way as he leaves? Or maybe he'll march straight over here and demand to talk to me in the privacy of a dressing room. Tingles rush up my spine at the thought of his large hands on my skin. But since I created a boundary, I won't be a tease. We can only be friends.

When my phone rings, the sprite allows me to grab it from my bag and re-situate onto the platform. I click the video option on and flip it towards the mirrors. Zola immediately squeals on the other end.

"Oh my Stars! Lou, you are ... wow! All you need are some wings, and you could rule the skies!"

"I can attach wings," the sprite peeps in a small, quiet voice.

"No, it's okay. I'd rather blend in with the crowd," I decline at the same time as Zola yells, "Yes! She needs wings!"

We both laugh, but I quickly compose myself to avoid accidental needle pricks.

"How's London?"

"So big. It'll take me years to visit every site I want to. I'm still jet lagged. Barely been outside my apartment. I share it with a girl from Paris. Can you believe it? Angelique said she'll bring me to her parents' place next month and give me a taste of the best food in France."

My insides squirm with jealousy—both towards London and Angelique for enjoying my best friend without me. I have to remember that Zola deserves happiness at

Quaint Brush. Some time apart won't destroy what we've built.

"I can't wait for you to visit. There are some hotties here too. Their accent is ..." She mimes a chef's kiss. "Though maybe you prefer an Aussie accent?" Her brows raise in question.

"About that ... I need your help with Jacob."

"Anything. Tell me where we are on the spectrum between burying his body and chopping up his surfboard." Her lips curl in disgust. "What he'd do?"

I drop my forehead into my hand and groan. "Nothing. He's done absolutely nothing."

"Oh, you *want* him to do something?" Zola winks dramatically. "I'm on it. Give me his number; I'll send him a little hint."

I wave one hand in the air. "No, no. Listen, Zola, I need you to convince me why Jacob is a terrible guy, the worst possible option."

She goes silent for a minute, face scrutinizing mine. When I don't add any more information, she sucks in a loud breath and starts, "You don't want to date a man who has a child."

I don't respond, although I've never been opposed to the idea. The opportunity hasn't presented itself with past boyfriends.

"He smells awful," Zola spits out randomly.

False. Jacob's scent is warm and comforting like summer rainstorms.

"You told me he doesn't have a home," she says.

"Go on," I urge, needing more substantial reasons.

"You like such opposite things. How can you date a surfer when you hate the water?"

I fail to mention how freeing my swim lesson had felt

with Jacob encouraging me every step of the way.

"He has crossed the street on a Tuesday before and we know what kind of omen that is, don't we, chica?" She scrunches up her nose in thought. "Um, oh, I know! There are extensive rumors about him. Some of them are bound to be true."

Those haven't phased me. Not that I've read many, but I know from experience how false the tabloids can be. "I need more." I sigh and gesture for her to continue.

"Okay, okay. Let me think." Zola stares off screen then bangs her hand on the table. "You said he's a surfing instructor. That's not a high-paying job *or* at the caliber your family would expect."

That only makes me like him more.

"Someone who teaches kids all day is not reaching their full potential because—"

"I don't agree," I interrupt. "His passion for the sport supports others who want to learn. Spreading knowledge and joy like that is admirable."

"Well, I'm running out of ideas, Lou. How about this: Jacob is terrible in bed," she says, unconvincingly.

I close my eyes as an involuntary shudder racks my whole body. A vivid image of Jacob, naked, lying flat on his back with one hand behind his head, smiling up at me like I'm his personal sun fills my mind.

"Fuuudge," I mutter, but Zola catches it.

"Oh, Lou. You like him a lot, don't you?" She moves her phone closer, as if that will decrease the expansive space between us. "What do you need? I can threaten him to leave town."

I shake my head as tears prick behind my eyes. These feelings weren't supposed to happen, but I hear Ivola's wretched voice like it's burned into my ears. '*Whatever you came here wanting to find ... you have to help each other find before midnight on the thirteenth or you'll be stripped of your powers forever.'*

"Let's focus on the party, Lou," Zola goes on, "and a strategy for tomorrow night. What's your goal?"

"To talk to Bennett Savion," I reply quickly, pushing away my impulsive thoughts saying, 'to ride Jacob until the sun rises.'

"Good, and why do you want to talk to him?"

I nod into the mirror, pumping myself up. "Because he has a clue about Ouma's cottage."

The sprite points to the shelf of wigs, the traditional accessory in upper society events on the East Coast, like it's common practice for members of Western Clubs to wear fancy hats. We all have our strange customs. The bright pink wig with bangs sits on a mannequin's head, front and center, with my name on it.

When the sprite flops it onto my head and I readjust it, a new brilliant idea forms that could also help with Jacob's custody problems.

CHAPTER SEVENTEEN

Jacob

I'm enduring the most blissful type of torture. The hotel Erik booked didn't have two separate rooms, so the manager magicked us a portable room divider, but I can clearly see Alouette's silhouette through the thin fabric. Her movements as she dresses for the gala—her body twisting and gliding—are captivating, impossible to ignore.

Fuck. I want to be the one to zip her into her dress. I could be the guy who clasps her necklace together then kisses my way down the chain until she giggles and swats me away. My fists clench and release for the hundredth time as I peel my gaze away. This must be what agony feels like.

I straighten my pink bowtie. I'm certain Alouette will be wearing some type of pink accessory. Though, will she choose bright pink or pastel? Either way, she'll turn every head whether she's in a pantsuit, dress, or clown outfit.

The lines of my rented tux are tailored to my body

perfectly, thanks to the charm that came with the order. It's been a few years since I've wiggled myself into one of these and would rather walk into the party in a wetsuit or swimmers.

From the other side of the makeshift barrier, she hums softly, with a voice that vibrates straight to my bones. Listening to her feels like she's carved a hole in my chest and yanked out my heart. Fuck, I have it bad. Why couldn't we have met ten years ago? Or even four? It would've saved me from severe heartbreak with Felicity. I've only been in love once, but when Nella made her public announcement to the world that we had a child together, Felicity couldn't handle the surprise. I had barely managed a goodbye before she vanished from my life forever. That's not a feeling I'd wish upon my greatest enemy.

"Um, Jacob?" Alouette's quiet voice peeps from the other side of the room. "Can you help?"

"Yeah, what's wrong, mate?"

"You have to swear to keep your eyes closed, though."

"Why?"

"Because I said so."

"Nah, I'm not feline it."

"Jacob!" She gasps in fake-shock. "Did you make a cat pun?"

"Meow-by. Meow-by not." Chuckling, I shake my head and snap my eyes shut. "How am I supposed to help ya?"

"You swear you can't see anything?" she asks, and I can feel the air flutter around my face like she's waving her hand by my nose.

"Oath, I swear."

"Okay, I'm gonna guide your hands to where my wings connect to my dress."

"Holy shit! Wings? Do I need to find a pair?"

"Don't worry, I brought you some."

I bite my lip, using every bit of strength to not open my eyes when she moves closer. Her perfume of wildflowers and berries hits me like a soft caress.

Fabric rustles against my hands, feathery and light. A vivid image overtakes my mind of running a single feather over Alouette's bare stomach, below the swell of her breasts. Slowly, I raise my hands and fumble with the fabric and buckle along her waist. Every part of me wants to prolong this for as long as possible.

"On the belt, there's a hook," she instructs softly, almost a whisper, "feel for a small metal loop."

After a few stumbles, I latch the wings on and immediately miss her when she steps away.

"Can I open my eyes now?"

"No."

I stay hyper-focused on her pitter patter footsteps that sound like raindrops on the carpet as she moves through the room.

"Are you peeking?" I ask, angling my head to where she makes sounds, like I'm a hound tracking her.

"You didn't tell me not to."

"Not fair," I groan.

"Don't worry. You look pretty with your bowtie," she teases, yet her voice holds almost a sultry note. "Wait, I need to straighten it."

Her hand gently adjusts my tie, then rises to flutter along the line of my jaw, lingering longer than necessary. I could paint a kiss along her fingertips. Once she straightens my bowtie, which I am certain was already straight, her hands drop to my chest. My breath hitches.

"Jacob..."

"Owlette?"

I swear, even with my eyes closed, I know what her face looks like right now. Hesitant but wanting. Will she work up the courage to grasp what she desires? I'm right here, available, and certainly willing.

She sighs, then backs up. "Where's your wig?"

I point to the chair next to me, then hear her climb on something.

"Careful, you might fall."

"I won't as long as you stay still."

"Mhm," is all I can manage to say since I'm guessing her boobs are directly in front of my eyes if she's balancing on a chair.

With delicate gentleness, she places the jet-black wig over my hair.

It's a good thing I shaved to a clean, fresh face today so my blond beard wouldn't clash. With only a few strokes of her hands, she's tucked my hair under the wig.

"Can you put your hand out to help me down? I don't want to rip my dress."

Her body weight presses into my palm as she steps down. I don't want her to let go.

"Would your grandma like parties like this? I bet she was a force to be reckoned with."

"Ouma loved life. From ice skating to leather crafting to bird watching and teacup collecting, she cherished each experience and took nothing for granted. Once we took an archery class together and got matching bruises on our forearms," she says, chuckling lightly. "When I was nineteen, she felt inspired by a documentary about murals and she woke me up at midnight just to drive her to a random alleyway so she could graffiti the wall. I swear I thought I was going to jail."

"Sounds like a cool person."

"It seemed like she was trying to get me out of my shell, to enlighten me to what else the world offered. But I was happy throwing pottery and reading."

"Your thrillers."

"Mhm, until Ouma dragged me to an erotica book club. Zola made fun of me for ages about the cucumber keychains they passed out."

"Did ya ... like that specific kind of book?"

"Only the ones with public sex scenes."

My cock twitches at the same time as my damned phone rings, much too loud for the mood in the room. I jump in place. "Blimey!"

"One second!" Something—maybe the room divider—scrapes along the carpet. "Okay, open your eyes."

My phone, displaying Erik's face, rests on the bed; I grab it, answering, "How's it goin', mate?"

"Nella arrived at the party," he says with a harsh, emergent voice. "It looks like she's up to somethin' crazy and try'na sabotage' ya."

"What do ya mean?"

"She's turned up with ya other exes."

"No!"

"And a social media influencer hasn't left their side. Looks like you're in for a whirlwind of a night."

"Why would she do this?!" I panic.

"Beats me. She's either certifiably insane, bro, or gotta crazy vendetta for ya."

It feels like spiders are crawling along my neck.

"By recruiting my other exes?"

"Yeah. Felicity and Sonya and another, I can't remember her name, but I sure do remember that face. So, four women you've screwed are all out there, ready to battle."

Lightheadedness overcomes me instantly. "Why? I've

given Nella everythin' she's asked for. I'm broke, mate. What else does she want from me?"

"Looks like she's going after the jugular too, mate. Not sure how ya goin' get outta this one. But it looks like somethin's gonna go down." Erik frowns. "I'll ask around and text ya when I learn more. Good luck, mate. You'll need it." He hangs up faster than I can process another question.

"Damn it!" I yell and kick the chair.

"You okay?"

I turn around.

Fuck. All the air is sucked from my lungs. The room disappears. Any moonlight shining through the window amplifies the evening's glow on Alouette's brown skin. My gaze sweeps upwards from the base of her black goth boots, buckles disappearing beneath her dress. Whoever chose her gown is a pure genius, deserving of medals and trophies and the entire lottery.

The thin, fitted dress hugs her curves in an elegant and sophisticated way. Of course, it's black with electric pink details. The hue I picked matches perfectly, and is the same color as her pop of lipstick—brave and striking. My chest squeezes with longing. I hope her reflection shows her the fiery passion I see in her, an inextinguishable flame.

Even though most people will be drawn to her magenta wig, I can't take my attention off her eyes. And those lips. I will not survive the night if I don't taste her. I swear to Luna Above if she doesn't initiate a kiss, I will. Guaranteed. But how am I supposed to do that with four of my exes in the same room?

CHAPTER EIGHTEEN

Alouette

We walk the red carpet, arm and arm, outside of the Museum of Science and Animal Studies. I try to ignore the paparazzi cameras flashing and focus on the moody music that has a crimson sharp edge of autumn.

"Names?" a staff member asks.

"Jacob Talksihnn, and Alouette—"

"Talksihnn." I keep my eyes on the attendee when I feel Jacob's gaze dip to study my face.

Please play along. Don't deny it. Crap, I should've asked him if this was okay.

"The list shows *unnamed* as your plus one." They inspect my wings with obvious intrigue, then set their sights on Jacob.

"Great, now you have her name." Jacob places his free hand over the one I have wrapped around his arm; a silent cue he'll play along.

As he guides me through the grand double doors, only my wings are extended, otherwise we wouldn't both fit. We walk down the long, dark corridor, lined with framed moths and butterflies like at home. Honestly, it makes me a little nauseous. Even on a date, I'm surrounded by the haunting pressure of my family. No matter where I go, their influence finds me.

"So you're a Talksihnn tonight?" Jacob leans close to whisper as we keep distance between the couple ahead.

"Hope that's okay." I glance up, heartbeat hammering wildly.

"How are we playin' this, mate?" He grins, amused by this adventure. "You're my sister or ...?"

"Wife." I swallow, as the chatter ahead grows louder. "It'll help us both."

All he does is nod, calm ... unphased. I can't decide if his demeanor is good or bad. If he thought about the idea of us being an item, wouldn't his face be flushed? Regardless, I'm milking this for as long as possible since it feels like heaven to shed my last name.

I savor the spot where our bodies connect, wishing we had fewer layers between us. Regardless of the confidence Jacob carries, I know he'd be more comfortable in swim trunks than in this tux—even though his appearance tonight could inspire sonnets. Was it his idea to smudge black eyeliner under his eyes? It matches his dark wig almost too well.

The hallway opens to an expansive gallery where at least one hundred people mingle and chat in their expensive outfits. A huge banner drapes across the elevator window that reads: *Unified Charity Auction Gala*. After completing some research last night, I learned that this annual event invites both high ranking Typs and Fuzers of prestige and wealth to raise money for several programs.

"Look, her earrings are down to her shoulders," I whisper. "And that fairy has a crown. Is she a princess?"

A low grumble of acknowledgement comes from Jacob's chest as he also scans the room. Does he know some of the other celebs?

"You're the most captivating person here, Alouette. You're stealin' everyone's attention."

Heat scorches my skin and climbs up my neck.

"And that makes you growl?" I glance up at his face, where his brows are pulled together.

"I didn't growl."

"Oh yes you did, now, like this." I do my best impression, which makes him smirk.

As I step further into the room, I'm met with a cool, spacious area decorated with elaborate architectural details. The air feels hushed and respectful and important, with soft lighting along the perimeter. On one side, tucked away in shadows, are several artifacts, specimens, and fossils I recognize as replicates from the Nkosi museum back home. However, they don't take center stage tonight.

Spotlights illuminate rows of tables laden with tablets for participants to bid during the silent auction. Behind us, three high-top counters present a wide variety of beverages, each bartender dressed in rainbow uniforms. The far wall, though, is what grabs my attention. Rising from floor to ceiling over at least three stories, a massive glass wall stands tall. On the other side, a greenhouse holds more types of plants than I could count, full of birds and bugs.

Every little inkling in my body wants to set the birds

free. I wave to a toucan who compliments my dress with a clear ruffle of his feathers.

"I need to tell you something before we make too many intros." Softly, Jacob pulls me away from a speaker and leans towards my ear.

I feel his breath on my neck, but he doesn't speak. He waits. And waits.

"Jacob?"

He stands so close I have to crane my neck up. His face looks like he's in pain, as if he's holding in a sneeze.

"Uh, are you okay?"

"Fuckin' hell, little owl, your hair smells perfect." He shakes his head like he's in a trance. "Sorry ... anyways, I was gonna say that my ex is here tonight."

"Where? What does she look like?" I glance behind him and do my best to not pin each woman around our age with little dagger glares. "What color wig would she wear?"

He rubs a hand down behind his neck. "Actually. Four of them. Nella, Sonya, Posh, and ... Felicity."

I take a step back, my boots clunking into a chair. "Are you kitten me?"

"Did you say *kitten*?"

I throw my hands up in the air. "Yeah, how am I supposed to compete with four other women? This is insane!"

"Compete?" Jacob comes behind me, his front gently pressed against my back. I swear he's debating about wrapping his arms around me. It's crazy that I'm disappointed when he stays still. "I'm flattered, little owl. That ya consider me worth competin' over," he says, his breath caressing my neck. "But you'd win the gold anyways. You're empathetic, artistic, and passionate. Don't sell yourself short."

"If I didn't know better, Mr. Talksihnn, I think you might like me a little."

He huffs, a half-frustrated sound; I turn around and gaze up at his diamond eyes.

"I *can't* like ya, Mrs. Talksihnn. But if I were allowed, then yeah, maybe you'd be right." He gulps. I hate how turned on I am from a simple throat bob. "Let's make a fun little wager tonight." He says it like a command, still quiet enough for only me to hear. "Every time someone brings up my centerfold piece in Surfers International, I'll owe ya a cheeseburger."

As heads turn our way, curiously wondering who snatched up the famous Mackin' Master, a vibrant tingle of courage washes over me like a magical mist. Maybe it is a spell cast by an onlooker, but tonight I want to be brave.

"Okay. And every time you introduce me as your wife, I'll ... owe you a kiss. A real one."

His eyes blaze with a fiery heat, dark and full of need. "Deal," he agrees before I can change my mind or create any stipulations to our arrangement.

"What do I need to know about your exes? How long were you with each one? Are they models or surfers or A-listers? Will they knife me? Should I get on their good side or act possessive? Do you want to talk to them alone? Do you still love them?"

"Slow down. Tonight, I'm yours and you're mine. Don't worry about them, be yourself. We have three goals: talk to Bennett, talk to the custody lawyer, and ... look at me, little owl."

He snags my full attention again when he grips my chin and angles my face directly towards his. Fuck, that's sexy.

"The third goal?" I ask breathlessly.

"Introducing you as my wife as many times as possible, babe."

I swallow when he reaches down to take my hand in his, then I say, "You called me babe."

"Well, I am your husband. And maybe I can be your night hawk later."

"I need to write all these nicknames down. I bet you have a label maker."

"You *wish* you could get your hands on my label maker. Lolly the Labeler is private property."

Softly, he tugs me towards an elder nymph couple, both wearing yellow wigs atop their antlers. They clang their cocktail glasses together until the male notices our rapid incoming, like we're a tidal wave out of control.

"Well, isn't this Jacob Talksihnn from Down Under? Good to see you, sir," the nymph says, sticking his tree-like hand forward for a shake.

"Yes, g'day Senator. Have you met my stunning wife, Alouette?" he says quickly, like the words would burn his tongue if he didn't spout them out.

My cheeks flush as I lean forward, barely believing that we're going through with this scheme.

"Pleased to meet you," the female next to the Senator says with a toothy smile.

Before I can shake her hand, he pulls me to the next couple nearby.

"Good evening. This is *my* wife. Alouette, meet Arora Adeline Fae Isling of Cranberry Falls. Arora, this is *my* wife."

"So, I've heard." She glances between us, a sparkle in her purple eyes.

"So sorry, mates. But we need to make our rounds. You know how it is. We'll swing back later." With a devilish grin, Jacob tugs me to more couples. I had expected him to exaggerate the word 'wife,' but his focus lies on the possessive word, '*my*.' Like he's proud and showing off what he claims. I would've hated that with any past boyfriend. When Jacob does it, a longing tension clamps tightly deep in my core.

On our way to the makeshift bar, Jacob repeatedly points at me, stopping to tell each person the same thing:

"*My* wife ..."

"Susanna. Alouette, *my* wife ..."

"Harold, meet *my* wife."

"G'day. This is *my* wife."

I roll my eyes but can't help but smile at his giddiness. I whisper, "I never said *when* you'd get these kisses."

He wiggles his eyebrows ridiculously and points a finger at me. "I think I'm more interested in *where*? Will there be an audience?"

My mouth drops to a perfectly shaped O as I slap his shoulder gently, letting my hand linger a little longer than necessary. "You weren't serious about that, right?" I ask, hoping I'm wrong. My traitorous body decides now is the best time for kegel exercises as my muscles clamp and release, making me wet. Holy Goddess! Some creatures in attendance might be able to sniff out my aroused pheromones. I also pray to Luna that no guest here has a mind reading spell because all they'll gather from my thoughts are images of Jacob touching me, kissing me, worshipping me.

This is an epic disaster.

Leaning on the bar, covered by a long black tablecloth, Jacob orders the same cocktail Marquis got me on my birthday. How does he remember that? While we wait for the bartender to mix our order, I drink in Jacob's appearance, feeling instantly guilty for being shallow enough to want him for his body. Then, I remind myself how even in serious situations, he's tinged with playfulness, how he's persistent, and selflessly sacrificed all his money to support his child.

Jacob passes me the cocktail and our hands brush tenderly. The air is charged between us like lightning about to strike. He takes a sip from his glass, eyes on me over the rim, then his attention flickers behind my shoulder.

"There he is. THE Bennett Savion just arrived," Jacob says. "And he's already got everyone's attention."

"Any bodyguards with him?" I ask before peeking.

"The two meat heads near the doors, but not around him. Let's watch for a few minutes and see how he interacts with others."

Trying not to look suspicious, I slip closer to Jacob and lean against him slightly to get a better view.

"Wantin' to get cozy?"

"Shut up. I'm trying to see him better."

"Sure, sure." He chuckles. "Doesn't look like he came with a date."

For the hundredth time after searching Bennett Savion online, I try to imagine how well he knew Ouma.

"Let's get a little closer." Jacob places his hand on the small of my back and I'm on the verge of bursting.

We overhear Bennett Savion quietly discussing the rise in magical storms and the devastation it has caused some small towns along the coast. Does he know Calypsa has suffered from one of those?

Right when I'm about to interrupt his conversation, a bright light flashes in my face.

"Tina from Talkin' Toxic here. Smile for the camera, honey. You look like a lost doe. Oh, my followers are gonna eat this up," a woman says in a high-pitched voice from behind the blinding lights. "Keep your arm around her. Perfect, like that." As more cameras flash, I shield my eyes and drop my head. Because Jacob is by my side, everything will be alright. I can take on the world with his support.

"What do you think about Jake's upcoming reunion tonight, Miss Nkosi?"

"Talksihnn. Her name is Alouette Talksihnn."

The cameras stop and Tina goes silent. Then a calamitous flurry erupts as they all shove forward, chaotically bumping into us.

"Watch it, mate!" Jacob pulls me to safety.

Cameras flash, and people scream questions about our marriage at us, but Bennett's bodyguards quickly force them away. All around, white spots flood my vision.

"You okay?" Jacob hovers over me, inspecting my belt, now hanging crooked, which means my wings are bent.

"Yeah. You didn't have to do that though, Jacob. It's going to be all over the internet that we're married."

"Excuse me, did they say Alouette? Alouette Nkosi?" a deep, gravely male voice asks.

Once my vision clears, I see Bennett Savion standing before me; his eyes glassy under spectacles, his mouth parted. His brown skin is darker than mine and worn, smile creases are etched into his skin.

"Yes, that's me. Well, Alouette Talksihnn," I say, refraining from glancing at Jacob again.

"Oh, child. It's you!" Bennett Savion's voice breaks, and he takes his glasses off so they hang over his sartorial tux. "Please, would you humor an old man and join me in private?" He glances around the open gallery then speaks into his watch.

His bodyguards join and usher me towards the giant glass wall. "This way, please."

"What's goin' on, mate?" Jacob hisses. "Hey, take your hands off her!"

There's no chance to refuse, flanked by two beefy men and Bennett Savion's cane, pushing softly against my boots from behind. A door magically forms and swings open, swallowing us whole.

Inside is a bird sanctuary; the air conditioning that was giving me gooseflesh vanishes and warmth floods the room. Thousands of squawks and chirps sing around us, which couldn't be heard from the gallery. At such a sight, witnessing exotic species from macaws to birds of paradise, kingfishers, and more, a euphoric sensation zips up through each chakra center of my body. This place is my personal ecstasy in a dome.

Until I notice Jacob on the other side of the closed door, knocking on the glass frantically.

"Wait! Let him in!"

"Not yet." Bennett Savion laboriously sits on a wooden bench, resting his cane at his side. "This conversation is between me and my granddaughter."

"What?"

My heart rate triples, and I stare at his features. Right when I saw him, something felt familiar. Now I realize he has Mom's eyes and nose. Not capable of words, I sink next to him and gape.

"Yes, I know dear. I'm sorry you had to find out this way."

"How do I know it's true?"

Bennett pulls out a picture from the inner pocket of his jacket. A younger version of him, sitting with a younger version of Ouma outside her cottage, a baby sitting between their laps. "It's the only picture I have of your mom as a child."

"Wh-Why didn't Ouma tell me?"

He smiles for the first time, a mouth full of dentures. "Oh, my dear Alouette, disappointing you was the only thing she feared. You were everything to her. After your mom cut us off from her life when she learned the truth about me, Tariji was afraid you'd do the same."

"But, what about Grandpa?"

"Ah, yes, Willis was a good man with the revered Nkosi name." Bennett nods slowly. "Long ago, I had nothing. I certainly didn't start out as council president. Willis could offer my Tariji everything. She was angry at me, you see. I never wanted to get married because I didn't believe in a social construct that gave men more power. When Willis popped into the picture, she serenaded him with attention to spite me. One thing led to another, their parents pressured her into marriage and poof, it was a done deal."

"I don't understand. Why didn't she break off the engagement and stay with you?"

"She wanted prestige and a legacy. Plus, she loved Willis too, in a different way. Your grandma never could've predicted that my name would eventually have more status than a Nkosi. You see, she was already pregnant with your mother when they became engaged. Tariji refused to tell either of us who the baby's father was until we both put the child in our wills. Willis knew he wasn't the father, but still took good care of my baby. He treated my Tariji well until he passed. Good man, Willis."

"But Ouma loved *you*?"

"That's what I choose to believe." He sighs. "Until her dying day." He nods slowly, deep in his memories. "Tariji always wanted to keep us a secret from the public. Didn't want to create a scandal for your mom."

I can barely believe what I'm hearing. "So ... when did Mom learn the truth?"

"We waited a year after Willis died, then we told her together." He bows his head. "It certainly came as quite a shock to her. You were in elementary school and that's when your parents decided to travel for work. Then Tariji became your full-time caregiver."

"Third grade. I was eight." I lean over, head between my knees, and breathe in deeply. "Mom knew this since I was eight?"

He rubs my back with boney, frail fingers. "You're okay. To understand the world, listen to the ..."

"... bird's silent flight," I finish and look up at him.

My heart shutters. All the little moments with Ouma bounce back in an echo of memories, now altered. He blinks, like he's capturing my expression as a keepsake.

I let this sink in. Endless questions weigh down the tip of my tongue. Why didn't Bennett reach out to me sooner? Why didn't Mom tell me this? A knife of betrayal wedges itself between my ribs. But Jacob's loud banging brings me back to what's at stake. And I don't have time to waste.

"Mr. Savion, I would love nothing more than to talk to you for the rest of the night, and I hope we can meet again soon to speak further, but I actually need something from you."

"Anything, dear." He clasps his hands on his lap.

"I'm looking for Ouma's missing cottage. When she died, her house disappeared. Do you have a key or clue?"

Patting his pockets, his brow furrows with concern. "I'm sorry, Alouette, but I don't have anything. I didn't know a house could move."

Kneeling before him, tears, hot and thick, well up, threatening to spill. "Please. I called my mom and she said you have the key. Was there any key Ouma may have mentioned?"

"The only thing that I can think of that feels relevant is Key Cove. It's a spot we used to picnic at, outside of Calypsa. It's close to the Black Cat Market, in case you've heard of it, by the waterfalls."

"Key Cove?"

"Yes, dear, but do stand up. You'll rip your dress down there." Gently, he pulls me back to the bench. "Here, give me your number. We can plan a lunch date next time I'm in town. Unfortunately, tomorrow I fly to San Diego. If I think of anything else, I'll message you right away."

Thud. Thud. Thud.

We glance to where a giant crack fractures the glass wall. On the other side, Jacob pounds a metal stool into the wall, face red, wig askew, sweat glistening on his forehead. He bangs harder, faster. I stand to run to him. To tell him to stop. That I'm safe. But the fissure grows and lengths. Until finally it snaps and a million jagged shards cascade down like icicles from a breath-taking action movie.

CHAPTER NINETEEN

Jacob

Someone's magic freezes the broken glass pieces in place, hovering thousands of deadly shards in the air. There's enough space between the cracks for the birds to soar out of their enclosed space and into the grand gallery. I rush towards Alouette. Her worried eyes study the birds and finally rest on me.

"Are you hurt?" I pull her into my chest and hug her fiercely. "Why'd they lock you in there? What'd he say to you?"

"I'm fine." Her voice drops. "He's my grandfather."

"That's ... wow!"

"Bennett and Ouma were together." Her eyes sink into mine and I feel her confusion. "Do you know what that means? I've never technically been a Nkosi. I'm a *Savion*." She pauses and runs a hand through her hair. "Now I don't know what to think."

"What do you need?" I wrap her in a hug, and she buries her face in my chest.

I can't hear her response. What if she wants to leave now? I scan the walls for a clock and spot a brown cuckoo, showing thirty minutes until midnight. There's no telling the last time I saw a legit cuckoo clock, which means the oracle's reading must be authentic. If so, I have half an hour for Alouette to kiss me. The way her eyes are clouded over has me questioning if coming here was a good idea.

"Wanna go back to the hotel?" I cup her face with both hands as her eyes fill with unshed tears.

"No." She sniffs and shakes her head. "I want you to meet him."

"Okay."

She double blinks and searches my face for a missing clue. "You agreed to that pretty fast."

"Yeah, true. But I did smash down a glass wall in front of him and you know how lasting impressions linger."

She laughs.

"If you want me to meet him, I can do that. I'm bloody great with presidents."

That earns me a side eye glare, but she takes my hand, leading me to the bench where Bennett sits, watching our exchange. His eyes sparkle with starlight which reminds me of Alouette, the only woman I'd want as a date tonight.

"G'day, sir. I'm Jacob Talksihnn," I say, holding out my hand.

"Yes, I've read all about your surfing career, young man, and quite a few other tidbits." He winks, obviously referring to Nella's wild claims and accusations. "If I may give a piece of advice ... as someone who has been in the spotlight too?"

"Of course, sir."

"How others perceive you is none of your business. Surround yourself with a small group of people who love you fiercely. That's all that matters."

"Yes, sir," I say, unsure how much I believe it. "And respectfully, I'd like to give *you* some advice."

He gestures openly with both hands to welcome what I have to say.

"Now that ya have Alouette in your life. Don't let 'er go. It'd be the biggest mistake ya could ever make."

"We agree on that, son." Bennett Savion, the bloody Fuzer president, bows his head at me. "Now, if you excuse me, I need to place some bets at the auction."

As he walks towards the bustle of people, where Fuzers are attempting to determine whose magic can summon the birds back or fix the glass wall, two bodyguards surround the president like a sandwich. With Alouette at my side, I stand dumbfounded at the scene that's unfolding into nothing short of comedic relief. Among the crowd, wigs are askew and bright birds perch atop the high-rise tables while the live band keeps playing as if nothing was amiss.

It doesn't take long for the glass to be repaired and some of the birds to be collected. The chaos winds down to a dull chatter again. Alouette's hand tangles with mine as she guides me away from the jungle and back into the crisp, air-conditioned room. People have clustered again, some near the auctioning station, others by the scientific skeleton displays that have been pushed to the perimeter.

Ready to follow Alouette's lead, I shield her against others to block her from curious gossipers. Everyone is curious about Bennett Savion's private conversation with the girl wearing broken wings; the woman I want to kiss desperately. But she's supposed to kiss me first.

I'm tired of playing games and hiding my feelings. I freeze, my heart seizing up unexpectedly. Alouette's arm is yanked back in surprise.

"Jacob, you okay?"

I clutch my chest. "I think so. My heart feels like it's about to explode and I might be freakin' out a bit."

"Why? Did glass cut you? Where does it hurt?"

"No, nothing like that." I press my hand into my temple. "Shit, I'm gonna say it. You need to kiss me by midnight so I can talk to Nella. That's what the oracle said."

She stares at me, face blank. What's going through her mind? Does she even want this? There are a thousand things I want to say, but she beats me to it.

"Okay, I'll do it," she states.

The pain, the nausea, the confusion all cease. My whole body is numb.

"How do you like to be kissed?" she asks, her gaze dipping to my lips. She looks nervous, but curious. "Do you like fast or wet or open mouth or closed?"

I raise both hands and back up a step. "No, this isn't right. I can't. Not like this. Fuck, I shouldn't have said anything."

"But you need this so you can talk to Nella. If I have to kiss you so you can find your happiness, then I'll do it. I think I can manage one kiss. It won't kill me."

Her pink lipstick gleams softly; her welcoming smile has me reconsidering my reservations. But it wouldn't be fair. Who wants their first kiss to be a transaction? And if I get my way, I'll want to kiss her a thousand times more. Starting out on a rocky wave won't glide us along into a smooth ride.

"No. Just..." I shake my head, making an X with my arms. "Forget I said anything."

"Jacob, you're shaking. Are you overheating again?" She slides a hand over the front of my jacket and slips it off. "Here, take this off."

No, she can't start taking my clothes off. I'm losing all

control. My cock hardens and I desperately want to press her against the wall and finally discover what she tastes like. Games aren't my style. She needs to know exactly what I'm thinking and feeling. I shrug off the jacket and let it pool in a puddle at my feet. Then I do exactly what my body longs for and back her step by step into the shadows.

Alouette's little gasp makes my dick strain harder against my pants.

"Look at me, little owl."

Her dark, ravenous eyes pin me in the most beautiful way. With every one of her breaths, her chest rises faster and more visibly.

"Listen to me. When we kiss for the first time, it's going to be because ya crave me. It'll be marked into your skin and memories for all time. I'm goin' to imprint myself on this gorgeous mouth of yours," I say, brushing my knuckles over her lips. "And don't ever take off my clothes again in public unless you're willin' to give a show, understand, Mrs. Talksihnn?"

I bask in the way her eyes widen. My fingers itch to run through her hair and show her I'm serious, but it's not the time.

"So the rumors are true?" A female behind me interrupts with a voice of polished stone. "You're married? Well, congratulations, Mr. Talksihnn, this will make your custody hearing much more positive on your end, having a two-caregiver home."

Regrettably, I take my eyes off Alouette and turn. A woman with a blue wig and glasses stands waiting. She is shorter than Alouette and at least ten years older than us both. She wears a trusting smile as an accessory to her navy suit and stiletto heels.

"I'm Ubika Nishal. I see you're in the middle of

something, but unfortunately I'm about to leave. Erik asked me to meet you and I owe him a favor."

I shake her hand too dramatically, almost breaking her bones. "Yes! That's me! That's us!"

"I spoke to your legal team last night. We will schedule a hearing date where Nella is required to attend to negotiate custody arrangements, or she will face charges. From the looks of your records, you've done everything right since you found out about your child and have faced substantial barriers. Almost every choice you've made has been responsible and proactive. And now that you have a wife, I'm assuming you won't be living in your van anymore?"

I nod, too fast, too excitedly. "Of course. Alouette has a house in Calypsa that has plenty of spare rooms," I blurt, unable to stop myself or pause. "Ms. Nishal, do you know anything else?"

"Nella's lawyers have agreed to hold court in Oakmar which is only two hours from Calypsa. I'm assuming they live near there."

"Oakmar. Yes, I could get a house there," I say to myself. "It's two hours inland ... no surfing ..."

"Mr. Talksihnn, let's take one step at a time. Don't rush into any major changes. I'll be in touch," she tells me, handing over a business card.

I'm in a daze when she walks away, her heels clicking along the hardwood floor in a beat that matches the drummer's rhythm of the band. When I turn to Alouette, my stomach somersaults. There's a deep aching part of me that yearns for her to understand how much this means to me. Her eyes crinkle with a smile that turns my world upside down. On impulse, I lift her and spin her in a circle, in disbelief at this miracle.

Her joyous laughter pours out, her pink wig slipping off. Her eyes shine like fireflies. This woman, destined to defy expectations, seems as happy as I am.

"Did you hear what she said!?" After I place her solidly on the floor, I keep my hands on her waist. "This is unbelievable!"

"Jacob ..." she says softly.

"I need to put her contact in my cell before I lose this."

"Jacob ..." Alouette's hand presses against my chest.

"Hmm?"

Suddenly, I'm pulled downward by her soft hands that are wrapped behind my neck. Alouette's lips move towards mine.

CHAPTER TWENTY

Alouette

I pull Jacob towards me and press my lips against his. They're soft and pillowy, warm and smooth. His large hands gather me closer. He's too tall and my heels don't give me enough height. As if he's reading my mind, Jacob wraps his hands under my legs and lifts me up like it's the most natural thing in the world. I wrap my legs around him, losing all self-control. He tastes like his raspberry margarita, sweet and delicious.

The intensity of how he returns my kiss—such longing and craving—sends a shockwave through my core. My back presses against the wall as he pins me. A low groan rumbles from his throat, and I swear I can taste and feel his overpowering desire like a tangible substance. Unable to help myself, I grind my center against his stomach, wishing his hard arousal was positioned exactly where I need the friction.

"Mmm, yes," he whispers when he breaks away and presses kisses against my neck.

His grip grows more possessive, tighter. I keep my hands clasped behind his neck and my ankles entwined behind his back. Every sweep of lips on my skin sends shivers up my spine. I desperately ache to tear off the rest of his tux and explore his body.

My skin heats and my entire body is hyperaware as Jacob trails more kisses over my jaw, then back to my mouth. His teeth playfully drag at my lower lip, and I moan into his mouth.

"Christ, little owl."

The deep, gravelly sound of his voice is a pure drug. I'm wet in moments and want his touch between my legs. What else can he do with his wicked mouth? I imagine toying with him in bed, stripping for him, his dark gaze burning through any hesitation.

Panting, I gasp for air before he drowns me in his kiss again. My pulse thunders. I rub against his stomach. Tingles travel up my body on complete overdrive. This feels like insanity. Not real. Another whimper escapes from my lips.

"Fuck, holy shit, fuck," he mumbles urgently.

We stare at each other, in deep and prolonged eye contact. Out of breath, he tries to communicate something without words, but I'm too lost in lust to understand. I need his lips on my neck again, his hands on my body.

"I'm gonna put ya down now, love," Jacob says gently, watching my reaction. "No matter how much I crave to have every soul here watch me take ya, if we don't stop now, I'd only create chaos."

"I don't care. Give me your disaster. I can manage some chaos," I breathe, but my feet are already planted back firmly on the ground.

At this angle I can better see the throbbing shape of his

cock pressing against his pants and ... oh my. Still wedged between him and the wall, Jacob's arm creates an arch over my head. His eyes are squeezed shut as he gathers his breath. Reaching up, I recenter his black wig and run a hand down his clean-shaven face. He looks different without the blonde stubble I've grown to adore. The black eyeliner he wears is more smeared than before, so I wipe a fingertip across his cheek to fix it.

Finally, he opens his eyes again. That blue-green sharpness staples me in place.

"You kissed me," he says, almost in awe.

"I did."

His genuine smile is one meant for photographs. For a snapshot to be kept eternally as a memory to cherish.

"Let's get out of here," he offers with hungry eyes.

I run a finger up his chest while my heart rate threatens to implode. "I thought you liked when people watch?"

"You're killin' me. Don't tempt me." Jacob holds my hand and glances over his shoulder.

For the first time, I peer around the pillar. A woman meets my eye, then nods our way, causing a couple of others to twist their heads and inspect us. One of them, with a violet wig and Latino features, turns straight towards us and heads closer.

"Fuck. Here we go. Buckle up," Jacob mutters, squeezing my hand.

I'm about to ask him what he means when all three women, looking like a sorority group, stride closer, exuding confidence. Jacob adjusts so his hip tucks me a bit behind him and his stance widens. It hits me: these are his exes.

The one with a violet wig leads the pack in the middle, her near-black eyes like coals. She wears too much blush and enough jewelry to function as an anchor.

To her right is a woman with speckled red freckles that adorn her face like paint splatters. Of the group, she's the most petite. Her radiant emerald gown contrasts nicely with her pale skin.

I ignore the snarl of the third, a girl with a skimpy dress who looks too young to have dated Jacob years ago. She wears a feather wig and has arched manicured brows.

"Jacob. Did you not know we'd be here?"

He sighs next to me and squeezes my hand once more. "G'day ladies. This is Alouette. Babe, meet my exes, Sonya, Felicity, and Posh."

He casually points to each, indicating that Sonya is the leader in purple, Felicity is the shy freckled one in the verdant dress, and Posh is the bitter-looking one who has already lashed out unnecessarily.

"So, Nella recruited you? Why?" he wonders. When I follow his gaze, his focus stays on Felicity, as if she's the only one he sees.

"We're here to keep you away from Nella. Don't ask where she is," Posh hisses, then flips a strand of her wig out of her eyes. "Your carelessness and irresponsibility have ruined her life. Us women stick together. It's easier when we all have something in common ... hating you."

Jacob shifts his stance, his attention still on Felicity. "Why, Tee?" he repeats. His nickname for her is like a dagger to the temple.

Felicity hasn't looked up yet. Her gaze remains fixed on the spotless floor, showing her reflection. I swear hurt lingers on her face. He never told me how long ago they broke up. It seems they still care for each other. What happened between them?

"Can we talk in private?" Felicity asks quietly.

Jacob steps closer to my side, but I place a hand on his

chest and reply for him, "I'll wait over by the firefly display."

I can feel Felicity's eyes scorch my hand where I claim him; not that I mean to. We're not even a real couple. Yet. But I'm starting to think we could be.

"You sure?" Jacob's brows twist tightly, but I nod and meander towards the tables along the far wall, tucked away from the guests.

There's a bench in the shadows calling my name. Maybe after everyone has downed a few more drinks, they won't notice if I finish out the party barefoot.

I sit, grateful to be away from his exes. They sure slapped me back to reality. It's hard to not track Jacob and Felicity's movements as they part from the others. They stand close, familiar with each other.

"Where are you from?" a tiny voice peeps from next to me.

The most petite elf I've ever met, smaller than my hand, sits cross-legged on the bench. Either her hair is royal blue, or her wig is a piece of custom art, because it looks natural, falling down to her ankles in waves.

"Calypsa," I reply, then glue my focus back on my date and his ex. "You?"

"Born and raised here, local ..." she pauses. "I don't usually do this, but I can see how frazzled you are. Want to eavesdrop on your man's conversation?"

"Excuse me?" I ask, but still don't take my eyes off Jacob as Felicity rubs her hand up and down his arm like she's comforting him.

Without explanation, I can suddenly hear Jacob's voice in my ear as if I were wearing headphones. Quickly, I glance around to see if anyone nearby can notice, but it seems to be a personal audio system. The elf next to me grins, apparently using magic of her own. My stomach flips with unease, but it's too good of an opportunity to pass up.

"I don't understand how you expect me to take ya seriously, Tee." Jacob's voice sounds harsh, edged with hurt. "Ya left. Without a goodbye. Now ya want a second chance?"

"I made a mistake, Jay. I've thought about you almost every day. Haven't you considered calling me?"

"No, Tee! Ya broke my heart." He crosses his arms and stares at something over her head. "Ya know how hard that summer was when my sisters all moved in together without invitin' me. Then I heard I might have a kid, and you bailed. Without a damned word. We could've talked about it. I don't even know what ya freaked out 'bout. Thought ya always loved kids?"

"I did!" Felicity moves toward him, but he backs away. "I do, but how was I going to face my friends and family when my fiancé had a child I didn't know about? Do you know how embarrassing that was?"

Fiancé? I suck in a breath and reach up to pull off the headphones, forgetting they aren't attached.

"Turn this off. Please," I beg the elf. "I don't want to hear anymore."

She shrugs and their voices are cut off. Again, I hear the gentle hum of nearby conversations, the clinking of glasses, and birds fluttering atop a nearby pillar.

My heart rams so hard in my chest that I press a palm against my sternum and push. Distraction. I desperately need a distraction. A new song plays, persuading a few couples to head to the dance floor. Rising, I turn my back towards Jacob so I don't invade their privacy more. He'd been engaged and I had no idea. It's a mind-boggling concept. At one point, he'd been willing to spend the rest of his life with that woman. Who am I to steal his name for a night?

Someone taps my shoulder. I notice the gold wig first, tied back at the base of the man's neck. I'd already noticed him earlier when we entered, since he's the only other Black guest here, other than Bennett Savion. "Want to dance?"

I'm not one to avoid dancing, no matter how ridiculous I may look.

"Sure, one second." I reach toward a staff member passing by with a tray of shots. I gulp the contents and it burns all the way down my throat.

The hem of the man's long cape brushes against my arm as he swivels to the dance floor. I know vampires don't exist, but this mystery man definitely emits that dark, alluring vibe.

My hips find the rhythm of the music, which makes my wings jiggle on my back awkwardly. They may not be heavy, but they're sitting at a strange angle.

"Can you unhook these, Mister ...?"

"Hayes." He chuckles and helps unbuckle the wings. Carefully, he sets them on a nearby tabletop.

"Lou," I reply, not wanting anyone else to use my full name. It sounds too delicious on Jacob's tongue.

Hayes grabs my hand and whirls me around gracefully again. We move in a dizzying way until I run into his hard chest. I laugh, unable to remember the last time I danced with a guy. Sure, Zola and I danced all the time, but we've also been busy. The movements feel as freeing as flying would.

"This beat isn't meant for dancing," I say, unable to keep a laugh in at his outrageously dramatic moves.

"Of course it is."

I'm swung around, dipped, and lose all sense of where the ground is. Hayes's chuckle comes from somewhere close. The room swirls in a swipe of colors. I'm soaring, encircled by music. When I'm rooted back on my feet and skid to a halt, Hayes is smiling at me, so close I can smell the fresh minty on his breath..

Except it's not Jacob's mouth it's coming from.

Maybe he was once engaged to Felicity, but that was in the past. It doesn't mean I have to sit back and let her take the guy I like because they have a history. The only logical action is to tell him how I feel.

Hayes is ready to twirl me again, but I put up my hand to stop him. "I'm sorry, but actually, I came with someone. I should've led with that."

"I know. I had to get a taste. Everyone's been whispering about the gorgeous woman in wings." He bows and flashes sharp canines that are obviously fake. "Good night, Lou."

I curtsy in response, then turn to search for Jacob. Except, I'm interrupted by another stranger holding out his hand in offering. He's taller than Hayes, with sharp hazel eyes and a short brown wig.

"Dance with me," he commands in a tone I don't appreciate.

"Um, no thank you. I'm looking for someone."

The man's nose flares wide. "Me. You're looking for me and I'm right here."

"No, I'd rather sit this one out."

"Come on, sweetheart. I suggest you take me up on the offer." He stalks forward until my heels press against a stool.

"Excuse me. I said I'm not interested." I raise my voice

and wish a magical saltshaker would fly across the room and knock him out.

"Hey, back off, man," Hayes says from behind.

A wolfish sound emanates from the stranger, and as I question whether shifters actually do exist, Jacob sweeps between us. Facing me, he's obviously aware of the situation, but doesn't give the guy the time of day. He takes me in his arms to dance.

"Ya *kissed* me," Jacob repeats, with a clench of his jaw that's outrageously sexy.

"You already said that," I say, smiling.

"I'm confirmin' it happened."

To the beat of the music, Jacob twirls me across the floor. I stumble a thousand and one times. Yet he keeps me upright. I never take my eyes off him. His strong hand rests gently on my waist, guiding me through steps I don't know with effortless grace.

The chandelier's soft glow catches the warmth in his eyes, and my heart flutters. I breathe in his cologne, a subtle scent that mixes with the aroma of champagne and flowers filling the air. As the music swells, he holds me closer, and I feel as though we are the only two people in the room. In this moment, spinning in his arms, I silently wish the dance would never end.

As the song concludes, I guide him to a nearby bench. No one is within listening distance. Sitting face to face, our knees brush and a war of a thousand feelings rages within me.

"I'm sorry," we both say at the same time.

"For what? You didn't do anything," I tell him. "I eavesdropped on part of your conversation with your ex with someone's magic. I shouldn't have done that."

Jacob takes both my hands in his. "I don't remember half of our conversation, but whatever ya heard, please know that I'm done with her. Tee wanted to get back together, but I'm not interested, okay? Alouette, look at me ... There ya are." He runs his knuckles down my jaw line to my chin. "When Tee left, that break up played into my biggest fear, that my social image mattered to her most. But I know you're not like her. Please, let's try. You can't deny this energy between us."

My face heats and I swear I won't cry in front of him, not when others are close. Guilt threatens to suffocate me. He's being too nice when I haven't been honest.

"Do you know why I pretended my last name was Talksihnn?" I sniff, fighting the hot tears collecting.

"Tell me," he says, ready and willing to listen as he scoots closer.

I focus on his aqua eyes. Under the costume and wig, there's more than a surfer, more than a celebrity, more than a brother or a son or a Fuzer. He's a man with pain in his past and desires for his future. I hope we can forge a path together somehow, regardless of our differences.

"I hate living in the shadows of the Nkosi legacy. If I would've walked into this museum telling them who I was, do you know how many people would've approached me with questions about my parents and their studies? Or to ask me when I'll be joining their research team? I want a clean slate, where there aren't any expectations of me. Tonight was the first time I got to glimpse what that might feel like as someone different."

I pause and gauge his reaction. He nods, so I continue.

"I'm two hours from home, in a wig, unrecognizable. No one here knows who I am. It would've been smarter to create a random last name like Jones, but last night I considered that if the custody lawyer heard you were married, it could help your case. I got lucky that it worked out that way, but I should've asked your permission first. I know more than most the power of a name. I shouldn't have assumed I could borrow yours."

He leans over and kisses my forehead. "You're the tops, Owlette. And I promise, I'll help ya anyway I can. We'll find your grandma's cottage. I can feel it in here," he says, pounding his chest with his fist. "Tomorrow ... because tonight, there's something I have to do."

My breath catches in my throat as his hand gently cups my cheek. I close my eyes and savor the warmth of his touch. And then his lips are on mine again. A jolt of electricity courses through me. I return his need with my own and revel in the sweetness of the moment as the rest of the party fades away.

When we finally pull apart, I can't help the smile that spreads across my face. Jacob's eyes sparkle as he grins back. No words are needed—that kiss said everything.

CHAPTER TWENTY-ONE

Jacob

Our hotel room is filled with an intoxicating scent of vanilla and jasmine. The room-splitting divider is now propped against the wall. Lucky me. I glance between the two beds and curse silently. How the fuck I'll get any sleep tonight is beyond me. She'll be right there, in soft pajamas, or less, and I'll be figuring out ways to jack off in the bathroom without her noticing.

Alouette throws her wings onto the chair before kicking off her shoes, one by one. They each bang against the wall with a loud thud, and she winces with an apologetic look. I shrug it off, smirking.

"Bennett Savion suggested we investigate Key Cove," she says, already planning, when all I can do is think about taking her clothes off. I try to focus when she continues, "I want to go there tomorrow."

My guess would be that her grandma simply wanted

Alouette to learn the truth about her heritage, but it's not my place to say.

"And how could Mom never tell me who her real father was? Was she planning to keep it a secret forever?"

Alouette reaches for the upper clasp that fastens her dress at the base of her neck but fails with each reach, paired with a frustrated grunt or two.

"Here, let me help."

I cross the space between us in a single breath and free her from her prison of silky fabric. The way the black dress clings to her curves should be illegal, but I'm even more curious to see how deadly she looks without it.

"You're drooling." She chuckles, then slides her hair out of the way so it doesn't get caught.

I can't even answer as I stare at the few black freckles at the top of her spine calling my name. Slowly, I trace a finger over them, connecting them like a star constellation.

"I had a dream about you last night," she says.

My cock twitches, the ache unbearable. I swallow, painfully. "What kind of dream?"

"You know."

I lean closer. "Tell me about it."

She turns around so our bodies are flush against each other. "Just to be clear, I'm not sleeping with you … yet."

When both her lips roll in, and that little devious look flashes in her eyes, my dick presses even harder against my pants, trying to break free. Fuck. Every inch of my being wants to grasp her to me, strip her bare, whisper words into her skin.

"I have an idea, but don't you dare make fun of me," she says quietly.

"Never."

"Let's go on the balcony."

"Okay," I say. I'm willing to follow her into battle if she asked.

As we step onto the balcony, the cool August air envelops us, but my attention is captivated by her. She stands towards me with her back against the railing, one strap of her dress falling off her shoulder. The stars above are nothing in comparison to the glimmer of the moonbeams glistening on her shoulders. Her hair, gently lifted by the midnight breeze, dances with the shadows. I'm struck by how she embodies a confident bird perched high above the ground. As our gazes lock, her smile outshines every lantern on the street below.

"Come closer," she demands, her dark eyes shining with a need that matches my own.

I place my hands on her hips. "What do you want, Owlette?" I kiss her forehead with more tenderness than I thought I possessed.

This woman has destroyed me. I'd eat slugs for her. Crawl up a mountain with weights strapped to my ankles. Scuba dive with a box jellyfish. But it's too soon to tell her any of this.

"I was thinking of this idea earlier, but if it's too weird, say so," she says quietly.

"I'll do it. After all, you are my wife until the morning."

That gets a low chuckle that sends damn butterflies through my stomach.

"I want you to tell me more about yourself. With each new fact, I'll let you undo a button on my dress."

My erection is suddenly throbbing. Oh my goddess, she plans to murder me with this game.

"Out here?" I glance around at the neighboring balconies. Since the hotel is in a U shape, plenty of other guests could see us if they're still awake. "Are you sure?"

"Yes." Then she bites her bottom lip, unraveling any self-control I have remaining. Fuuuuuuck.

"Okay. What do you want to know?"

"Anything."

"My middle name is Blaine." I reach behind her and unclasp the top button. It falls loose a bit, making the front of her dress slip down a little. If she's wearing a bra, it certainly doesn't have any straps.

"More."

"Uh. Fuck, okay. Social media is my biggest enemy. I want it all destroyed. Privacy matters."

"Okay, go ahead." Her voice is full of something I can't name. Nervousness? Excitement?

I undo the next button, then quickly trail my fingers down her spine to count the rest. Three more. I might explode from desire.

"Another," she practically begs.

"When I can't sleep, I think about what Dakota likes. If she's into karate or drawing and which stuffed animal is her favorite."

Without checking, I flick the next button and the dress drops to her hips. I suck in a ragged inhale, then step back a little. My heel slams into a patio chair, which makes it screech across the concrete. The top of her breasts swell over her black strapless bra. I've seen her in swimsuits, but none of them gave this extra push up. I'm bloody starving for her. This is insane.

"More," she demands, eyes on fire.

"If I had to ask one person for help, it'd be my oldest sister."

She puts a hand up for me to stay where I am, then reaches behind her and fidgets with the buttons herself. It takes an eternity and an obscene amount of patience for me to stay rooted where I stand. My heart pounds erratically. I need her like I need oxygen. When the silk falls lower, I spot the perfect circle of her belly button. Every muscle tenses. I'm ready to lunge at her if given the signal.

"More," she whispers.

"The only thing more beautiful than a sunrise while riding the waves early is ... your smile. You have three different smiles. The first is soft and serene, when you are captivated by something and don't realize anyone's watching. The second is polite and only rises half way and the third one when your nose crinkles, that one's for me. At least that's what I tell myself, because I don't want to share."

"Mmmm," a moan slips out of her pretty mouth. "That might deserve another button."

Her arms twitch behind her back, making the dress drop to her bare feet. A matching, solid black thong rises high on her hips and accentuates her curves in the best possible way. I'm greedy. Desperate. Immobilized. Wired. Every part of me feels like I'm unhinged.

"You have two more secrets to spill, Mister Talksihnn."

Because two more pieces of her clothing remain. She wants two more secrets. Okay, get your shit together, man. But I can barely think. Can't form words.

"Uh ... I'm thinkin' of firin' Erik," I blurt, my breath coming heavier, faster.

Instantly, her bra plunges to the patio. Two of the most wondrous, edible, luscious breasts I've ever seen wait for me. I move forward, but she holds up a hand to stop me. Call a bloody gravedigger and lower me into the ground. I'm done.

As the breeze blows, her nipples stiffen to hard peaks, and I have to readjust my cock or I'll snap.

"Fuck. I'm a lost cause for ya, little owl. What are ya doin' to me?"

"One more, Jacob," she purrs, her thumbs stretching against the string at her hips. She pulls it out far, then lets go so it snaps against her skin.

My stomach sizzles. A burning sensation coils hotter in my veins. I need the refuge of her kiss before I break in two.

"I want you to be there when I meet Dakota."

She tugs her panties over her curvy hips until they tumble down her legs.

I'm not an architect of words. But I swear she's a damned masterpiece—a magical symphony of stardust. She smiles again as I salivate like a wild beast because she has decimated me. I stare at the V between her thighs and long to touch, feel, kiss. Fuck, this is torture.

"You okay?" she asks, brows knitted together but wearing a flirty smile.

I don't know how to answer. Some amount of time passes until I can choke out. "Can I kiss ya?"

"No, no ..." She laughs. "Don't rush, Jacob. I want this to be special. And I'm not having sex with you tonight. In fact, you're not allowed to touch me. Yet."

My head falls back and I stare up at the moon. "Fuck me dead, Owlette! Ya serious?" I straighten, crack my neck both ways, and rub my hands together. "Okay, okay, I can do this. I swear. Bring it on. What's next?"

I'm stiffer than a tree. She doesn't want me to touch her yet. So I won't. The fact that she's doing this for me, being so vulnerable, naked on the balcony where others can see her, is the hottest thing I've seen in my damned life.

Her left hip juts out a little, making a little space between her thighs, before she says, "Now I'll tell you a little bit about my dream last night after each piece of clothing you take off."

Thank the goddesses I already took off my wig, jacket, cufflinks, socks, and shoes inside when we first arrived. That leaves about seven articles of clothing. Way too many. I tear off my bow tie and waistcoat and toss them to the patio.

Her look of wild approval gives me gooseflesh.

"Suspenders look good on you, my little night hawk."

"Your dream?"

My hands itch to cup her breast. My lips tingle, needing to suck her nipples and bite her flesh. Ugh, I could scream at the top of my lungs right now. All this excessive pent-up energy threatens to explode.

"You and I were experimenting ... in a hammock ... hung from the pier by your van."

I swallow.

"In broad daylight."

"Alouette..." My voice sounds strained, deprived, and raw. Quickly, I rip off my suspenders and cummerbund. "That was two items. I need two details."

Her head tilts to the side and she waits. Fuck. I relish how much she's enjoying being in control, driving me crazy.

"I was wearing a swimsuit, laying on my back, perpendicular to how you're supposed to lay on a hammock, but my legs were impossibly flexible like a circus performer, fully out wide in the hammock. I mean, it's not a position I could ever get in—don't get hopeful—but it gave you a full view of me spread open for you."

"Tell me," I command, then a rough and intense rumble comes from deep in my chest.

There's no chance I can wait to hear more. I unzip my

pants, let them drop to the ground. Watch her gaze dip to my crotch. Savoring her delight, I tug my briefs to my knees until my cock springs free. Her gasp sends shivers up my spine. I can't even deal with the excitement in her widened eyes or how her lips part slightly as she takes in the sight of me.

I grip my cock in my hand and start stroking, slow and long and hard. Her breath hitches again, but she doesn't look away until I speak.

"Look at me, Alouette. Tell me your dream. And touch yourself for me."

She licks her lips as her hand drops between her legs, to the most treasured spot.

"First, take off your shirt." I can barely hear her over her heavy breathing.

I rip off my shirt in a scramble of stumbling movements until I'm as bare as her. The breeze tickles my skin, and I grind my teeth together. My hand finds my cock again and I push into my palm. With each passing second, her chest rises and falls harder and faster. Which gives me the most precious view of her tits bouncing.

"Keep going, Owlette. Tell me what I did to you."

"I ... oh ... you ran your finger along my inner thigh, from my knee to my ..."

"Say it."

"To my pussy. Your body blocked anyone from seeing me fully, but anyone who was paying attention could figure out what was happening."

"Ugh, goddess, yes." My eyes squeeze shut to picture it, but I can't leave her alone here in the moment. I pry them open, force myself to maintain eye contact. I refuse to even let my gaze drop to her fingers swirling around her clit.

"What next?"

"On the hammock, you slid your fingers into me. I still remember the look on your face when you felt how wet I was for you."

"Fuckin' christ, Alouette."

"You made me come harder than I ever have. And when I woke up, I had to use my toy, or I'd lose my mind." Her arms move faster, harder. The look on her face tells me she's getting close. "This morning ... oh ... in my bed ... I thought about you on top of me, looking down at me. Your chest ... oh ..."

"Keep going. Don't you dare stop." My chest seizes strenuously—I'm going to burst.

"Your chest was wide and strong above me and your cock pressed against my entrance and ... Oohh ... OH!" Her legs shake and her hips thrust forward until her knees buckle.

I leap forward to catch her as her orgasm spasms through. Her muscles twitch and quiver in my arms. I hold her tightly, skin on skin, until she rides the wave through and her body settles. Panting, she rests her cheek on my chest and takes a few deep breaths. I'm hyperaware of my cock pressing up against her stomach, but don't dare move.

"Jacob ..."

"Mhm?"

"We're naked. Together."

"Yes, we are." I try to steady my racing heart. "Ya okay?"

"Yeah," she says sleepily. "I'm ... good. But you ..."

"Don't worry about me. I'm gonna take care of it in the shower."

Her hand brushes up my inner thigh, but I stop her before she can touch my length. "Not tonight, love. I want this to be about you."

"But ... that's not fair." Her dark eyes show confusion, so I lean down and kiss her gently, with no urgency.

"I bet if you take a look out there, at the sky, ya'd feel pretty free right now, standin' naked and satisfied. I want ya to bask in this." I kiss her forehead, then back away.

Inside, I head to the shower with one thing in mind. I need to make sure my hammock is ready for future use.

CHAPTER TWENTY-TWO

Alouette

As we arrive at Key Cove, I part a curtain of emerald ferns to enter. Before us is a sanctuary cradled in the heart of the forest. Across the way, sunlight casts a golden glow on the moss-covered rocks that encircle a crystal-clear pool. Calm water reflects the sky, encircled by wildflowers swaying gently in the breeze.

As I step closer, my feet sink into the soft carpet of fallen leaves. It's like I've stumbled upon a realm untouched by time, a place where magic whispers between palm trees.

A sign reads: 'Moth and Butterfly Conservation.'

Sunbeams shine through the leaves like spotlights. Each one illuminates a different winged creature. I scan the floating jewels along the winding path. A Monarch swoops past with such grace that her movement reminds me of Jacob atop his surfboard.

Moss-covered logs line the path like the edges of a sidewalk, guiding us around a loop. Jacob is so tall he has to duck under some of the hanging flowers. We follow the dirt path until it leads to a row of huts lined by a tiny brook.

Beside me, Jacob stays quiet, as he has all morning. I wonder if he regrets last night's balcony escapades. I haven't had the courage to ask him his thoughts. Maybe he needs time to process, but I can't get his kisses off my mind. Or how his piercing eyes studied me like I was a gift. Or how many times the knot in his throat bobbed. Now, every time he makes a little sigh, there's a buzz in my gut anticipating what he's about to say.

But he soldiers on in silence, each time breaking a bit more of my soul. At this point, I'd be content with a written message in a bottle as our means of communication. What the Abyss is going through his head? Last night he had been ready to pounce on me like a jaguar, and now he's keeping a two-foot distance between our bodies. I've sent a text to Zola for advice, but she hasn't responded.

"How 'bout we split up?" Jacob doesn't meet my eyes as he wanders to the other side of the stream.

His withdrawal cuts me like broken glass. A young raven flaps its wings and lands close like she is encouraging me to tell him how I feel instead of waiting. My insides twist tight at the thought, so I ignore her and walk towards a woman who emerges from her hut.

"Welcome to Key Cove. Need incense?" she asks. "Only ten bucks a bottle."

"No. I'm looking for information. Did you happen to know Tariji Nkosi?"

"The winner of The Warner Award? Sorry to tell you, but she died earlier this year."

My shoulders sag and a heaviness returns to my chest. "I know. Did she ever visit this area?"

She nods. "All the time. She lived close to here, outside

Calypsa. Once I saw an episode of Fuzer Millionaires and they gave a tour of her massive mansion. It even had an art studio inside. Why are you interested in Tariji Nkoski?"

"I'm her granddaughter."

"No shit!" Her friendly smile widens in surprise. "I need to tell Yuri. You stay put," she says and bounces to the neighboring hut.

Across the clearing, Jacob's messing with a log, ignoring me again. Irritation snakes its way through my blood. Who in the Skies does he think he is to be so blatantly rude? How can guys flip a switch immediately? He watched me strip naked and now wants nothing to do with me? Anger festers, boiling in my center.

I march straight towards him. As if he can feel my enraged glare, he finally looks up and meets my eye. Worry and alarm cover his face as I pick up my pace. When we're inches from one another's face, the first thing that captures me is his eyes. They're more blue today, matching the azure sky.

"What's wrong?" he asks, both hands behind his back.

"Why are you acting so weird? Ever since we woke up, you've barely said a word to me."

"I didn't realize. Guess I was stuck in my head." Red-faced, Jacob brings out a wrapped box from behind his back and presents it to me. "I was hopin' to give it to ya later."

"What?" I stare at the black box with a pink ribbon around it, my two favorite colors.

"I bought ya a present while ya slept last night," he explains, voice soft and uncertain. "It didn't cost much, so it's nothin' fancy like ya have at home. If ya don't like it, I can return it."

"Jacob ..." I say, but he places it in my hand before I can object.

"Go ahead."

My heart somersaults in the most perplexing manner. When I unwrap the box and tuck the ribbon into my purse to save, what lies inside is so thoughtful that I want to take a picture of it to send to Zola.

I cradle the mahogany music box, marveling at its intricate carvings. A great horned owl covers the lid, and the sides depict a forest scene with other birds in flight. Inside, pink velvet lines the box. I wind the golden key, and a lullaby I recognize tinkles out as a small owl figurine spins. The scent of wood polish lingers, and I'm struck by how sweet Jacob is, finding something suited to me, a magical piece of art.

"Wow, Jacob, this is …"

"I'm sorry," he interrupts and steps closer. "I've been … distracted … since I woke up this morning." He scrubs a hand down his face and averts his gaze. "Alouette … I …" He fidgets with his hands as his forehead wrinkles. "I got an email from the custody lawyer …"

That was a turn I hadn't expected, and a bad feeling creeps up my neck like a violent vibration.

"She already found out I lied about bein' married, and I don't know how to respond. I've been fucked up all day and worried sick. And I've lost half my followers overnight. I swear I wasn't tryin' to ignore ya. Listen, ya deserve the world. And there's no chance I'm lettin' some other guy sweep ya off your feet in a dance. I've been thinkin' all mornin' how to convince ya to be my girlfriend while being terrified 'bout all the other shit." He sucks in a steadying breath. "In all my relationships, I felt … differently … than how I do 'bout ya. So, I'm not sure how to do this. Tell me the best way to say sorry so I don't mess this up."

Witnessing him ramble, watching him shuffle on his

feet, his head bowed, might be the cutest thing I've ever seen. I reach out to comfort him. Right when I lean into his chest, tension flows from his body. There's an overall feeling of weightlessness that feels too good to be true.

"Jacob Blaine?" I raise onto my tiptoes. "Will you be my boyfriend?"

His prominent cheekbones raise in the largest smile I've witnessed to date. He extends both arms around my back and gathers me in close. In his embrace, I feel energized. Thrilled to start this new chapter together, I beam up at him until he expresses his feelings with his lips. I relish in his taste, welcome in his animated zest, and cheer internally that we're trying this thing between us.

"Don't think I only want ya cuz of last night," he says quickly. "What ya did on the balcony was ... fuckin' intoxicatin' ... but ya know what drew me to ya? It's the way ya see the beauty in the world and how much passion ya carry in your heart. I can't stand it, Owlette. Every second we're together, I need to touch ya, kiss ya. It's absolute torment, I swear. I'll be yours if you're only mine, understand?"

A wave of warmth washes over me. I want to whoop loudly, dance in place, fling my arms open wide. Instead, I draw in a deep breath to calm the drumming in my chest. High on adrenaline, I cover him in kisses. If I had lipstick on, he'd be painted pink. This must be what it feels like to fly.

"Yes, Jacob, yes!" I sigh. "And thank you for the music box. I didn't get you anything, though."

"That's clawful!" His eyebrows wiggle wickedly. "Are you fur-real?"

I don't let myself laugh. "Stop it."

"No way. It's paw-sitively shocking that ya haven't smiled yet 'cause I happen to be quite hiss-terical."

"Wow. You're feline yourself today, huh?"

"It'd be a cat-astrophe not to," he says and I roll my eyes, pretending to not be amused.

I help him stand so we can walk through the cove hand in hand. He rattles on and on about how he couldn't sleep last night, how he texted three of his sisters asking for advice on how to confess his feelings and how he was a wreck during the whole two-hour drive home.

At the last hut, the door remains open where a tattoo artist with dreadlocks works on his own leg, his machine's buzz blending with the sound of rustling leaves. The scent of antiseptic hangs in the air as I admire the intricate artwork etched onto his beige skin. I notice his designs instantly. They're all various sizes and colors, in antique, barrel, and skeleton shapes.

"Hey, I'm Yuri. I heard you know Ouma? She said you'd be coming around asking, but I assumed I'd see you months ago and forgot all about you."

I freeze, paralyzed for a moment. My thoughts scatter and I can't think straight. Finally, my efforts have paid off. All the hurdles have led to this moment.

"You called her Ouma too?"

"Sure, she treated me like a grandson since I've been in and out of the foster system. Bought all my teacups from her."

I'm floored. Literally, I might collapse. Had Ouma helped me sell some pieces? She'd always encouraged me to walk the path of my dream, but I never expected her to spread my art throughout the community.

My hands shake. "Um, do you have one of the teacups by chance?"

"Yeah, one sec." Yuri turns around, fumbles through a crate behind him and withdraws one.

I recognize my unique style immediately. To be sure, I flip it over and see my initials scrawled under the glaze. If Ouma wasn't embarrassed to share artwork by a Nkosi, then I shouldn't be either. Maybe I don't need to change my name but simply embrace that I'll always be different from the rest of my family.

"Did Ouma happen to leave you a letter or a message for me?" I scan the collection of keys on his forearm again, beautifully done.

"For sure, but get a tattoo first?"

"I'll get this raven," Jacob says casually and sits in the chair, already ready to be stuck a thousand times with a needle.

"Really?" I ask, intrigued by his selection.

"Yeah, been wantin' to get somethin'," Jacob remarks.

"Well, hold on, man. I'm not a traditional artist," Yuri says and flicks his wrist; the needle gun moves on its own without him holding it. "Because of my spell, I have to do pairs only. My magic gives an answer the other seeks once the tattoos are both complete. If you want one dude, she'd need to get one too."

"Tell me how the magic works first," I say, handing the teacup back. I don't want to feel like it's a scam. "Do we tell you our questions before the tattoo, or—"

"No, you'll know the answer right after it's done. Like a clear image in your mind," Yuri explains. "Every customer I've asked has explained it like a 'knowing'."

"Okay, I'll get that black rose and moth combo. On this page."

"Cool. Ouma came here often with her beau for picnics to watch the moths together."

A strange sensation whips through me, envy and elation. I'm glad she enjoyed her years by spending time with Bennett. Yet, I wish she had trusted our bond enough to tell me her secrets.

"I'll go first." I poke Jacob until he slides out of the chair and stands next to me, holding my hand.

What do I want to know the answer to most? If Jacob and I will stay together? Will we find Jacob's daughter before the next ceremony? Will we get our magic back?

"Where do you want it?" Yuri asks.

"My forearm." I flip it over so my inner wrist is exposed.

"Here?" Yuri lays the stencil down at the perfect spot.

A strained "Mhm," escapes my lips, my nerves racking my system.

After a few more extended minutes that last an eternity and his quick warning, the needle bites into my skin with a stinging buzz. It's an odd mix of sharp pain and dull vibration, ebbing and flowing as Yuri works. My skin feels hot and tender. Each prick is both discomfort and anticipation as the image slowly becomes part of me. I breathe through it, time blurring.

"Distract me," I beg Jacob.

"Would ya ever do what we did last night in a forest?"

Yuri whistles low. "Man, he gets right down to it."

My cheeks flush warm. "Maybe. Depends on which forest and the time of day."

Jacob's jaw clenches. Each time he makes that slightest movement is like turning on the ignition to my hormones.

"How about in a department store fittin' room?"

Yuri chuckles again. "Quit making me laugh, bro."

"Maybe. Where have you done something like that before?"

He blanches and runs a hand through his hair. "Ya want to know?"

"No, not really." I chuckle. "Where would you want to … with me?"

"Everywhere. Anywhere. Here. Now. Tomorrow. On a plane. Church basement durin' a service. Library stacks after hours with all the lights on. An office with all the blinds open."

"I need to write these down, man." Yuri laughs again.

There's a high chance I like Jacob way too much. The desire to kiss him, confide in him, be constantly by his side whispering to him about all my secrets and fears, and be there to support him on his lowest days is unlike anything I've ever experienced

"Alright, outline is done. Did you want shading?"

I glance at the design and fall in love with it. Nothing needs changed. It's absolute perfection. "No, I adore it like this. It's for Ouma."

"When did you say I'll get an answer?" Jacob asks. "I don't feel anything yet."

"After yours is done. Then you'll both receive a message."

"What question do you want answered?" I ask Jacob.

CHAPTER TWENTY-THREE

Jacob

We exchange spots so I can sit in the tattoo chair. Sunlight pours down in beams through the tree branches, and I can see thousands of tiny specs of dust floating in a single ray. Quiet bird songs trickle around us, but soon Yuri's buzzing gun overpowers their noise.

The question I magically need answered by this spell is how to meet Dakota asap.

"Here." Yuri pulls out an envelope. "Ouma's letter."

Alouette grabs it, tearing open the seal. I watch her eyes zoom over the page as Yuri leans over my exposed chest.

"Ready, man?"

"Oath, mate."

"Alright. Buckle up. Women tend to tolerate the pain better. Let's see what you're made of." Yuri grins.

The initial poke of the needle surprises me, but isn't too

bad. Afraid to move in the slightest, I don't say a word as I watch Alouette read the letter.

My mind feels like mush when I'm around her. Half the time I have these grand moments of inspiration where I feel the urge to compare her to a sunrise. Then the next second, I can only gape at her, desire flooding through me with pure, primal lust. It's as if her energy makes me a better man while somehow also stripping me to the caveman who only grunts. It should be outlawed how much I'm addicted to her.

When Alouette finally looks up, her gaze scans my bare chest with appreciation, then she meets my eyes.

"Want me to read it to you?" she asks.

I nod slightly, pretty sure I'll be holding my breath during the duration of the tattoo. I clench my fist tight as the pain worsens the longer he draws.

"It says, to my sweet little owl, I'm assuming you've learned about your origins by now. Yes, Bennett Savion is your grandfather. I apologize from the depths of my soul that I wasn't strong enough to tell you myself. I couldn't bear the possibility of you responding like your mother. Going through that once was hard enough, but twice would break me. Bennett is a good man. Trust him."

She pauses and I can tell a heavy weight has lifted off her shoulders. Alouette stands straighter, prouder, ready to battle anything. I'm proud of her for being brave enough to share this letter with me. If I wasn't being stabbed a hundred times, I'd crush her in a hug.

"You don't have to keep going," I gently urge.

"I want to. I may skip a few lines here and there. Next she says … remember, it doesn't matter what others want you to accomplish," she continues, her eyes full of unshed tears. "It's your life. Your passions. Your dreams. Your time here on this earth. Choose to spend it in the way that brings you the most joy. My greatest wish for you, Lou, is to experience the deepest love imaginable someday. Whether that is love for your pottery or a ... partner ... Never stop hunting for that glitter of happiness that will warm you from the inside out."

Would she ever consider me as a real partner? How quickly would I drop Marquis for her?

"From up here, in the clouds, I can feel you're searching for my cottage. Have you been wondering where it ran off to? Please don't go alone. My cottage is on Thornwitch Isle, a short boat ride off of Calypsa's coast."

"We've been there!" I interrupt, but she holds a finger to her lips, continuing.

"That land is protected and can't be built upon or sold, so I knew my home would not be tampered with after I left. I wanted it to be surrounded by nature and bugs and never be at risk of demolition. It is yours, Lou. I've signed the deed over to your name."

Alouette stops there and folds the paper. "I don't want to share the rest. But I guess I already have my answer. You didn't need to get a tattoo after all. She already told me what I had asked."

Yuri shakes his head. "Nah, wait."

"Almost done?" I wince, promising myself to never get one of these again.

"Did you want shading?"

"Not if she didn't," I reply.

"Okay, then ... finished!"

As soon as Yuri draws the needle away, pain sears through my skull. I gasp, my hands fly to my temples. My eyes squeeze shut and I bend over in half.

"Holy Mother!" I scream.

Alouette scrambles to me. "You okay? What do you see?"

"Dakota is blonde, like me. I see the back of her hair. She's sittin' on a wooden patio or deck, outside in the forest, safe and calm. Can't see her face, but I know she's starin' at a sign in the woods. It says, 'Historic Property Site.'"

"Ow! What in the?!" Alouette doubles over as if she's about to vomit. I'm unable to help as she groans in misery, clutching her head.

"That's where Ouma's cottage is!" she says through forced breaths. "I'm inside of it, looking out the window, and I see the same sign." After a few shaky inhales, Alouette stands, wobbles a little, then blinks a few times.

"Why would Dakota be at your cottage?"

"I don't know, but let's go! It'll take us at least an hour to get to the shoreline. What if there aren't any boats available?"

"I'll text Cheyenne now and beg for one to be ready."

Yuri holds a mirror up. "Want to see your new ink?"

"No, mate. Gotta run."

Having already paid him, we grab our bags and rush away from the booths.

"Come on!" Alouette speeds ahead, her smaller size making it far easier to maneuver around people.

My shoes crunch over brittle leaves as I launch myself towards the path. Leap over logs. Zip past trees. I almost slip a dozen times but trample down the trail after her. The breeze tastes different, a flavor of hope and thrill tinges it now. But my heart ticks like a clock changing its pace. Faster. Faster.

Can't believe I get to meet my little girl soon.

Suddenly, my phone rings. Nella's face appears. What

the ... I don't even have her contact in my cell. A rush of unease comes over me and my chest clamps tight.

Mid-sprint, I answer, keeping my voice as formal as I can. "Jacob Talksihnn here."

"What did you do?" Nella screams and I don't recognize her voice in the slightest. "Where is she?!"

I stop and almost collide with a tree, then brace myself against the trunk.

"What are ya talkin' bout?"

"Dakota's gone! How could you take her from me!? Bring her back. Now!"

Shivers run up my arms and my heart feels like a stampede. I don't know how to be a parent or protect her. I can't think. Can't move. How am I supposed to fix this? How am I supposed to keep Dakota safe if I don't know anything about her?

"I didn't take her, Nella. I swear. I don't even know where ya live. I didn't even know her name! Why would ya think I've taken her?"

"She's gone." Her cries turn hysterical. "She left a note."

"Read it."

"It's in her handwriting. Says *'going to daddy's.'* If you don't have her, then who does? What the fuck, Jacob!? Who has my baby?"

My jaw clenches painfully and I spring back into action by darting after Alouette again, then I command Nella, "Call the cops. Send them to Thornwitch Isle by the historic site. There should be a small house. I think she's there."

"How could you possibly know that if you're not with her!?"

"Do it! Now! I'm on my way."

"Jacob ..." a sob rips through the line. "They won't be able to get to her. There's a huge storm headed that way.

Haven't you heard? It's the biggest magical storm the coast has ever experienced. Showed up on the radar an hour ago. Been all over the news."

Terror twists my gut like venom and vicious promises. I'm too far away. Who will protect Dakota? How could I let my magic be taken? If I were any type of father, I would have chosen to always have a spell of protection in my pocket. My baby girl needs me and I'm useless.

"Jacob!" Alouette yells from far ahead. "Help me, please!"

CHAPTER TWENTY-FOUR

Alouette

High above, a metal cage is strung between two trees with dozens of trapped birds, all flailing about. I know we need to keep running, but I can't leave them. How could someone be so cruel?

Jacob arrives behind me, out of breath and with a wild appearance. He reaches to tug me along, but I point up. He follows my gaze to the animals in distress, then shakes his head urgently.

"We can't help them. I have to get to Dakota," he says adamantly.

"Please! five minutes," I plead.

His expression is profound, something made of sonnets that stand the test of time. He rubs a hand over his beard, then glances around at the trees. "Fuck. Okay. Climb up my back. Hurry."

When he crouches low, I do as he says, balancing myself as he rises to his full height.

"Stand on my shoulders, then reach for that branch."

I slip on my first attempt.

"Careful!"

With a hefty amount of struggling, I manage to cling to the branch. Pull myself up. Every muscle strains. Cursing under my breath, I rise to the branch and pray to not fall. The knot of the rope is tied three times, so I use my teeth to loosen it. Bite and gnaw. Pieces of hemp stick to my tongue, so I spit a bunch out. I pull and yank. As the birds squawk to the point of madness, the knot loosens.

"Calm down, babies. Don't break a wing," I say, lowering the rope as softly as I can.

Below, Jacob jumps up, grabs the cage and lowers it to the earth. After a simple flip of the door, they burst free, soaring in every direction. Some disappear, but a few remain behind, watching us as if to show their appreciation.

I scale down the tree until Jacob gives me his shoulders as a stepping stool. We work pretty well as a team.

"Thank you, Jacob."

"All good, mate," he says to me as a crow pecks at his shirt. "Let's go!"

Then Ms. Grim also swoops by my face. "Hey, stop that."

More birds dive like we're their targets. For a moment, I'm worried they've been possessed until they collectively latch their beaks and claws on my clothes and lift. Higher. I'm hovering over the ground.

"Woah! What the ...?"

"Alouette! Are you okaaaaa– hey! What are ya doin'?"

They hoist Jacob up, rising next to me. We're elevated higher with each unified flap of the birds' wings. A mixture of pure shock and thrilling excitement shoot through me like a potent drug. I'm flying.

Struggling to control my body, the birds increase their speed as they soar higher towards the tomb gray clouds.

"Thornwitch Isle, Ms. Grim. Hurry!" I scream into the wind stinging my face.

My eyes water, but I force them to stay open. We fly faster than imaginable over the green treetops growing smaller and smaller. In the distance, the sky drastically splits between robin-egg blue and the darkest gray possible. A storm approaches, heralded by a foghorn's warning and the lighthouse's flashing signal.

Each time the birds' movements make me dip a little, I let out an involuntary gasp, but never doubt them.

"Ms. Grim, can you drop us at the cottage's exact location?"

I shudder at the execrable storm. As the island approaches, palm trees rustle. A strong, briny scent slashes through the wind to where we fly, followed by an attack of thrashing leaves. One smacks straight into my face and scratches my skin.

Ferocious, violent hisses whip like a hurricane. My heart thrums heavier, faster, in my chest. What if they drop Jacob into the ocean? Could he survive a fall from forty feet? The first flash of menacing lightning streaks across the sky —the most obvious omen.

"We need to land!" I scream, unsure if Jacob can hear or if the birds will listen.

I have no control of my limbs as the savage wind pushes me. Please don't land in the waves. Please. Rain falls but not as a mere drizzle. It pelts me like coins being chucked from the clouds. I squeeze my eyes shut. There's no other option than to dangle and trust the birds until we're back on solid ground.

I need a distraction. Ahead, Jacob's birds struggle with his weight as they tire. What if they drop him from too high? I should've told him how I feel. That I want to teach him the next steps to pottery and watch horror movies with him, while eating pizza, cuddled on the couch. And hold his hand while telling off Marquis how he has no right to dictate my love life. *Love*? Is this love?

My shoes smack against something hard. Then I fall to my hands and knees before I can let out a scream. Finally, on the ground. Thank Skies.

I'd kiss the sand if we had more time. The magic here feels corrupt; I can almost taste the toxicity in the air. Only a few yards away, sits Ouma's cottage. It's here!

"Fuck, I was dead as a cactus up there." Jacob's voice comes from behind, then I feel his hands all over me, checking me for injuries. "You hurt?" He takes both my cheeks in his big, warm palms and I've never felt safer than when his eyes darken as he checks me.

"I'm okay," I breathe, hypnotized by the cottage.

"You mosssssst definitely are not fine," a hoarse voice snarls, "but itssssss funny you think sssssso."

Ivola Steinbeck, the private investigator ghost who stole our magic, floats above. Her features look more human than spirit now, which gives me an eerie shudder.

Jacob barks something at Ivola but the world fades away. Ouma's cottage is here. We found it! All I can hear are the buzzing bees, the swishing plants, the quiet squeak as the rocking chairs on the front patio sway on their hinges. The last time I sat there was with Ouma before her diagnosis, when we drank margaritas. She'd tell me stories about her past travels.

Unwilling to take my eyes off the cottage, I follow the serpentine ivy dripping with magic, twisting up the pillars. I can picture the box we stored in our secret spot, the one overflowing with ticket stubs of shows we went to, admission receipts to carnivals, and other little mementos of our shared precious memories.

My nerves catch up to me. What if the inside has been damaged by the storms? Or raided? What if Ouma's belongings are gone?

In the pit of my stomach, a coiling tension takes hold. I step forward, only to be thrown backwards. My back thuds against a tree, nearly knocking the wind from my lungs.

"Why can't I get closer? What's this shield?"

Next to Ivola, Jacob uselessly pounds his fists against the invisible wall. I follow his gaze until it settles on a short blonde girl crouched on the patio, her back to us. It almost looks like she's leaning from exhaustion against the siding of the house. Dakota...

"I needed to get my body back. At firsssssst adult ssssspiritssssss sssssolved the problem. But the children? They have the mosssssst energy to sssssteal." Ivola licks her lips; her tongue noticeably forked down the middle as it slips out. "That'sssss why Fuzerssssss don't mature into their magic until they're sssssseventeen. Because kids have too much wild power. Itssssss not sssssssafe to give them sssssspells."

"DAKOTA!" Jacob screams, his voice scratching and hitching.

"Because of that little girl, I'm sssstrong now," she sneers. "You may as well sssstop trying to break in. The sssssseal won't budge."

My gut wrenches and heaves. I need to help him.

"DAKOTA!" he shouts.

"Let the girl go!" I plead and march towards Ivola.

"No. I need her to refuel in a few dayssssss. The unnatural magic I'm using keepssssss draining my energy to make those ssssssstorms."

Jacob wears a haunted, far-away, panicked look as he paces between the trees. His hair is amuck from running his hands through it. I hate this.

"Take me instead," I say, too quietly, as the pouring rain smacks into puddles and branches. I clear my throat and try again. "Take me instead! Use my energy and let the girl go."

Jacob stares at me, hands at his sides, shoulders slumped. He won't protest. Because he loves Dakota with every inch of his being. I understand that intensity because that's how I feel about Jacob. It may have snuck up on me, but there's no point in denying it anymore.

I'd rather have him live his happily ever after than suffer. Maybe one day I'll break free from Ivola's clutches.

"Take me instead," I repeat.

"Don't need you," Ivola hisses. "Your magic is already depleted. You're an empty tank. A vesssssel. Hollow and usssselessssss."

I drop my head and stare at the ground where an ant hill towers to my shin. A thousand little ants work together in harmony for their united goal. I wish I had a thousand workers at my disposal. It's a bit too late to regret my introverted personality, where I've collected no more than a handful of friends. What I need is someone who has support in numbers, power, and strength.

Bennett Savion.

But he's too far away to help. Even if he answered my call, what good can he possibly do from the other side of the country?

"I'll do anything. Please," Jacob begs Ivola.

Numbers and power. The answer is at the tip of my fingertips, taunting me. Numbers and power.

"Jacob!" I run to his side. "Do you have cell service out here?"

He checks quicky. "Yeah, why?"

"Log into your social media."

His forehead creases, then he taps away, fingers shaking. "Now what?"

I glance at his screen. 10k followers. Plus, if we tag Nella, a fraction of her 200k will see it. Raising the phone so we're both on the screen, I press 'record.'

"This is Alouette Nkosi and Jacob Talksihnn. Some of you have heard that I lied about being married to Jacob. You're right. I did. Please don't punish him. He needs your help. Jacob's daughter has been kidnapped by a ghost. She stripped us of our magic, and we can't get to her. We need every Fuzer who lives near Calypsa to come to Thornwitch Isle to help us free her. Any spell you have may be helpful. Tell all your friends and hurry because the storm is coming!"

CHAPTER TWENTY-FIVE

Jacob

Hours pass in agony. No Fuzer army has come to help us. Either the storm is blocking their access or they think I'm an asshole.

On my hands and knees, sweating, and drenched with rain, I continue to dig in the mud. There's a chance I've dislocated my shoulder, but I dig through the shocking pain. After pounding against the invisible shield for Crone-knows-how long, I've resorted to this last idea.

"Dakota!" I scream for the millionth time, throat raw and thick.

She hasn't responded once. My mind flickers through worse-case scenarios repeatedly. My little Dakota's mind warped and controlled by that ghost bitch. Is she scared? Hurt? I ache to wrap her in a protective blanket and hug her.

Alouette digs beside me, fingers caked in muck, dirt smeared across her face, her hands acting as shovels. We're both shaking and a lingering silence hangs heavily between us.

My back strains and my arms burn from fatigue. My chest feels like it'll cave in at any second. Somewhere, a strangled sob makes my vision swim. Me. I'm crying, adding to the rain already dripping down my cheeks. I cover my face with both hands and lean forward until my forehead collapses into the mud.

"Come on! Let me in!" I scream at the deranged Ivola, who floats higher, out of reach.

Alouette leans me against a tree trunk to support my weak body. Her pained expression clouds her eyes. She shakes her head slowly, confirming my suspicion that we'll never be able to penetrate this shield without magic. I don't know what else to do. Alouette leans against my chest, but I'm too numb to comfort her.

"I don't understand. I thought people would come help," she says weakly, voice quaking. Water cascades over her shoulders and her clothes cling to her drenched body.

How could Alouette still stay by my side when I'm failing?

"Go find shelter," I mumble, barely able to hear my voice. "I'm not leavin' Dakota."

"I'm staying."

All remaining hope drains out of me. I can't even keep Alouette safe. Sitting against the tree, catching my breath, my shoulders slacken in surrender.

Her phone rings. I'm surprised the battery isn't dead after she had called so many people for help.

"Hello?" She tries to cover the phone from the rain. "Marquis?"

"... you two ... together? ... I'll kill Jake ... if you ..."

"Marquis! Stop it. We need help." A long pause, then

she asks, "What?" She pushes the phone closer to her ear. The longer she listens, the wider her eyes grow.

I should ask questions, but my head pounds and heaviness drowns out everything else.

"He said he'll never speak to you again ... And ..." Her eyes fill with tears, a sight that's a dagger to my chest.

I try to put on a brave face and pull her closer. "I choose you, got it? He can throw a tantrum all he wants. I bet he'll come 'round eventually, but until then, I don't care what he says because I'm not goin' anywhere."

Alouette smiles and sniffs. I hate seeing her spirit wither. Her body seems to shrink in like she's retreating. She droops her head and whispers to the mud, "Oh Goddess ... please, send someone to help."

She keeps mumbling, but I can't process what she's saying, so I stare at the water droplets descending her beautiful face. We've lost and we're defenseless against Ivola and her destruction.

Depressing cold rain pelts my skin, but I no longer care. Slumped against the rough bark of an ancient tree, I stare blankly at the forest floor. Droplets gush from leaf to leaf. What's the point of trying anymore? I've failed, each attempt leaving me more battered and broken than before. Now, surrounded by the indifferent wilderness, I feel my last ember of hope flicker and die. The forest will go on, the rain will eventually stop, but I ... I am done. Let the muddy earth claim me. Dakota deserves a parent who can keep her safe and rescue her when in distress.

I close my eyes, succumbing to the weight of my despair, as the relentless rain washes away the last of my dreams.

CHAPTER TWENTY-SIX

Alouette

I'm devastated. My only idea had backfired. About an hour ago, I watched the last of Jacob's spark disappear from his soul. The darkness surrounding us is only a reminder of our defeat.

Have I been obsessed with priorities that don't matter? For years I'd whined about the Nkosi name tormenting me. It'd been a complaint stemmed from privilege and entitlement.

I suck in a breath and burrow my cheek further into Jacob's chest. Ever since he sunk into the mud and gave up, he's barely moved a muscle. At least the rain has calmed, so I can actually see Ouma's cottage again.

Still inaccessible, it glows from the inside out with a light from both upper and lower stories. The stone exterior by the bay window is exactly how I remember. It's too bad the flowers along the cobblestone pavement that leads to the front door are all smashed from the deluge.

As I stare at the cottage crumbling among the pines, a

wave of memories crashes over me. The musty scent of wet wood drags me back to summer days spent in isolation, chasing fleeting moments of joy that always seemed out of reach—until Ouma became my primary caregiver.

I long to hear the deep creak of the old porch swing, now just splinters from the wind's destruction. This cottage is supposed to be my sanctuary. I let my head fall into my hands.

Once upon a time, Ouma had told me stories on the worn rug by the fireplace. Her comforting voice has faded, replaced by hollow echoes. As I sit here, the crushing weight of grief bears down on me, burying the last remnants of childhood. I wipe away another tear and realize the rain has stopped. Yet it feels like I'll never be dry again.

"Jacob? What are we going to do?"

I'm in a dazed state of awareness where I can't fully believe this is happening. Why isn't Nella here with the police yet? How has everything fallen apart so quickly?

No. I refuse to give up. Because if the Nkosi legacy has gifted me anything at all, it's the trait of perseverance. No one in my family became a famous scientist by throwing in the towel. I may not want to follow their footsteps exactly, but I still have their tenacity in my blood.

"Finally give up, sssssweathearts?" Ivola dives towards us like a pelican swooping in for its next meal.

We both raise our hands to block her dagger teeth and try to swat her away. She looks corporal, but my hand goes straight through her body. Interesting. Ivola isn't as strong as she thinks. Her unnatural powers must have limitations if she has to steal magic. We need something powerful enough to undo her spell. If an army of Fuzers refuse to come to us, then we need something huge, or ... giant ...

The leprechaun!

I stagger to my feet, shoes squishing in the mud, and cup my hands around my mouth. "Kolen!"

"What are ya doin'? It's useless. No one's gonna help," Jacob mumbles, both bitterness and embarrassment lacing his tone.

"Kolen! I know you're out there! I'm offering a trade!"

Jacob only shakes his head. Part of me is angry that he's given up. He must care more about his own child than I do, so why isn't he doing more? That's when I notice the gray pallor of his skin, darker on his hands and wrist and slowly creeping its way up his forearms like a living virus.

"No," I gasp.

His veins turn crimson and the gray rash spreads too fast, too high. He grunts in agony and leans his head back on the tree. I glance down at a hole in the ground. Sure enough, a couple of toxic beetles skitter out, then crawl up his boots.

"Aah!" I stomp on his foot to crush the first.

I stomp again to kill the second. Its guts and juices spill out, oozing crimson and black fluid that is deadly to the touch.

Jacob's breaths turn shallow and labored.

"Kolen!" I scream again and again. "Kolen!"

A ground-shaking stomp approaches from afar. Then another. They grow closer and louder, shaking the trees.

"Kolen! We're over here!"

"No, you can't do that!" Ivola screeches, fluttering around in a panic. "That's not fair." She holds her hands out as if to cast another protective spell around the cottage, but no sparks appear.

The leprechaun's massive green head emerges from the treetops. He groans, loud and slow. "Trade?"

"Yes. Bring that little girl and this man to safety in Calypsa. What do you want in exchange?"

"Your most big fear." He licks his lips greedily over his pointed teeth.

Before, I would've admitted that my worst fear was swimming in the ocean or never living up to everyone's expectations of what I should be doing with my life. But Jacob has helped me overcome both. I still have progress to make, but they're no longer what I'm most concerned about.

I swallow the rocklike sensation lodged in my throat and stare at Jacob. "Living without *him*. That would be my biggest fear. To trudge through life day after day without him."

"Deal." Kolen nods.

"No!" Ivola zooms back and forth in the air as if she can block his massive strength.

In one heavy swipe, Kolen's fist shatters the dome in an ear-splitting crack. Gold glitter drizzles down in an ironically beautiful arch. Jacob's gray hand reaches towards the cottage door. My heart races frantically as his eyes droop and his cracked lips part.

Ivola soars away, above the treetops, howling and bawling until her voice blends with the wind.

A small, feminine squeal breaks what's left of my courage. Tears fall down my face.

"Alouette," Jacob whispers. "You shouldn't have ..."

"Jacob," I say, choking on my own sobs, knowing this may be the last time we see each other.

I hold his hand in mine and kiss the toxic gray, not caring anymore if he's a man doused in poison. He's mine. I'm his. For a moment longer.

"I don't think my soul was ever looking for the cottage,"

I say, sobbing. "Do you want to know what the rest of Ouma's letter said? The part I didn't read?"

Jacob nods, barely moving as his head falls to the side, weak. He's dying. I can barely breathe.

I recite the poem Ouma had written:

> "Moths to flame, we circle near,
> Hearts once poisoned now sincere.
> Letting go of toxic fear,
> Love's light makes the path clear.
> In each other's arms we've found,
> Trust and joy, our lives unbound."

The corner of his mouth quirks up, but it doesn't form a full smile. The gray poison has spread to his neck and moves towards his ears.

I press my hand against his cheek, too cold to the touch. "This whole time I've been looking for love, Jacob. I've been looking for you."

"I ..." Jacob wheezes and the sound snaps me in two. "I ... love ... you."

Time stands still as my mind races, processing what he said. Is this real? A tidal wave of emotions crashes into me.

Watching him deteriorate before my eyes is the ultimate torture. I might laugh from irony or cry or both. He loves me. Jacob *loves* me. Part of me wants to pinch myself, to make sure this isn't some noxious fantasy.

Fear spreads through my chest. This is the man I've fallen for, being vulnerable in a crisis of epic proportion. I need to be strong for him. I want to bask in his words, but I can't. Because he's dying. A blonde figure swooshes past in my periphery until Kolen's giant hand scoops her up. She screams as she's lifted high in the air.

Dakota.

Jacob can't open his eyes, but I feel him try to see his daughter. My heart breaks for him. I have no idea if he'll survive the trek. Kolen grabs Jacob before I can say goodbye. Words fail me, however, I know one thing for certain—I love Jacob too, with every fiber of my soul.

CHAPTER TWENTY-SEVEN

Jacob

I wake stiff and confused to the smell of spiced cider and light strands hanging from the endless black above. I sit up, pushing off hard rock and hear whispered conversation nearby. I follow the sound, my sights crossing over abandoned vendor booths, faintly lit by soft lanterns attached to rock walls that climb endlessly. Wait. Am I back at the Black Cat Market? How did I get here?

Patting myself down, I realize I'm in clothes that aren't mine with a strange white ointment coating my skin. There's a potent magic and power in the air.

A breeze whisps from above, reminding me that somewhere this cave opens to the sky. What time is it? What day is it? How long have I been here? From the empty darkness, a pair of eyes appears and glares straight at me as if it can see my soul.

"Hello?" I stand on shaky legs and almost topple over.

"You're still weak."

"Who are you? Why am I here?" I raise both fists, my mind on high alert.

"You recall nothing?" the voice asks from the darkness. Is it human? The tone screeches against my nerves.

Racking my brain, I collect the fragments of what I last remember, sorting it out from the outlandish dreams and nightmares still invading my conscious. A massive green hand. Thunder. Lightning. Pain. A screaming child.

"Dakota!" I leap forward and scan the open space. "Where is she?"

"She's fine," the voice soothes, stepping closer but the darkness still cloaks them.

"Who are you? Show yourself!"

"We've been entertaining her while you were ... recovering."

"I want to see her!" I launch forward, frantically searching, turning in a circle, hoping to catch a glance of the blonde hair I have imagined. "Where is she!? And where's Alouette?"

The voice sighs, but that makes me panic even more.

"Tell me!" I scream.

The silhouette steps from the cloaked darkness and becomes clear as someone rises to full height. A beam of light shines on their face as they move forward. I squint to meet their unique purple and silver eyes. It's the oracle.

"Kwiin Rory!"

"Did she kiss you before the clock struck midnight?"

"Answer my question," I snap, but then all the fight drains from me and I practically beg, "Please."

"Which one?"

"Stop playing games! What's goin' on?"

They nod, paired with a telling frown. "A leprechaun named Kolen brought you and Dakota here a few days ago.

Our healers attended to you both. Your blood was full of toxins, most likely from a plant or nasty bug. You were minutes from death. I'm surprised you survived at all. I should go and tell them you're awake."

"No, wait!" I lunge forward, closing the space between us. "There were only two of us?"

"Yes, I'm sorry. I don't know what happened to your swan girl, but she isn't here."

The scene of us desperately digging outside the cottage flickers in my mind like a broken, scratched film. Pieces of the puzzle don't add up. How did Dakota arrive at that cottage? Did Ivola kidnap her or was Dakota already on Thornwitch Isle?

"Can you lead me to my daughter, mate?"

"No ..."

I cut him off. "Why?!" I yell.

He throws up his hands to surrender. "You look horrible. I don't think you'll make the walk. You might pass out."

"I'm fine. I need to see her."

From behind me, footsteps echo off the vases of flowers and skull decorations. Is it her? Am I about to see Dakota for the first time?

"Dad?" a little voice asks, sweeter than ice cream.

I whirl around. My heart is in my throat at the sight of her. There she is, perfect in every way. From what I remember of Nella's appearance, there is barely any resemblance, simply a miniature and feminine version of me as a kid. She actually looks a lot like my younger sister, Jess. Her bright blue eyes—wide and round—are the color of the ocean on a summer day. A smatter of tanned freckles —from too many hours outside—mirrors mine. Long, thick blonde hair cascades over her shoulder down to her waist. I've never seen anyone more beautiful.

"Dakota?" I ask, frozen in place.

She rolls in her pink, plump lips and fidgets her hands with the hem of her shirt. Maybe she's recently gone through a growth spurt because her clothes are a size too small as her gangly arms hang out of her sleeves like noodles. Bug bites and tiny scratches cover her knees and shins which makes an intense protective outrage wash over me like a tsunami. Every instinct rises in my core to hunt down and murder whatever caused her injuries.

"You can call me Koda," she says, smiling, then hops over like we've known each other for the last ten years. "You snore louder than the cats purr. Hopefully you're not allergic because their hair is all over your clothes. One even laid her paw over your mouth once. I think she was trying to silence you, maybe kill you. It was hilarious. Once you talked in your sleep, but she didn't move at all. Do you have a cat at home? I love animals but my favorite is turtles. Once I asked Mom for a turtle, but she said no because I'd have to take care of it, and I forget when I'm playing. It might be a good idea because I lose things a lot too. Can you imagine waking up and stepping on your pet turtle by accident? Or not being able to find it because it's hiding in a pile of laundry? Now that would be hilarious. I wonder what I'd name my turtle?"

She smiles and I'm mesmerized. Fully entranced. Giggling, she sits on the boulder next to me and asks, "What would you name a turtle if you had one?"

"Uh ... I ... I kind of do have one. His name is Taco."

She claps her hands together and bounces on her butt. "Taco the turtle! That's perfect. Do you think he'd eat a taco if we fed it to him? Where does he live? I don't know much about the restaurants around here but back home, there's a place called Three Broomsticks that has the best tacos you'll ever eat. I'll bring you there sometime but you gotta let me have a soda. Don't tell Mom, she never lets me have caffeine which is stupid because I sneak in candy all the time and she doesn't know that." Her hands clamp over her mouth. "Never mind, I didn't say that. Am I gonna get in trouble? Are you the kind of dad who will yell at me?"

"No," I say, laughing and shaking my head. "Never. Koda, I ... are you okay? Have they been taking care of you?"

She waves a hand dismissively. "Dad, or should I call you Papi? Don't worry about me. I'm ten years old. It was a little scary when we got here because you didn't look good, so I've had to wait forever to tell you my favorite color is pink." Then she stands, as if her little dynamite energy won't allow her to sit still any longer. "I like art a lot. Every kind of art. Once I made you a bracelet; but I didn't bring it with me in case I'd lose it. I know exactly where it is on my dresser, right where I left the note to Mom that I was going to find you." She pauses again.

My pulse races, unable to comprehend that she's right here, that she looks like me, that she's so full of spunk and life that I could cry.

"Mom's gonna be mad, but I don't know if she'll yell at me or you. I think she will be here soon." Koda leaps over the skeleton decorations on the ground like they're toys. "I wonder if she brought me a sandwich. The food here isn't good. Rory tried to give me avocado toast. Have you ever eaten that? Sal at school said that Australians like vegemite. Have you had that before?"

"Yeah, I have." Every part of me wants to wrap her in a hug, squeeze her tight and never let go.

This girl is a firecracker. She skips along and continues

to talk a mile a minute about the most random things that are the most precious pieces of information I'll store as treasure.

"Kolen is my new best friend, but don't tell Sal. I can't believe how green he is, greener than a lime. He let me play on his top hat, but I can't show you the trick I practiced because he left a few hours ago. Maybe we can leave now too and meet Mom on the trail. This place is too dark, and I love to hike. Do you love to hike? I bet you'd carry me on your back if I asked you to. I've been waiting my whole life to ask that question, would you?"

I drop to my knees in front of her and hold her small hands in mine. My chest tightens from our first ever contact. "Yes, I'll carry ya to the moon and back if ya want me to, Koda. I'm sorry I'm so late to meet you. I have a thousand questions, but I want ya to know that I love you so much. Remember that, okay. No matter what happens, I love you."

"Yeah, Mom told me that already. I didn't know you were my dad until three months ago, when Sal showed me something on his phone. I'm not allowed to get a phone yet and the picture of a surfer was super confusing. When I asked Mom, she told me about you, and I've been mad at her for a while, but then was happy again since it was my birthday and she planned a big party and I got so many presents. Then I heard her talk to someone on the phone about not ever meeting you and I got mad again, so I packed my stuff in my backpack, especially my blanket, because even though I'm not a little kid anymore I can't sleep without my blanket. I think it's magic. Do you have magic? Mom said I might one day."

"You have every type of magic that matters. Right in here," I say, hovering my pointed finger over her heart.

"Whether you're a Fuzer or a Typ we can figure out later. Be you, Koda. Always."

She surges forward, wrapping both her arms around the back of my neck and pressing her lips to my cheek. A loud, squishy smack finishes her kiss faster than a blink, then she pulls away. "Come on, you need to meet Quentin and Xavier. They're ginormous. Bigger than a house!"

She tugs my hand forcefully. I turn to my side to give Alouette an amused wink, forgetting she isn't there. Fuck. I have to find her. But there's no chance I'm leaving Koda until Nella arrives.

Ahead, light shines through the cave opening. Down the tunnel, daylight and trees welcome me to a turned page in my life. Two colossal bats swoop playfully between sun rays, scooping up bugs from the soil each time they meet the earth. Koda skitters with glee towards them, and I reach forward, wanting to protest, but suck in a breath instead. This wondrous girl has survived ten years without my guidance and protection. It's not my place to enforce rules.

I'll never get to be the one to make her wear a helmet when she rides a bike for the first time. Or teach her that markers are for drawing on paper instead of walls. I've missed all the years nagging her to put her seat belt on and remember to brush her teeth. But I'll be there in the future, to volunteer for each school excursion. I'll work five jobs if necessary to sign her up for any art class she wants, and to read her every book she loves until I lose my voice. I'll be there even when she's sick of me.

One of the bats flattens itself on the ground. I can feel myself cringe when Koda climbs atop its back.

"Come on, Dad! It's so fun and not scary at all!"

That's *my* girl. She's fearless. I've had enough flying to last me a lifetime but nod anyways and slide onto the neighboring bat who lowers itself for me. Its skin is cold and hard, which reminds me of a dragon. Maybe they share genetics.

"Just one minute," I say, unable to hold back my concern.

"Ready? Go!"

Her bat rises, flapping its titanic wings. The movement is like a stingray in the water. Maybe Koda will let me teach her how to surf. If Alouette was brave enough to enter the water, I bet she might even participate in a surfing lesson to encourage Koda.

Shit ... Alouette is in danger. How am I celebrating and enjoying this time when she might be under Ivola's control? The possible scenarios flipping through my mind feel like a punch to the gut.

"Okay, Koda, come down, please."

She obeys with the largest grin spread across her baby cheeks. It's obvious how she's in the middle of a transition. Half her face is still young and innocent, but her adult teeth have grown in.

"Wasn't that cool?"

A female voice hollers from the forest. Koda's eyes bulge and she scrambles off the bat, then gestures for me to follow suit.

"It's Mom!" She pulls at the bottom of her shirt and rushes over to stand next to me.

"It's okay. I've got ya."

"You're not scared?" She looks up at me in wonder.

"Nah, we're good. Trust me?"

Koda nods, which melts my heart on the spot.

"Dakota?!"

"We're over here!" I yell back, projecting my voice through cupped hands.

A flurry of stomps crunch over leaves and a group of hikers arrive. Nella looks different from the filtered photos she posts online. Glancing between her and Dakota, it's obvious the only trait they share is a fragile nose shape and a rounded bone structure.

"My Bluebird!" Nella drops to her knees and spreads her arms out wide.

Whatever hesitancy Koda felt is ripped away as she sprints into her mom's arms and crashes into her chest. Sounds of cries and laughter mix as I watch them. A pair that knows everything about each other—whether they sleep on the right or left side of the bed, if they like cake with milk or water, and their favorite tv shows. I desperately long for that connection.

In the distance, the hikers sit in a circle on some rocks, unpacking their lunch. After a few minutes of me standing there awkwardly, as Nella reprimands Koda with an obscene attack of kisses to the face, I finally clear my throat.

Nella glances up, then rises to stand. "Jacob," she deadpans.

"Nella. How's it going, mate?"

"You haven't lost your accent, I see," she says, glaring. "How could you tell her to run away from home!?"

I shake my head and lift both hands to surrender. "No, I swear I—" I say at the same time as Koda chimes in, "No, Mommy, Dad didn't know."

"Dad? But you don't know him." Nella rubs her hand over her forehead and clenches her eyes shut.

"But he is my dad. And I want to get to know him," Dakota says.

I phrase my next words cautiously. "All I've wanted is to be a part of her life," I begin calmly. "I don't have any more money to give ya right now, but I will. Let's work this out for her. I promise, all I want is to be in her life."

"Being a parent is hard. It's not a game. It's sacrifice and—"

I cut her off, "I'll do anythin'."

Her face drops. "Anything?" Nella tucks Koda behind her back.

"Yes. I'll move to Oakmar. I'll give ya the majority of my paychecks. We'll watch her whenever ya wanna go on holiday or a date. I'll drive her to school, and we'll help with homework."

"We?"

I swear internally. Alouette. "Yeah, me and my ... my person. And speaking of her, I need to go. She's in trouble. Now that Koda is ..."

She snaps, cutting me off, "Koda?" Nella's gaze whips over to our daughter. "You gave him a nickname to call you?"

She nods silent and proud. "I want something special with Dad and it's important to me, Mommy. Please listen to him. I like all of what he's saying."

Nella sighs, then nods to the group behind me. "Ubika, can you bring the papers?"

Wait. What? The custody lawyer is with the hikers? She joins us with a large folder and pen in hand.

"I've drafted this on your behalf, Mr. Talksihnn. It sounds like you're in a hurry, so we may have to go over it another time. You can sign it and I'll be in touch. The basic concept is that Nella is agreeing to meet to discuss custody and your rights. There will be a lot of details and negotiations to consider later. I wanted to have this in writing and knew Ms. Franklin would be most willing when reunited with Dakota."

We both sign, and I can't believe my luck. There's a chance Koda will be in my life after all. I'd do anything to make that happen ... except abandon Alouette. She needs me, and I can't stay here any longer.

"Koda, can we talk in private?" I point to a huddle of trees.

"Yeah, I'll race you." Her brows wiggle in a little dance, then she prances in front of me.

Nella smiles softly, then meets my eyes. I nod and turn my back on my past, ready for what's coming.

"Where do you have to go, Dad? I can come too! And I have so much to show you and tell you."

I crouch to her level again. "I want to hear about everythin' and I want to see all of it. But right now, I need ya to stay with your mom 'cause there's someone I care about who needs me. After I find her, I'll return as soon as I can. We can play and I'll introduce ya to Taco sometime, okay?"

She scrunches up her nose. "Okay. Makes sense. Do you *loooooove* your girlfriend?" Her whole body wiggles like she's dancing.

"Soooooo much!" I say, wiggling my head to copy her. "And I love you too. Always and forever. Even more than ya like the color pink."

Her jaw drops in mockery. "Not possible! Hey, Dad, what's *your* favorite color?"

"Today? It's pink."

"Oh, good, then Quentin will let you ride him."

"Excuse me?"

"You have to go somewhere fast, right?" She points to the bat. "Quentin said he'd take you."

"He said that for real or pretend?"

"For real. He also says you don't weigh much so it'll be easy, as long as you don't fall off."

I can't tell if she's playing a game or can actually communicate with animals.

"Then, I accept. Tell him thank you."

"Oh, he knows." Koda jumps into my chest again in an adorable hug. "What's her name, Dad? The one that needs you to rescue her?"

"Her name is Alouette. But she's the one who rescued *me*."

I force myself away from my daughter and climb atop the bat's back. Without a word, it rises higher and higher. For as long as possible, I keep my eyes trained on her marigold hair until Koda's out of view.

CHAPTER TWENTY-EIGHT

Alouette

After a few nights wallowing inside Ouma's cottage, I'm all out of hope. I'll never see Jacob again. Though, if he and Dakota are safe, wherever they are, then my sacrifice will be worth it. At least I'm out of harm's way after Ivola left. She said she preferred taking energy from children, so once Dakota was gone, she had no reason to stay.

Bundles of dried herbs dangle from gnarled wooden beams overhead, their earthy fragrances a sad reminder of my grandma. For the hundredth time, my eyes are drawn to the hearth, where her bread would bake. I investigate Ouma's collection of teacups full of expired fairy dust, vials of trapped moonlight, and bowls of decayed flowers.

With a sigh, I face the harsh reality: the cottage's magical energy is gone, and the emptiness it left weighs heavily on my soul. Once a center of mystical energy, my safe place now stands as a hollow shell—a fading memory of what one was.

This cottage was more than my home—it was an extension of my being, where I felt most comfortable. The realization comes crashing down that when Ouma died, I didn't only lose her, but also a part of myself. When this cottage disappeared, I no longer had the place where I had always felt most accepted.

Maybe my home isn't this place, but with the people who accept me wholly. How will I ever find that feeling again without Jacob by my side?

I have every intention of staying here for the rest of my life. I'll live off the land, find a way to survive among nature.

Eventually, I'll need to tidy up the space, starting with tearing down the cobwebs that drape from blackened beams overhead, then dust the shelves lining the walls, all covered with mildewed tomes.

In one corner, the threadbare cushion lies empty, where Ouma's cat used to sleep, its surface now moth-eaten and faded. A life of solitude won't be the worst of options. Of course, Marquis will need to be updated. I wonder if I'll be off his hit-list now that I've given up Jacob. That thought sends a piercing pain through my chest.

And the monthly ceremony taking place tonight ... If I perform the ritual alone, will Luna still grant me a new spell? I could be an outlaw, a Fuzer living on the edge, until the end of my days.

There's a knock on the door. When I peek outside the window, there's a group of people with backpacks all glancing around curiously. The door creaks loudly when I open it.

"Um. Hello?" I ask.

"Hey, are you the one who posted the SOS video?" a woman asks, her eyes moving past me to inspect the cottage.

"Uh, a few days ago."

"Yeah, this was the fastest we could get here."

"Well. The crisis is over, but thanks for your trouble," I tell them, then shift to close the door.

The woman blocks it with her hand and pushes her way inside. "Actually, we're exhausted from looking for you. Mind if we sit for a bit?"

I gesture to the room. "Sure, go ahead," I mumble, but don't want to host or entertain a group of strangers. "I need some air. I'll be back in a few minutes."

Outside, the scent of sea salt is carried on the wind. I'll have to reorient myself with how far inland I am. As I meander around the backyard, I continue to stare at the wet soil and broken tree limbs laid scattered across the garden. Maybe it'd be wise to recruit these visitors to help me clean before they leave. Tears well up, blocking my vision right before I run into something hard and firm.

"Alouette," a deep timber vibrates, one that invades my soul.

I freeze. Clench my eyes shut. Jacob can't be here. It's impossible. The leprechaun may devour him if I break my vow.

"Are you real?" I ask with a shaky breath.

"You tell me."

A finger tips my chin up, my heart fluttering with anticipation. His warm breath whispers across my cheek. Gently, his lips touch mine—soft, sweet, and full of emotion. Time slows. I savor the warmth of his hands on my back, the faint scent of him that's my new addiction.

Opening my eyes, my joy reflects in his gaze.

"You're here?"

"I am," Jacob says, smiling, while slowly rubbing his hands up and down my back.

"How?" I glance behind him. "Is Dakota safe? Are you hurt? What about the poison? Where's the leprechaun?"

He chuckles and tucks a loose strand of my wild hair behind my ear. "Koda is with her mom, not a scratch on her. Healers got the poison out after a few rough days. I'm still a little dizzy sometimes, but I'll survive, thanks to you." His hands still, and his smile flattens. "Little Owl..."

"Don't ever do that to me again!" Emotions unraveling, I shove his chest. "YOU. ALMOST. DIED!" Tears collect, hot and heavy, and I barely hang onto control to keep them from falling. "Do you know what that did to me? Seeing you suffer like that?" Another shove. "It b-broke me! Felt like you cracked and snapped every bone in my body! Like you sucked out all my air and severed my heart! I can't survive that again."

A tiny lift at the corner of his mouth jerks up. "I think you might like me a little bit."

I cross my arms tightly, hoping to hide how my heart is threatening to burst from my body. Pretty sure my lips quiver as tears threaten to pour.

"Oh, babe, it's okay. Come here." Jacob's large hand wraps behind the back of my head and he scoops me towards his chest.

I bury my face in his shirt and brutally sob. Imagine the ugliest cry anyone has ever cried since the dawn of humanity. Snot runs and drips. With every snort and gasp, I release the terror and worry I've stored. I fully believed I'd never see his sweet smile again. Yet here he is. When I've calmed down and wiped away the tears, I step back to see his aqua eyes clearly.

"What about my vow to Kolen?"

"I triple checked with some experts. Apparently, leprechauns are notorious for being all talk and no action."

He kisses my forehead, then my lips. This man is fully delectable. "I love the way your brows crease right here when you're serious."

My heart flutters like raven wings when he looks at me like that. His smile helps me believe I can soar, that I'm capable of flying into the vast blue. His arms are my nest, a safe haven where I can rest after a long day's flight. Ouma's cottage isn't my home. It's wherever he is. With Jacob, I'm no longer earthbound.

"Jacob?"

"Yes, Alouette?"

I tug him past the overgrown bushes and wilting flowers to the back door. Inside, my blankets are still in a messy pile from where I shoved them off this morning. After closing the door behind me, I pull both curtains wide open so sunlight shines in through the windows.

Jacob glances around for only a moment, then his eyes are fixed back on me. "People are here? How is it possible that you have guests? I thought you were a prisoner and rushed to come save you." The disbelieving chuckle is adorable as he rubs his beard.

I shake my head. "They came to help. A little too late. I guess our video actually worked. Dozens showed up. But I don't want to talk about them right now."

"What do ya want to talk 'bout?" He cups the side of my face with so much adoration it's basically heart wrenching.

"I don't want to talk at all," I say, quietly, only wanting to indulge in him.

At my confession, his eyes darken to the deepest sea blue. Never have I been in love. Until now. Anticipation and nerves braid together in a confusing jumble.

"Owlette ... I can see ya thinkin'. Relax." He leans down and kisses my neck, which sends a tingle of little shockwaves straight up my spine. "What do ya want? No pressure. No rush."

Unwilling to wait, I gaze into his hungry eyes. "I want you. Now. Every piece that you're willing to give." I let out a loud, frustrated huff. "Goddess, I'm not making any sense. What I'm trying to say is with you, I feel whole."

His lips crash into mine again, fiery and passionate, hotter than the Sols. We're moving across the room. My heels collide with the door as he presses me against it. A loud cheer from the other side makes Jacob pull away for a moment and smirk.

"You're sure about this?" He nods to make it clear he's referring to the company out there, who will be witnesses to every sound.

"Yes. Don't stop kissing me. Don't stop ever."

And then I'm being devoured, quite thoroughly. No kiss has felt this layered, this meaningful, full of such depth and desire. My ass and back slam against the door again. This time. I force myself to intentionally block out the cheers from the others and pay attention to only Jacob. His tongue dancing with mine. His intense enthusiasm. His hands in my hair.

"Fuck, Owlette, if ya moan like that again, I'm not gonna be patient enough to draw this out."

His voice, turned rough and raspy around the edges, makes my nipples pinch tight and rub against my bra.

"What do ya like?"

"To be told." I gasp when his mouth claims my collar bone like a famished dog, pushing my shirt off my shoulder. "Can you ... oh ... can you tell me what to do? The whole time?"

A tearing sound comes from my sleeve and Jacob reels back, eyes wide and pupils fully dilated. "Oh, shit, I ruined your ..." His ravenous expression takes me in, how my lips are swollen and belong to him, only him. "Fuck it. I don't care."

Jacob reaches forward with both hands. I watch his biceps flex under his strong hold, not knowing what he's doing. With a solid grunt, he shreds my shirt in one large rip. A breeze from the window combs against my skin and my tiny hairs all bristle.

"Holy Abyss. How do ya get more stunnin' each time I look at you?" His voice sounds pained, primal, strained to its limits. "Ya want me to tell ya what to do?"

I nod once and his hands flex at his sides. "Unclip your bra."

I do.

His lips part on a sharp inhale. He scrubs a hand down his face again. "Goddess, help me. Turn around."

Obeying, I place both palms flat on the door separating us from the people on the other side of the threshold—a door without a lock.

"Did I tell ya to lean forward? No, little owl, I did not. Stand straight and drop your pants."

I shimmy out of them, able to feel his fierce stare against my heated skin, following the path of my pants as they slip down my thighs. Over my knees. Past my ankles. I kick them off one foot at a time and don't dare turn around.

"Always barefoot," he says, chuckling.

I thirst for his touch. Now that I've granted him full control, I want to beg him to be the one to pull off my panties. His body presses against my back. Skin on skin. He's naked already.

"Oooh." I shudder pleasantly. "Jacob ..."

"I love when ya say my name like that," he mumbles

low, his bare chest vibrating against my back. "Now grab my cock."

Barely able to blow out a deep breath, I bite my lip to center myself. I reach behind my hip where his dick is pressed up against my ass. It's so hard and thick. I reposition to get a good grasp and stroke up and down. Once. Twice.

He swipes a solo finger under my breasts. I shiver, then press my ass against him.

"Ah, feelin' greedy?" He presses his mouth against the back of my head. "Faster, Alouette. Harder."

Wanting him to feel overwhelmed with pleasure, I handle him at a punishing pace, with a vigorous hold.

"FUCK!"

His body falls forward until his palms are the ones that slam loudly above my head. I'm gloriously pinned, his heavy weight pushing my front against the door.

"Jacob ..." I force out his name, breathlessly craving more. "Please."

"Your turn to make demands?" he rasps, then tugs my underwear off until they flop to my feet. "Spread these and let go of me."

My legs part for him like he's using a remote to direct my body.

"Further," he mutters through gritted teeth.

The absence of his erection in my hand is a loss I wasn't expecting to mourn. But the sensation of his whole front pressed against my ass makes my heart beat wildly. This is what I've been waiting for. He collects my hair and moves it over one shoulder, so his hot breath tickles my neck.

"So beautiful. I wanna take my time with ya nice and slow. But I also wanna fuck ya until ya can't walk. Which one will it be?"

"Whatever you want."

His capable hand runs down my spine, unhurried. Leisurely. As hot as this is, there's a tender vulnerability within every move, look, and electric touch. I feel utterly cherished by him.

"I want …" He plants a trail of kisses down my back, then continues, "… to make ya …" His lips trail over my curves as he lowers himself further and further to the ground until he's sitting between my legs. "…scream my name for all those people out there to hear, understand?"

I have no warning before he scoots under me, his lips sweeping against my clit. Another elated moan flies free. I've never asked for oral before, but if this preview is the way Jacob performs, I'll be begging for it nightly. Tension coils taut and I buck against his mouth.

He murmurs some snarky command, but I no longer care. Apparently, I didn't listen because he disciplines me with both hands clutching my thighs tightly so that I can't escape. His tongue is a gift from a mystical holy paradise. The way he swirls it in the most perfect spot should be a sin.

I tremble.

He sucks.

I shake.

"Oooh! Jacob!" I try to step away, but he cages me with his strength.

"Nuh uh, don't run from me," he orders into my skin, then comes up for a breath. "Come, Alouette. It's okay. I've got ya."

My breath charges, swift and dynamic. Heat surges. Muscles spasm. I can't tolerate it. Damn. Everything feels too good. He inserts one finger, and that's all it takes to push me over the edge. I clench around him and my entire body …

CHAPTER TWENTY-NINE

Jacob

Convulses. Alouette thrashes against my mouth. She tastes of divine sunlight drizzled with delicious pineapple juice. A wild orgasm splits her down the middle until her moans explode in ragged breaths; the single most sexy fuckin' sound I've ever heard.

The chatter on the other side of the door quiets, telling me the strangers are aware of her pleasure. And I'm the one lucky enough to give it. The thought of someone else possibly wanting her, knowing she's choosing me, makes my cock impossibly harder.

"Woah ..." On shaky legs, she steps even closer to the door, away from my grasp, and leans against the wood. "I ... I may have blacked out for a second."

"You okay? Need water?"

She shakes her head with a wicked grin, then scoots down to join me on the floor. "Your turn."

I wipe my mouth clean with the back of my hand and memorize her arsenic gaze. Every nerve fires with the need to touch more of her, move closer, kiss her endlessly, fuck her until we're both consumed.

A knock comes from the other side of the door. "Uh, Miss Nkosi, are you okay in there?"

"Yup!" she chirps out stupid-fast. "All good."

"You need something?"

"Nope! No, thanks," she stumbles on her words, giggling and wide eyed. "Perfectly fine."

"Right, okay. Well, if you want us to leave early, I can—"

She shoots me an evil grin. "I'll be out soon, and we can all go to the mainland to Calypsa's ceremony after lunch."

Fuuuuck. She's keeping an audience for my benefit. My heart hammers in my chest, wanting to break free. My skin grows hot and there's a fluttery sensation in my chest. She runs her fingertips over my thighs, and I become hypersensitive to her touch. A shiver racks my entire body as she strokes my cock again. My heartbeat pounds so loudly, it could be heard across the ocean. My hands ache with the need to explore her more, to memorize every spot that makes her quiver.

I imagine her in various positions around the room, her concentration on me exhilarating, like a drug I'm growing more and more addicted to each time she strokes me harder.

I reposition, still sitting, my back against the door. It's so hot how her hungry eyes flicker between mine and my dick, which stands at attention in her honor. She tilts her head slightly as she studies my reaction when she slows down and releases the tight hold. Fuck, is she aware of how much she unspirals me?

"You're gonna suck me now, babe. Face me. Yup, like that. Get in Balasana but stick your ass in the air. Mhm, like that. Now spread your legs. I want to smell your arousal from here."

Her throat bobs as she nods and continues to stare at my dick like I'm her favorite dessert after a year of fasting. In this position, I get the perfect view of her breasts hanging. This, right here, right now, might make it as my all-time best moment once I reach my death bed.

"Eyes on me the whole time, got it? Good girl. Start with only the tip. But make that suction tight."

Desire tingles in my veins. She lowers her mouth so tantalizingly slow that I might erupt from impatience. Finally, her lips wrap around my tip ... only one maddening inch. I throw my head back against the door with a bang.

"Oh, that was a loud one. Your turn for a shot!" someone yells from the other side.

I can't pay attention to their laughing shouts as Alouette skims her tongue around me. She sweeps it under as her hand rubs up and down. Up and down. Fuuuuuck. My legs tense to the point of becoming rocks. Like I demanded, she doesn't take me deeper. The prolonged eye contact shreds away any barriers between us.

"Good girl, Owlette. But I can't wait longer. Deeper now. As much as ya can."

She shifts forward, ass rising, mouth moving along me. I groan, clenching my eyes shut. Fuck. So warm. So wet. So good. And damn, she's messy. Sucking and slurping, and I can't get enough. Needing purchase on something, I grip her hair, but don't pull. She moans. The sound makes me thrust up into her mouth.

"Fuck, sorry, babe. You okay?"

She moans again, moving deeper. Oh my Goddess. She'll be the end of me. I'm dying. Can't survive this. My breathing grows erratic as she squeezes my balls. Her grip grows more possessive, more intense. Everything tightens. I open my eyes to browns, watching me for commands.

Need to warn her.

"Babe. Now. I'm gonna—"

I'm about to pull out to release when her hands wrap behind my back to keep herself firmly planted.

"Holy shit!"

The build up is too much. Everything clenches. And then ... my whole body racks and seizes in ecstasy. Raw bliss. I shoot straight into her mouth, down her throat. Alouette never pulls away. She swallows all that I have to give, and I've never felt or seen anything more erotic. I ride it out, her dark eyes glued on mine until she slowly slips off my used cock and wipes her mouth.

"Can I move?" she asks earnestly, open and willing to do anything I say. "I want you to hold me."

I reach out, a smile spreading across my face. "Oh, babe, come here."

She crawls over and curls into me. With her soft, bushy hair pressed against my chest, I slowly massage wherever I can reach and feel her breath against my skin. The sticky afternoon air wafts through an open window, but it's a refreshing relief after such an intense moment.

After a few minutes of us both settling, she admits, "I'm scared 'bout what might happen at the ceremony tonight."

I kiss the top of her head. "I won't let anything come between us. We'll figure out the next steps."

"Since we both found what we were looking for, we should get new magic, right?"

"I hope so."

"What if there were underlying rules we didn't know about? Like what if you need partial custody of Dakota before tonight?" She talks faster, spinning in her thoughts.

"Hey, look at me." I pause as she re-situates. "Do ya see fear in my eyes?"

"No."

"That's right. Because as long as we have each other, the rest can figure itself out. Whether we have magic or not. We're in this together. I'll keep fightin' to see Dakota and I'll do it with ya by my side."

"Even when the tabloids eventually learn about Bennett and link me to a Savion scandal?"

"How others tell our story is their perspective, that doesn't mean it's real or true. You have never been and never will be a disappointment, no matter what family claims ya."

She nods, eyes strong and determined. "I know that now. I can be proud of my name without following in my family's footsteps, whether I choose Nkosi or Savion. Either one has blessings and curses. I know I have value and you helped me figure that out."

"Does that make me the hero?"

"No way. I'm the heroine. You're the side character who give the best oral on this planet."

"Oh, is that right?"

"Yeah, I'll have to brag about you to Zola. But don't let that go to your head, the big one or little one."

I chuckle. "Oath."

She pecks my lips softly, then gives me a dirty look. "I do have one request before we get changed to leave."

"See ... I knew you'd want to make some demands."

"I want you to go out there and get me some water."

I bite my lip. "Like this? *Before* I get dressed?"

"Yes, sir. I want them all to know who made me scream and that I'm the only one who gets to have you."

"Hmm, I could get used to being called sir. Alright. Be right back. Ice or no ice?"

She laughs. "We don't have a freezer."

"No ice it is." I rise to a stand, nude and satiated. "Wish me luck."

Alouette disappears through the doorway. Totally nude, I turn the doorknob, then swing it open.

CHAPTER THIRTY

Alouette

Back in Calypsa, Jacob and I step into the moonlit clearing. The air is full of magic, old and new, and a cool breeze carries the scent of the sea from beyond the dunes. It reminds me that the ocean erases footprints, always offering a clean slate.

All around me, Fuzers of every age stand at attention while the Typs watch in anticipation. My heart buzzes chaotically with nerves.

Decorative lanterns bob between the palm trees, casting a warm glow over the food trucks lining the street. Some vendors have tents full of products and I glimpse a few familiar faces.

Near the center of the clearing, a bonfire crackles, spitting embers into the night sky. My bare feet sink into the cool sand as we make our way through the crowd. Everywhere I look, there is power and the love of enchantments. A teen, still maturing into their strength, conjures butterflies from thin air, much to the delight of children.

We pause at a table laden with sweets. The scent of honey and cinnamon makes my mouth water. I reach for a moonberry tart at the same time as Jacob. He shoots me a tender smile and pulls away, offering it to me.

"Pretty crowded tonight," Jacob says, his voice melodic and low, only for me to hear.

I know he's trying to distract me from the possibility that our magic may not function when it's our turn at the ceremony. I nod, still worried. He chuckles, a sound I've logged to memory, and presses the tart into my hand. "Our magic will return. I can feel it."

As if on cue, a hush falls over the gathering. I turn to see a council member in a hooded robe step onto the makeshift stage at the center of the clearing. They raise their arms, and I feel a thrill of excitement run through me. When they turn, a shocked gasp carries across the crowd.

"What is it?" Jacob scans the area for a threat.

I already see what's caused the commotion. Bennett Savion drops his hood and smiles out at the gathering. The president hasn't conducted a ceremony in years. Is he here for me? As if reading my mind, my grandfather meets my eye and nods slightly, a silent promise that eases my racing heart—if only a little bit.

I squeeze Jacob's hand to direct his attention to the stage.

"Oh," is all he manages to say.

Silence washes over the crowd, and the background music fades away. Bennett holds up the traditional bowl of stones, all representing spells chosen last month. One of those is mine, the ability to read at super speed.

One at a time, the Fuzers will step up to the front and

slash open their palms, enabling their magic from the past month to drain from their veins. We'll recite our new chosen power, which will mark the stone with a fresh magical spell lasting thirty days. Once the new stone is placed on our open cut, it'll grant us the requested power until next month's ceremony. It is quick, easy, and almost painless, as long as the Typs approve our selections.

For the hundredth time, I glance around for Marquis. He had promised he'd be here to support me. If my magic doesn't return, I need to know he has my back and always will.

"Welcome to the monthly Fuzer declaration ceremony on this thirteenth of August, 2025. Thank you for receiving me as your council member tonight. We will go alphabetically as per tradition. First, Deekla Georgette Anderson," Bennett calls, and an older woman steps forward.

I recognize her from the downtown craft store. To save everyone's time, she moves with fluid, experienced swiftness. With a quick slice of the dagger, blood splatters on her stone and a new symbol is etched into the surface.

"She has chosen for magic to do the labor of stocking her shelves in her shop," Bennett announces. "Any oppositions? Going once? Twice? It is approved! Congratulations, Deekla. It's lovely to have met you."

He flies through the list with ease as my thoughts swirl in chaos. Jacob has stayed quiet, but he still brushes his finger across mine every few minutes. I must trust we'll be okay. Ivola had said our powers would be stripped forever only if we didn't find what we were searching for. But we did. Everything has to be okay.

A guitarist, with the last name Matthews, casts a spell to tune his instruments automagically. Then, a businessman with the last name Moltel chooses a spell for free marketing for a month. The Typs debate their approval on that one for a minute, but ultimately agree.

My name is due soon. Nkosi—the middle of the group. Halfway through has always been the perfect placement; during the first half, I pay attention to others' spells, then the second half, Zola brings me a marg to celebrate.

That's when my phone pings with the tone specifically saved for my best friend. Her face appears on my screen. There's no time to chat, but I answer anyways. Zola's dark brown eyes sparkle with warmth and support. Seeing her brings a lightness to my chest.

"Don't look at me like that, Lou," she says with an excited grin. "I'm not hanging up. And before you ask, I chose a spell to not have to clean my paint brushes. Think of all the time it'll save!"

A hundred questions swirl in my mind about London, but I can't stop tapping my foot or fidgeting my hands long enough to organize a coherent thought.

"Just put me in your pocket. Oh shit, they're already on a 'Nalson?' I called just in time."

Realizing Bennett Savion already got to the "N's," I let out a much-needed breath.

"If I do this, will it help at all?" Jacob leans down and brushes his lips against mine.

"Ew, I can basically hear you groping my bestie!" Zola pipes from my pocket.

"There's that smile." Jacob rubs his knuckles against my mouth. "After this is over, I definitely have some gropin' ideas in mind."

We both laugh, but I pull away. Too many concerns battle against each other. What if my magic doesn't return?

What if mine works but Jacob's doesn't? Why wasn't Ivola more specific?

If my last name was officially Savion, I'd have a few more minutes to decide on my spell. No, I am a Nkosi. With every blessing, there are equal challenges. I'm choosing to accept who I am. Now it's time to stop caring about other people's opinions of my choices. Whether it's my parents who expect me to change careers, neighbors who are surprised that I'm an artist, or Marquis for disapproving of my relationship with Jacob. It shouldn't matter. My life is exactly that—mine. Regardless of if my name is Alouette Nkosi, Alouette Savion, or maybe even one day Alouette Talksihnn, I'll be authentic to who I am. Expectations be damned.

"Alouette Mae Nkosi," Bennett calls from the stage. I think he's going to end there, but his mouth opens again. "Who was my clever conversationalist at a recent charity. I'm sure many of you have seen our picture together on various platforms. My request to the media tonight"—he looks to the corner where cameras flash in the darkness—"is to give this woman space and only approach my staff with your inquiries."

Slowly, I pivot. Everyone is watching me with curiosity. My heart rate triples, and my heels are glued to the street. I've done this a hundred times. Step towards the stage. One foot at a time.

"I'll walk ya up." Jacob pulls on my arm. I move unsteadily, chin up, asking Ouma for strength if my magic has indeed abandoned me forever.

"Did you know I love holiday romcoms?" Jacob confesses. "Yeah, the cheesier, the better. I'll binge watch twelve hours in a row about bakers and realtors fallin' in love in a small town. Hey, don't laugh at me, it's cute, right? Admit I'm adorable."

I can't answer. My eyes are locked on Bennett's.

We arrive at the front without tripping. Bennett sets a cool, smooth stone in my hand. I grab a fresh knife from the unused pile and slash my palm across the scarred line. Blood trickles down my wrist and I stare at the crimson flow. The familiar sensation doesn't happen, the zing of energy of my last spell whooshing out of my body.

Emptiness follows. Magic ceases to exist. I feel like I'm suffocating. How am I supposed to live without magic running through my veins?

Then the clouds shift, and stars twinkle brightly. A soft gust of wind caresses my face and a bird I can't identify soars above. As it nears, I feel Ouma's energy in the depths of my soul.

To understand the world, listen to the bird's silent flight. It'll be okay. Believe and trust in myself. Everything will be okay.

I whisper my spell to Bennett. His smile grows, showing all his teeth, and he pats Jacob's shoulder.

"Alouette's choice of magic is to keep one selected individual's name out of any public eye over the next month. Any oppositions? Going once? Twice?" Bennett lifts his chin higher. "It is approved. Congratulations Miss Nkosi; it's lovely to have seen you again."

Suddenly, the whole beach fades away. Gasping, I clamp a hand against my chest where a strong dazzling heat blazes like an inferno. Awe twists through my entire body and I feel like I'm floating. Never have I experienced this sensation. I'm speechless, but spontaneous laughter pours out of me. A flood of magic rips through my muscles like a tsunami, like it was blocked by a massive damn, trying to break free for weeks. I hear myself squeal with delight, as if I'm an observer outside my body. My skin tingles until my bare feet touch the solid sand again.

It's back!

Reality returns in a bustle of soft murmurs, waves crashing, and Jacob's ever-steady hand on my waist.

"Woah, you okay, babe?" he asks, wonder alight in his eyes. "Ya fuckin' floated!"

"I did?"

"Yeah, how do ya feel?"

Behind him, Bennett Savion is already calling someone else on stage like everything is going according to plan, as if I hadn't had an out of this world experience.

"It's back!" I rise onto my tiptoes and smash my mouth against his. "My magic is here!"

Jacob tastes of peppermint gum. He grabs me tightly, pressing me closer until all I can think about is getting him alone somewhere. All my anxiety has vanished. What remains is my love for him, excitement for the future. Quickly, I whisper an incantation that has automagically popped into my bank of knowledge, one that will prevent any reporter or tabloid or social media gossip from saying or writing Jacob's name. He'll be free from any scrutiny for a month.

"Let's get out of here," I say to Jacob, only focused on where our bodies connect.

He chuckles into my neck. "Aren't you forgetting somethin'?"

Oh, yeah. Whoops. I reach into my pocket to talk to Zola, but she had already hung up. I send a text across the sea that I'll call her soon. Plus, she will want to know the gritty details of every little act I plan to do to Jacob tonight.

"No, babe. I still need to pick a spell." Jacob smiles, nodding to the stage. "T comes after N, remember?"

"Oh, crap!" I palm my forehead. "I'm sorry. I wasn't thinking."

His lips find mine again. And again. "It's all good, babe. But I wanna go up alone. Stay here for me. My spell is a surprise." He sighs and reaches out to rub the crease formed between my brows. "Trust me. It's a good thing."

"Okay ... I'll be by the taco truck."

As I wait, I stare at the moon and concentrate on the force flowing through my blood.

"Interesting choice in spell."

I turn to Marquis's smirk and the feeling of home washes over me, including a dozen memories as children. And then our last conversation pushes through my stream of thoughts. Can I forgive him?

The air hums with the unknown. "We need to talk," I say, "... about Jacob."

"The asshat? Why waste our words on him?"

"Hey! He's your best friend."

"No. *Was*. He *was* my best friend. Then he slept with my baby sister, so I never want to see his face again."

"Not that it's any of your business, but we have NOT slept together."

Marquis glances up fast, meeting my eyes with renewed hope.

"Yet," I add.

He groans and kicks the sand like a toddler throwing a tantrum. "Lou, I can't do this. How would I ever talk to him again knowing he ... he'll eventually hurt you. He's fucked up four or five relationships. Obviously, you know one is international news and his life is being dragged through the mud. I don't want you to suffer through his mistakes, Lou. I love you too much to sit back and witness you go through the devastation of having your name sullied like you're not a real person."

During his speech, I may not have taken a single breath. This entire time I'd assumed Marquis was protecting his best friend from *me* and my lowly status. But that was far from the truth.

"Listen to me, because I'm only going to say this once," I begin, facing my brother, glaring into his eyes. "There's never a guarantee that we won't hurt each other. The future is unpredictable. We have no control over what others think, but we'll support each other through it, every step of the way. I'm not going to persuade you to accept our relationship. Ultimately, it's *your* choice. *You* get to choose whether or not to stay in our lives. Whether or not to give up on your best friend. Whether or not to accept me and my choices as an adult. I'm not a child, Marquis. Trust that I know what I'm doing. Trust that I can choose my own path even if it's not what *you* or Mom and Dad or the whole world envisioned for me. Please," I pause, straighten my back and take both his hands. When I swallow, a ball of nerves gets lodged in my throat. "Please, Marquis. If you don't accept me for who I am, what I choose, then things will change between us. Walls and shields will go up. We'll distance ourselves. I don't want that. Can you at least try? I love him. I love Jacob."

Eyes watering, Marquis pulls my hands closer and wraps me in a hug. "You're in love?" he asks over my shoulder. "Why didn't you say that to begin with? I remember when I realized I fell in love with Van."

"I know. You called me that night," I say, my voice breaking with emotion.

He half snorts, half cries. "Admit you told me before Zola so I can rub it in her face."

Pulling away, I slap his shoulder. "Marquis! How rude!"

"Ha! I'm right! What's her email? I gotta brag about this."

I swat his phone away. "You don't have her number?"

"That queen blocked me."

"Oh my Goddess ..." I can't help but smile, then I bring my attention back to the stage.

Somehow, I'd missed Jacob's entire turn. He's already walking towards me, a pep in his step. Thank Luna Above. That can only mean one thing: His magic has also returned.

Everything really is going to be okay. At least I think so until Jacob and Marquis square off in front of me, barely any space between their glaring stares.

Goddess, I hate this. The festival lights flash across Marquis's face, and I see that look—the same one he got right before he broke a kid's nose in high school for talking trash about me. My hands are shaking. I want to scream at both of them, to remind them of why they're best friends, but the words stick in my throat. The fury in their eyes scare me. Tears start to build because I don't want to lose either of them. The crowd moves around us like we're invisible, but I feel like I'm going to throw up. My chest hurts. This isn't fair. I don't want to be caught between two people I love preparing to tear each other apart. I can't breathe. I can't choose. Please, *please* don't make me choose.

Marquis, still looking absolutely furious, is the first to speak. "Do you love her?"

Jacob shifts his weight on his feet, like he wasn't expecting that question. But, without hesitation, he nods once, not glancing away for even a heartbeat.

Marquis makes this half grunt-half sigh sound and

crosses his arms over his chest. "And if you break her heart?"

"I won't."

Marquis takes a step forward. "But if you do—"

Jacob holds up both hands. "Then you'll have no choice but to kick my ass."

"That's right." My brother's voice barely softens; a minute change only noticeable to me, yet the meaning behind it is profound. "No games?"

Whatever nonverbal conversation they have is weighed with a history I may never understand. But after that specific question, Jacob's entire body relaxes, like it was code for something. His shoulders lower and his face loosens.

"No games," Jacob confirms, sticking out one hand for Marquis to shake.

Marquis stares at his hand, pensive, considering, until he finally reaches out and takes it. Before I know it, he crushes Jacob into a chest-on-chest hug and wraps a loving arm around his back. "Fuck you, ya piece of shit, fallin' in love? Are ya out of your mind?"

All the tension stored in my body simply vanishes. Tears well behind my eyelids, and there's a sudden lightness that feels similar to flying. After they pull away, I wipe a few tears from my cheek. Their relationship will survive and I still have my brother. Win-win. I thank the stars that it turned out this way.

"Alright, I'm actually meeting the council rep in that tent," Marquis says, clapping his hands together awkwardly. "They said Mr. Savion wants to talk to me about something. So, I'll meet up with you two later?"

Crap. In all the madness, I never told Marquis the news about our biological grandfather. Well, it's better he learn it from the source. Plus, it'll give him time to process before we break apart all the details together later.

Marquis saunters off without a second glance and it's almost as if the confrontation a few moments ago never happened.

"Babe, ya ready to get out of here?" Jacob rubs his hands up and down my sides softly.

Our intense eye contact is layered with deep yearning. I moisten my lips and move closer, wanting to be in his arms. Jacob kisses me with the tenderness of a committed man. Appreciation fills me. Gratitude for this ceremony. For my magic. For Jacob's help in finding the cottage. For all the events in the last few weeks that brought us closer together. Safety and acceptance. That's what I feel when he kisses me. This is someone I can plan a future with, someone I can commit to and fight side by side with against hardships thrown at us.

"So ... what's your surprise spell of the month?" I ask.

CHAPTER THIRTY-ONE

Jacob

We stand on the cool sand, me behind Alouette with my arms wrapped around her waist while we both stare out into the darkness. The gentle lapping of waves provides a soothing backdrop to the chatter around us. The night sky stretches without end, full of twinkling stars that shimmer in celebration. I can't help but smile as I take in the scene—faces reflecting warmth and excitement. The scent of grilled seafood wafts through the air, making my mouth water. But no sensory experience here compares to the sight of Alouette under the soft light of lanterns. She tilts her head back and to the side. Our eyes meet, and my heart swells with an overwhelming love.

"Did you hear me? What spell did you pick?" she repeats, rising on her tiptoes.

I can't kiss her too intensely now or I'll get carried away and never stop.

"For your cottage to travel wherever you go for the next month."

Her jaw drops. "What? I expected it'd be about Dakota."

"Nah, I'd need to run decisions like that by Nella first. And I have no idea when the hearings will be, or where. It could be next year, for all I know. But this way ya have freedom to travel anywhere. You could visit Zola in London. And maybe if I am granted visitation rights, you could come with me to Oakmar. That's me simply lookin' out for my best interests, since the cottage may be slightly comfier than my van."

Her nose screws up in that adorable way and I'm obsessed. "Are you inviting yourself to sleep at my place, sir?"

"Oh, it's official. The 'sir' will definitely work for me."

I imagine her bent over in front of me, beggin' *'please, sir'* as I enter her from behind.

"By the way, I invited some people, and they just arrived," Alouette says with a conspiratorial look at her phone.

"Who?" I glance around when she points behind me, heart racing.

My breath hitches. Koda walks hand in hand with Nella. It's way past her bedtime, but I don't care. I tug Alouette in their direction. Each time my feet sink in the sand, slowing us down, I curse time itself for having such power. As if in slow motion, Koda runs, her arms open wide, ready to leap into my arms.

At the last moment, I crouch down and she slams her chest into mine. "Hi, Dad! Mommy said I could come see you before we go home!"

Her warmth reminds me that she's real. She's safe. And she wants me in her life. A tear trickles down my face, and when Koda finally pulls away, she giggles, then wipes it away.

"Are you a daddy that cries a lot? I cry all the time. Once when a ladybug died. That was the saddest. I tried to scoop it up with a leaf but couldn't and I cried all day. Another time was when Sal stepped on my toe at recess. It hurt, and no one even noticed. Oh yeah, and I sobbed last week when I watched that movie about the baby dolphin who was trying to find its way home but got lost. Why are you sad?"

"I'm not sad, mate. I'm super happy. So happy that I can't hold it in and there's extra to spill out."

"Oh, okay, that makes sense. Are you coming to my house? I'll show you the secret hideaway treehouse that Grandad built for me last summer. But you have to be good at climbing. Are you strong or are ladders your nemesis?"

I hug her again, inhaling her childhood scent of starlight and joy, wishing I could capture it and save it in a bottle for later.

"How did you learn the word nemesis?" I wonder, glancing at Nella over Koda's shoulder to gauge how she's processing our interaction.

Nella seems ... mildly amused. At least she's here. Did Alouette bribe her to show up?

"Mommy gave me a rip off calendar that has a word of the day. Wanna know why? I love words. I was the Spelling Bee Champion in third grade, and I love word searches and madlibs and crosswords. Words are like mini puzzles. Don't worry, I'll teach you soon."

"I can't wait. Hey, guess what? This is my girlfriend." I point up to Alouette and hope she doesn't mind the label. "Babe, what do ya want Koda to call you?"

"Lou is perfect," she says, smiling. "Do you want me to call you Koda or Dakota?"

She tilts her head, letting the soft waves of blonde fall over her shoulders. "Dakota. Like Mommy does."

"Okay, Miss Dakota, if it's okay with your parents, I can show you a mural painter over there while your parents talk."

I nod, and Alouette sends me a rare wink with my daughter in tow. The two halves of my heart are already bonding and it's almost too much to process.

"So …" Nella shifts on her feet and crosses her arms, keeping her sights on our daughter.

"Thanks for being here. I bet that wasn't easy for ya," I say, shoving my hands in my pocket.

"You'd be right. But um, after long-winded voicemails, then page long texts from Lou, I thought I owed it to you to let Dakota say goodbye before we head home." Nella twists her sneaker into the sand. "Thanks for finding Dakota. She means the world to me. I couldn't survive without her." Her voice crack. "I … I can't believe she ran away."

It's not my place to hug her, and after two years of online mistreatment and public manipulation, on top of years of forcing me to be an absent parent, I have little desire to comfort Nella.

She sniffs and meets my eyes. "I may have been too hard on you."

I let out a deep sigh and feel some tension release. It's nice to hear, but I always knew I didn't need her approval or adoration from thousands of people to feel worthy of affection. Nella's opinion of me will matter little, regardless of the progress I make. Part of me still wants to be viewed as the golden boy, the one who can do no wrong and wins the hearts of fans across the globe. But deep down, I know I can let that go.

"I'm sorry for what ya had to go through alone," I tell

her. "I'll never fully comprehend the challenges ya faced during pregnancy or with a child as a single mom. I literally know nothin' 'bout ya, but I'm willin' to learn and work together. How 'bout we start over? I'll support ya in any way I can. All I want is to keep Koda in my life in a way that's fair to all three of us. Please, Nella."

"Okay, Jake. I'm willing to work together. Don't set any expectations about friendship, though. I need this to go slow."

"I want what's best for our girl. We'll take one day at a time."

Her head bobs slowly, eyes full of an emotion I can't name. It's hard to read Nella. "Okay, one day at a time."

"That's fuckin' excellent! Oh, whoops!" I cover my mouth.

"Don't worry, she's heard my sister use every curse word under the sun already."

"Well, on my side, she has nine aunts."

Nella barks a single, explosive laugh. "You have *nine* sisters?"

"Jen, Jules and Jess, Ashley and Havanna, Beks, Stef, and Mils."

"That was only eight."

That gets a smile out of me. Most people don't catch that.

"Well? Who's the nineth?" Nella prods.

"Let's say she has a shell and lives in a tank."

"You consider a turtle a sister?"

I take out my phone to show her, having to swipe through pictures of sunrises and Alouette first. When my pictures land on Tootles, the fifty-year-old sea turtle my mom still takes care of, Nella grins.

"Meet Tootles," I say, pointing.

Nella chuckles, a foreign sound to me, and then swipes through her own pictures. "This is Dakota on her second birthday."

I grab the phone to study her little face covered in chocolate ice cream. Never has a picture been so perfect. If I look at any more of these, I'll turn into a crying ball of mush.

"I'd love if you can send me some of those."

"Some of what?" Koda's voice bounces closer.

"Your dad wants to see baby pictures of you, but not right now. It's late and we need to drive home in the morning."

"Oh man, but Mom, they're gonna shoot off fireworks soon."

"When you're seventeen, you'll come to these every month."

That snags my attention. My gaze darts between Koda and Nella. "Is she ... like me?"

"Yeah, we ran a DNA test. She got your magical genes. So, I guess I have some research to do."

Alouette joins us, a hot dog in hand that smells way too good for basic American food. She chomps down and makes a tiny, satisfied moan sound that sends my brainwaves criss-crossing sporadically.

"Give your dad a hug, Bluebird."

"Fine!"

Koda scowls, then half-hugs me quickly before stomping towards the parking lot. It seems I have a lot of versions of that little one to catch up on. Once they're out of view, Alouette rests her head against my chest.

Among the flustering activity around us, my vision only sees her. "You brought 'em here. For me."

She nods with a little smirk.

"You are an amazin' woman, Alouette Mae … I love ya. So fuckin' much."

She bites her bottom lip. "I love you too. More than I thought possible."

Her words hang in the air, electrifying the space between us. My heart races as I absorb every detail of her face. As I stand frozen in place, our eyes meet, and I realize everything has changed.

"Wanna get out of here?" she asks.

The only response I can think of is to nod. "I have some ideas of where."

CHAPTER THIRTY-TWO

Alouette

Only a few yards away from our current hiding spot, surfers carry their boards towards the sunrise and early waves. The first morning light bathes the shoreline ahead. Cocooned by long grass, Jacob kisses my neck. I'm only halfway paying attention to the beautiful water because he trails his tongue over my sweet spot. I can barely savor the way the pelicans swoop towards the sea.

Maybe it wasn't the smartest choice to wear a dress to the beach instead of a swimsuit. I let him take me here, hoping I know what's about to take place. Too much time has passed without this man being inside me. I hope that sex with Jacob will feel like flying, like a bird diving, soaring free.

Damn. Why does he have to be a master with his tongue?

"I told you, Owlette. If ya moan like that again, then our first time will be here, on this beach, right now."

So, I lock onto his eyes and beg for him to understand how much I need that to be true. Jacob's blond hair is pulled into a wet bun, still dripping droplets down his temple. Nearby, the surfers have reached the water and splash into the cold. Jacob nips my exposed throat, and I realize I'll most likely miss all their epic tricks. Goddess, he will never disappoint.

"Did you hear me?" Jacob asks, love lacing his voice. "That was moan number seven. So, this is happening, little owl."

"Mhm." I whimper as his hand moves under my dress. My chest tightens at the extreme feelings I have for him. I may have only been with a few guys in my life, but I know this is love—*real* love. If he doesn't have sex with me soon, I'll lose all my sanity.

"These towels okay? Or do you want to straddle me?" Jacob asks, pulling away to meet my gaze.

"Oh, babe! Why are ya cryin'?" He wipes a tear from my cheek.

"I'm feeling a bit overwhelmed. I want this. I want you. This is the perfect place. I'm a bit overcome with ... how much I care for you. It's scary."

"Yeah, I get that."

It's impressive how he rarely tries to change my mind or fix things, but listens to what I have to say.

"Do ya wanna do ... this ... another time?"

"Absolutely not," I say, composing myself and running a hand up his chest.

As he pulls my dress over my head, he gasps, realizing I'm not wearing anything underneath.

"Lay down," he growls, his eyes on fire. "Now."

Flattening onto my back, I release a giant breath and stare at the puffy white clouds. Divine beauty stares back, luminous and refreshing while the sound of waves crash close by.

Jacob shimmies out of his shorts and surprises me by not wearing anything underneath either.

"You little deviant."

His smile lights up my world. I wish I could spend all my waking hours with Jacob, looking at me with such sincerity.

"Alouette, …" He spreads my knees and positions himself between my legs. With both hands by my ears, he leans in and kisses my forehead, my jawline, my lips, then whispers, "I love ya so much it hurts sometimes." The tip of his cock presses against my entrance. Absolutely maddening. "What do ya want first? Oh, wait, I remember. You like being told what to do, isn't that right, little owl?"

I nod, transfixed by his body, the curve of his shoulders above me, and the weight he presses against me, grounding me.

Barely moving at all, Jacob rotates his hips so the tip of his cock eases around my folds. He's not even inside of me, but the torturous sensation of how drenched I am where we meet tells me how much my body is aching for him to thrust inside.

He lets out an agonizing breath. "Alouette, babe, you're dripping for me. Look at this, fuck," he says, eyes dropping to my pussy. He takes his thumb and rubs my clit as his cock continues to slip over my entrance.

I arch my back, hoping to bring him in, but the man is in control. This. Him. I want this forever. His eyes are blown, so dark, so aroused. I'd do anything he commands.

"Ready?" His voice comes out a deeper timbre than I've ever heard from him.

"Yeah," I barely manage, body alert and tingling.

He pushes in.

First only a little. "Woah!" I gasp, and my hands slap against his wrists. Clinging on for dear life.

"Hold on, I got ya." He slides out a little. "Okay?"

I nod and brace myself for more.

"Again?" he whispers into my mouth.

I nod again, not wanting my voice to tremble if I speak.

His lips distract me. Claim me as he thrusts in again. A little deeper ...

"Oh my Goddess!" I dig my heels into the sand.

"Fuck!" he grumbles. "How do you feel this damned good?"

His face is scrunched and twisted, like he's barely able to contain himself.

"Relax, babe."

I exhale, and he eases in further. Further. Fuller. My walls clench around him and I have no words. No thoughts. This is the most extraordinary magic I've ever experienced. I can feel another wave of emotion cresting, about to cascade over me.

I'm totally in tune to how he's spreading me, every part of me aware of where our bodies meet. My vision locks onto Jacob's soul, his essence in his eyes, full of adoration for me.

"You okay?" he groans.

I nod. "Touch me," I gasp.

His fingers start at my nipples, pinching until I writhe up against him, giving us more friction. His cock buries deeper, hitting a new spot.

"Holy ... shit!"

Jacob grabs his bag and shoves it under my ass until I'm propped up.

"Right there, yes. Yes! That's deep."

"Not gonna ... last long ... like this... Ugh. Fuck. I can feel ya pulsin' round me."

He slams home again and again and all I want is more. My fingers dig into his back. His muscles are all flaring. I'm in ecstasy and have to close my eyes when he pounds into me harder and harder.

"Fuck, you're made for me."

His fingers work down my stomach and settle on my clit again. He rubs up and down with expertise, each movement matching the rhythm of his thrusts. Sweat beads on his forehead, and his arms bulge tighter than I've ever seen. How can it be this good? How can I simultaneously feel whole yet also feel like I'm about to shatter into a thousand pieces?

I move into a Setu Bandha Sarvangasana and drive my hips up and down against him with all my strength.

"Uuuuuuh! Baaaabe!" He throws his head back and holds my ass up. "Uuuaaaah!"

His deep, throaty growl undoes me. The force and power of him plunging into me again and again sends me over the edge. My back arches high. He groans. Thrusting over and over. I scream. Everything inside me lashes out.

Need more. "Faster!"

A ripple of violent utopia surges through me, head to toe, as the orgasm washes over me.

Freedom.

When I open my eyes, Jacob's watching me. All I can see are the darkest blue flecks in his eyes that resemble the deepest part of the sea as he moves faster. Harder. His groaning sounds make me clasp onto his arms tightly.

My body is mush, spent, but I need to make him feel as good as he did for me.

"Now …" I pant, my whole body in his control as he holds me. "Please."

Jacob's entire body tenses. A roar breaks through him as everything fractures within me. His body is a piece of art, urgent, needy, desperate. He sends me over the edge again until I feel his warmth fill me up.

Breathing deeply, eyes clenched shut, Jacob lowers me to the towels, his head hovering over my shoulder, about to collapse. I can feel his dick still twitch inside me, but I can't respond.

Decimated. Panting, his arms shaking, chest heaving, Jacob meets my eyes and smiles.

"Well, we know how to do it, don't we, mate?"

I can barely breathe; can barely nod. "Mhm," I manage, pulling him to lie flush against my chest, wanting to feel his full weight on top of me.

We lay there for a long time, his dick still spasming inside me, reminding me that I want this connection to last forever. Eventually, he rolls off, lying next to me. We stare up at the wispy clouds together and he reaches to hold my hand.

"That was …" he starts.

"… like flying …"

I can feel his smile without looking over.

"Exactly," he sighs, "Being with ya is like soarin', and I never want to land."

EPILOGUE

Spring 2026

Alouette

We stand in a small circle, surrounded by tombstones in Calypsa's historic graveyard. The afternoon sun shines down, gifting Dakota with more freckles before the upcoming summer season. I swear she's grown a foot since last autumn.

On my left, Zola squeezes one hand while Jacob holds the other. I've dreaded and looked forward to this day for months. Marquis—dressed in only a speedo after losing a drink game last night—stands beside the headstone that reads Tariji Nkosi, giving his speech.

My brother's innocent glare, laced with whimsical amusement, doesn't scare me in the slightest. Next to him, Grandpa Bennett stands stoically to celebrate his own true love. We already had a funeral for Ouma last year, but we decided to do another one with Grandpa by our sides.

"... and lastly, Ouma laid the foundation for my love of Dryococelus Australis, and I owe my entire career to what she taught me." Marquis's nose wrinkles. "I don't have much else to say, but I'll always miss you and your clever puns. Love you."

Marquis steps away, then crosses his arms, sulking from his unfortunate wardrobe. My turn is next, yet I can't move. There are too many things left unsaid, too many future stories she'll miss.

That's precisely when Ms. Grim lands atop the smooth marble, feathers so black they almost look blue in the light. Her beady eyes hold depth and wisdom that feels familiar. And it seems she's trying to tell me something. That's when it clicks. Ms. Grim appeared on my window the day after Ouma died. What if she was sent to comfort and guide me during my grief? Does Ouma talk with her when she visits the skies? Maybe she can relay this message, so Ouma knows we're here celebrating her life. The idea gives me newfound courage to seize this unique moment.

Letting out a deep breath, I step in front of the others. Grandpa moves closer, his arm wrapping behind my back.

"Ouma was ... she was magic through and through. From her deranged cackle to the way she beat anyone in chess and how she knew from such a young age that I was an artist. Not once did she point me toward a path that wasn't my calling. I'll always be grateful for that support, Ouma. If you can hear me, thank you, from the bottom of my heart. You knew what I needed before I did." I glance at Jacob, who's watching me intently, and remember part of the letter Ouma had written to me.

'My greatest wish for you is to experience the deepest love imaginable some day. Whether that is love for your pottery or a

... partner ... Never stop hunting for that glitter of happiness that will warm you from the inside out.'

I found that joy in Jacob. Sure, I'm well aware I don't need a man to feel fulfilled, but that doesn't stop our love from feeling like a wonder. Ouma had known somehow that I wasn't searching for a new career, but to be fully accepted as who I am. Jacob has given me that gift, with leftovers to spare. I have every intention of making this relationship work long term, through the ups and downs.

He nods; a silent encouragement to finish my eulogy. "I love you Ouma. I'll feel you in every bird that soars by, freer than any other creature. Thank you for encouraging me to fly."

Zola wipes a tear from her eye, then claps softly with her fingertips. Grandpa places a teacup I made recently, full of flowers, next to the grave. We don't see him often because of all his responsibilities, but he has promised to retire in the next couple of years then "follow us around until he becomes a nuisance."

Dakota is clearly not paying attention, her focus is set on some large trees by the iron gate. I bet my entire paycheck that she'll find a way to climb one the second Jacob turns his back. Not that he'd forbid it. In fact, he'll chase her up to see who can reach the top fastest. I can never win against those two athletes.

Since Dakota lives in Oakmar, that's where Jacob wanted to be. When Mom and Dad donated their property to the centaur staff, I packed everything that mattered, which was basically the contents of my pottery studio. Some days, when Jacob's not working as a personal trainer at the local gym, he'll swing by and bring me lunch from our favorite taco truck down the street.

Because Jacob now has partial custody of Dakota, he

wanted to be close by so he could pick her up from school without a two-hour commute each way. Which wasn't an issue for me in the beginning, since Ouma's cottage followed my location.

After that first month was done and Jacob changed his magical spell, I learned I didn't need his power to contain the cottage. Apparently, it was pleasantly comfortable in a sunflower field fifteen minutes from Dakota's school. We installed over a hundred bird feeders on our land, and now our property is a common spot for rare birds.

Life has changed for the better. If someone had told me almost a year ago that I'd be in a relationship with the man I saw surfing in the RipSilver competition on Kitesville Beach, I would've laughed.

Yet, I'm about to take everything one step further to a forever with my man. Back at Jacob's side, I rise up to whisper in his ear, "Before we head to Cheyenne's, can we talk over there? In private?"

One brow arches. "Am I in trouble? Or are you wearing that lace outfit I bought you and wanting to give the ghosts a show?"

I nudge him playfully. "Shut up. I don't know why you spent a hundred bucks on that thing. It barely covers anything."

"Exactly." His hand falls to the small of my back as he guides me behind a wide tree.

Before I can ask my question, Jacob's lips are on mine, claiming me as the one who has the key to his heart. His low voice rumbles darkly into our shared breath. No, no. If we go too far, I'll ask for more. I always do.

"Jacob," I say, laughing, pulling away, but his mouth finds my neck.

"What is it, little owl? What do ya need?"

I gasp as his tongue does that swirl thing that makes my knees tremble. "Move in with me."

He stops. Backs up until he can see my face. "Ya sure?"

"Yeah. You've only begged me about 574 times. I think I'm ready."

"Really? Truly? I can get out of my stupid lease?"

"Well, you still have three months on it. Maybe you could sublet it to save money or—"

He attacks me again, mouth to mouth, his tongue so sweet and full of desire that I accidentally make the sound that drives him wild.

"Yes," he says, his hands in my hair as he gives me air to study my face. "A thousand times yes. I wanted to do this months ago."

"I'm well aware. Now you can. I feel it in my bones. I'm ready."

"Okay, only on one condition."

"Which is?"

His smile makes butterflies flutter through my stomach. "Shake on it." He raises his bare foot, waiting for mine. With an exasperated sigh at how ridiculous he is, I respond with my one bare foot and touch my big toe to the tip of his.

We're simply two different people with wild souls that met during a time when the frantic winds blew so strongly, it connected the skies with the sea—a woman of flight and a man of the water aren't supposed to belong together, but who care about *'shoulds'* and *'should nots'* ... not us.

Prequel to THE WICKED BLUE
A SHORT STORY

By Cassie Swindon

CHAPTER ONE

How can I paint the taste of saltwater? I swipe more colors from my palate to stroke the beach I'm overlooking. How will the viewer experience the taste of the sea?

I've been raised to fear the waters and detest the merfolk who lurk Below. Yet I find myself licking my lips to savor a little flavor from the forbidden.

Standing on my balcony, gazing at the crimson horizon, wind whips my hair. Sometimes I have a strange compulsion to lean forward, slightly too far over the balcony's edge. Do the wind nymphs detect the confusing longing that teases me to test the boundaries and dip my toes in the waves once? If I fall over this balcony, will those nymphs catch me and carry me to the tides to please my soul?

I brush another curve on my canvas, then try to move a stray hair out of my face with my forearm. Otherwise, my hands would be responsible for a cluster of pinks and oranges smeared across my forehead.

Bending sideways, I survey the landscape from a

different angle. What would it be like to sail on a ship to where the sky kisses the luminous blues? I may never have been aboard a boat, but I can still envision every shade the ocean would have to offer, from navy to cerulean to teal and cobalt.

I finish painting. I wait for Sampson's design in which he promised me the same colors for his latest fashion genius. I glance around my studio, past the other two easels and the mess across my bed to where my best friend sits at a desk. His back is turned towards me as he furiously scribbles his vision on paper.

"Done yet?" I set down my palate and try not to trip over the half-hazard books strewn around my rug.

"Don't rush me, Eribelle," Sampson mumbles, but I can hear the smile in his voice. That's good news. If he's smiling, he likes what he has created. "And don't brag that you finished first."

I have half a mind to throw a pillow at his back but wouldn't want to mess up his drawing. He groans, then flips the pencil over to erase something. In his frantic movements, he accidentally knocks eyeliner and eyeshadow onto the floor. Among my disastrous domain, they may be lost forever more.

"Done!" He twirls around fast in the spinny chair, holding his paper to his chest so I can't see. "Show me yours first."

"No way!" I block his view to the balcony where my painting is drying. "This was your idea, so you go first."

He huffs. A burst of air blows a long lock of brown hair puff up for a moment. "Fine. But it'll be better when its finished, I swear."

As he turns it towards me, I gasp, and walk towards the beautiful outfit he drew. "Sampson! It's perfect!"

"I hate that word. Nothing is supposed to be perfect. In fact, maybe I'll rip the seam a little once you put it on to teach you a thing or two."

"You wouldn't dare!" I grab his notebook.

The intricate detail of the outfit for my upcoming twenty-first birthday is breathtaking. Sampson used shades belonging to the sea: indigo, denim and berry. Blues shift and slide against each other in both contrast and balance.

"If I wear this, Dad will arrest you." I choose to, in fact, throw the pillow in question to his head.

"Hey! The crop top isn't *that* tight. And it'll let you throw up your arms while dancing without any precious treasure falling out."

I agree. But it's the high-rise skirt that I can't take my eyes off of– a piece made from liquid heaven. The way the fabric glides mirrors the fluidity of the ocean. It's as if Sampson knows the one and only secret, I've kept from him–my longing to explore the sea. Yet, he's also my only confidant who understands the harsh punishment Dad would lash out at if I were to be caught in the waters.

I should have better sense than to wish to explore the Below. Apparently, my stupid genes have won in a battle against my survival instincts because I'm seriously considering changing my plans tonight and taking the risk.

"So...? You like it?" Sampson's biting his nail, while his knees are curled into his chest.

"No! I love it! Don't change a single thing." I point to the blue skirt. "What material do you have in mind? This looks like silk."

"I'll surprise you." He winks and takes his notebook back. "Well, Sugar Pants, what time are you leaving?"

I dramatically collapse on Sampson's lap. "Do I *have* to go?"

"Eribelle, Eribelle, Eribelle..." he starts with an outrageous fake accent, "you, m'lady are the most popular, most anticipated person at the ball tonight. Of course, you have to go, unless..." Sampson loops and twists my hair into an updo with mastery skill, despite my odd angle of hanging off his lap. "Unless you are planning any shenanigans. I think I can get on board with shenanigans, especially if they involve Kilka milkshakes."

Sampson taps the Taj99 device on his wrist and pushes a few buttons until a milkshake recipe is projected against my wall, with a high level of alcohol mix required.

"Holy Abyss, Sampson, do you plan on killing me with that?" I topple off his lap onto the floor and begin cleaning up some of the mess. "If I drink that much, I might even make out with *you* tonight."

He makes a gag face and rolls his eyes. "Fine, I'll go easy on the Kilka this time." Sampson slaps my ass while he moves towards my bedroom door. "You need to get ready and I need to find a snack, which I won't be sharing."

"You have so much hatred."

"I said what I said." He glides out the door, humming a recent Talia Sanchez song that echoes down the hallway.

Alone, I groan and check the time on my own Taj99. Only an hour until the guests expect my grand entrance. Maybe I can convince Dad to let me skip this event. Not even a second goes by until I laugh away at that possibility. Possible buyers from Khajit, Gonia and even Ozaron will be in attendance, and they all expect to see Finley Erickson's famous daughter– the only human known to have blue eyes. If Dad has any chance of selling more yachts than last year, I should play my part.

A strong cinnamon aroma wafts through my doorway

and footsteps thud against the hardwood, growing louder with each step.

"Damn it." I quickly crawl to toss a blanket over my most recent painting and shove my paintbrushes under my bed.

"Eribelle?" Dad's voice booms like a giant. "What are you doing spread out on the floor like that?"

I bend into a yoga pose, one foot and one hand off the ground, then take a centering breath.

"Ah, that's my girl. It's always good to brag about your flexibility."

I almost puke. Maybe I should. Then perhaps I can get out of this party if I fake an illness.

"I brought your favorite snack," Dad says, offering a cinnamon bun mid-air.

There's no point in correcting him with my intense chocolate obsession. Dad starts talking business and his expectations for my behavior tonight, but I tune him out and listen to the waves crashing into the pier outside. Seagulls squawk and the familiar shouts of fishermen greeting each other all blend into a painting in my mind. If I close my eyes, I can see the white foam making shapes on the seashells and footprints pushed into the sand. The textures, shapes, and colors all form an image of freedom.

"... Eribelle? So, what do you think?" Dad checks his Taj as an incoming message alerts him with a beep. "Can I count on you to do that, tonight?"

"Uh, yeah. Definitely."

"That's my good girl. I'm so lucky. You'll always be my biggest prize." Dad turns away, his shoulder width barely fitting through the doorway. "Oh, and if the mayor of Runlose cozies up to you, play along. We wouldn't want a repeat of last year, now do we?"

My insides turn to mush. Of course, I'm a prize. Of course, he backhandedly threatens me. Of course, I'm forced to attend another boring event with a silent competition of whose wallet is bigger than whose. Of course, I'll be used by Dad to make more sales.

As his footsteps fade away, I shove a bit of a delicious cinnamon roll in my mouth. Sugar coats my lips, but it's not as if I'll be putting on lipstick anymore. There's no way in Abyss I'm going tonight. I leave the rest of the dessert for Sampson to finish off when he returns. But by then, I'll be gone. I can't send him a Taj message because if there's one thing Sampson sucks at, it's lying.

Quickly, I tug on the straps of a backpack. It's buckle sticks on something under my bed. I yank and pull until it comes flying at me and I somersault backwards. As I shove a few essentials inside the bag, our three suns setting change the shape of the shadows within my room. I follow their rays to the open doors leading to my balcony. Running out the front door of Dad's estate isn't an option. Too many of his employees will ask why I haven't yet changed into a ballgown. Or they'd take the opportunity to politely congratulate me on my appearance on the new billboard downtown. I'd have to flash another fake smile and gently bob my head until they'd eventually mosey away.

I carefully move my still-wet painting inside in case this fierce wind is followed by a storm later. My balcony doors lock from the inside once closed so if close them, there's no turning back. I suck in a deep breath and shut them softly.

Warmth caresses my cheeks when I step out of the shade. Carefully, I peek over the edge. Heights haven't ever scared me, but I've also never considered scaling the side of a four-story mansion before. Voices holler and laugh far below. If I fall, there aren't any wind nymphs to save me. This could be the most moronic choice I've ever made.

Heart pounding, I straddle the railing and wipe my sweaty hands on my t-shirt. Hoverboards rush by below but thankfully no rider has noticed me yet. I say a useless prayer to whatever Goddess might be watching over me and swing my legs over. The stone exterior creates divots for someone experienced to latch their fingertips and toes on, but I'm no professional.

My shoe slides off its spot.

"Fuck!"

The muscles in my arms scream in protest. I manage to balance and gather my breath. *I can't fall. Keep going. Don't fall.* At a torturous speed, I scale down one stone at a time and somehow stay alive. Left foot. Right foot. Left arm. Right arm. Sweat drips down my temple. My pulse races.

Finally, my sneakers hit the pavement and my knees buckle. Shaking, my trembling hands hover over the street. I gulp and give myself three moments of panic. One. *I can't believe I did that.* Two. *If Dad finds out...* Three. *Sampson will think I'm a rockstar.*

Pressing off the ground, I straighten, walking taller, more confident than ever before. With each step, the waves pounding against the boulders roar louder. I'm almost there. A couple holding hands passes by me without a glance in my direction. They are both captivated by the cheery song blasting from their Taj. I start walking to the beat with a bounce in my step, believing for the first time that I'll swim in the ocean that has called me my entire life.

Why have I been such a coward? I should've tried this long ago. A bird swoops low, white wings outstretched, then lands to my right. Some of my classmates at university have rambled on when drunk or high about wanting to be a bird to soar through the open skies. I've never understood that desire. If given the chance, I'd be any sea creature besides a merfolk– perhaps a dolphin. I'd glide in the murky depths to experience a new life, where no one could tell me how to act or what to say or wear.

At last, the sounds from the bars down the street dissolve into distant hums and thumping beats. Ahead, the suns dip lower, ready to skim the horizon. My gaze locks onto a sail and I wonder if they're headed to Ozaron, the city famous for its art and deep forests. Slipping my shoes off, I wiggle my toes in the sand. Do I dare enter? I scan for any signs of creepy merfolk spying on me. No one.

I toss my backpack where it'll remain dry then slowly wade in the water. Ankles deep. I hold my breath. Water reaches my knees. Nothing catastrophic has happened yet. Maybe all the years of fears being carved into my mind were pointless.

I cringe. If Dad ever knew my thoughts, he'd ...well, he wouldn't listen to my pleas for the finances necessary to attend art school.

The water reaches my hips and I bask in the sensation of being halfway submerged. As corrupted as the merfolk are, I still wonder what it'd be like to live like them– under the sea. Do they have any form of art that could survive the elements of the wicked deep?

"ERIBELLE!" The familiar voice skids like scissors sliding against metal. "ERIBELLE! Get out of the water!" Sampson yells again and again, his calls growing louder and closer.

I should've explained to him, but this may be my only chance. Headfirst, I dive under. The icy cold doesn't hit me as harshly as I expected. Instead, it's almost soothing, like

I've always been meant to swim. But it's not where I belong since I can't paint here.

Sampson's muffled demands come from Above and I almost turn around. Unfortunately, I can't hold my breath forever, so I swim as far as possible then breech to suck in a lungful of air. The waves rock me and water splashes my cheeks. I smile. Perfection. I don't care if Sampson hates that word. This moment, right here, during the last moments of the setting suns, drenched from head to toe in the ocean is my perfect paradise.

Another scream comes from further out. In a small canoe, a woman bends over the side grabbing at the water like a lunatic. What is she doing? Did her hand get caught in her fishing net? I swim closer, faster, ready to help.

"Nate!" She peers over the side with wide eyes. "Nate!"

Immediately, I freeze. A high pitched sound rings in my ears. Shit. Someone has fallen overboard. I dip under but don't see a sinking body nearby.

"Hey!" I yell but the lady doesn't hear me. "Hey!"

"Nate! No, no, they took him."

My heart stops. They? I glance back to the shore. Sampson is jumping up and down, waving both hands in the air and wildly pointing behind me.

I spin. Bright scales shimmer. Merfolk. Terror clenches my gut. I don't stand a chance of outswimming them. If I can pull myself into the canoe, maybe the two of us can paddle back faster.

"Hey! Help me up!"

In a daze, the woman stands, paying me no attention and stares at the sky. I guess I'm on my own. Struggling, I heave myself into the boat despite it rocking back and forth.

"Nate," she sits on a crate and mumbles the name again and again, "Nate, my Nate."

Regret floods me before I act but I slap the stranger's face. She whirls at me, noticing me for the first time.

"Take an oar!" I say, while paddling myself. "Come on!"

We move in a circle, the waves rocking us. What the Abyss was I thinking coming out here?

"Hey! I place my hands on either side of her face and stare into her brown eyes. "You need to row. We're going to land. And you need to row now, understand?"

Slowly, she nods, tears running down her face. As she picks up an oar, slippery pale arms slide over the side of the canoe. Arms made of nightmares wrap tightly around my boatmate's waist.

Screaming. Someone's screaming. It might be me.

I clutch the oar and smack the merman's arms until he let's go.

A loud horn blares and bright headlights blind me for a few seconds. The merfolk all instantly swim away. We're safe–for now. Shielding my eyes, I catch the name of the yacht drifting towards us, '*The Eribelle.*' Dad's boat. Double triple fucking shit.

Read all of Eribelle's story, read '**The Wicked Blue**,' a gender reversal spin of Little Mermaid. This adult fantasy romance has two points of view, so prepare yourself for Axton, the merman warrior and protector of the Queen of Nerida.

COMING SOON

A soul sucking demon
&
A demon hunter

ABOUT CASSIE SWINDON

Cassie Swindon loathes wet socks, leaf blower machines, tight hugs, and rickety fans. Things she might murder for: a free massage, cuddles from a kitten, chocolate milkshakes, and long naps. Some of her favorite activities include decorating for the holidays, playing board games, and avoiding phone calls. She has four more ideas for upcoming books so sign up for her newsletter below.

Check out free short stories as prequels to my upcoming works in progress and also sign up for my newsletter here: https://cassieswindon.com/

- facebook.com/cassie.swindon.3
- x.com/CassieSwindon
- instagram.com/cassie_swindon_author
- bookbub.com/profile/cassie-swindon
- amazon.com/stores/author/B091N72414
- goodreads.com/cassieswindonauthor
- tiktok.com/@cassieswindon

www.ingramcontent.com/pod-product-compliance
Lightning Source LLC
LaVergne TN
LVHW010310070526
838199LV00065B/5505